Becky Bexley
the Child Genius
3

Student Fun and a Mammoth Discussion

Diana Holbourn

Discussion of Such Topics as Scams, Rumours,
Arguments and the Main Causes of Car Accidents,
and Fun at University

Windy
Seaside
Publishing

Cover design, book design and formatting by Gareth Southwell (art.garethsouthwell.com)

First edition September 2023

ISBN (paperback): 978-1-7391809-6-6
ISBN (ebook): 978-1-7391809-7-3

First published 2023 by Windy Seaside Publishing

Contents

Chapter 1

Becky Instigates Some Disruptive Fun in the Psychology Department One Day

Becky Bexley was a child genius who was at a university that wasn't really very good. But there were a lot of intelligent, thoughtful students there, and she made a lot of friends, despite the fact that there was an age gap of about eight years between her and most of the students on her psychology and media studies courses. They often had long discussions together, and also quite a bit of fun.

One afternoon in the middle of her first year there, Becky and about a dozen of her fellow psychology students were waiting for one of their tutors to come and lead one of their weekly seminars, where they would discuss what they were learning on his course, express opinions about it, and ask for help if they needed it. They were sitting in a fairly small study room.

The tutor was late. After five minutes they began to get a bit restless, wondering if he'd turn up. A few minutes later they were still waiting.

They began to get engrossed in conversation. One of them, Kirsty, said, "Not long ago I heard a programme on the radio about early psychology where they got onto the subject of how Freud and others did research into how to treat severe mental illness, and they mentioned some French psychologist, and then suddenly they started playing opera, part of a song from an old opera about someone who was mad, or at least something to do with madness, which the programme makers must have thought was appropriate, or at least attention-grabbing, hoping it would make the programme more interesting so people would be less likely to get bored of it and turn off. I think that's why they use sound effects like that. But I hate opera! When it came on I thought, 'Yuck!' I got distracted from what they were saying, thinking about how yucky it was, and I was tempted to turn the radio off immediately."

"Way to ruin a decent programme!" said one of the other students, James. Then he observed, "Playing a tune about someone who was supposed to have gone mad in the middle of a sensitive psychology programme doesn't sound very politically correct, does it!"

They giggled.

Becky had an amusing idea, and said, "Hey imagine if some famous psychologist invented a theory, and people believed it just because he was famous and because he'd invented some other theory before that gave him a good reputation because some people praised it and said it had helped some people. Imagine if the new theory was that the music that people like says a lot about them and what their psychological needs and desires are. Imagine if he said people who like opera are people who are really fed up of life, but don't dare say so because they feel repressed, and they'd like to shriek and scream and yell, but don't dare in normal life, so they go to opera to hear others doing it as a kind of substitute because it comforts them, because it makes them feel as if they're not alone in wanting to do it, so they can feel as if they're kindred spirits with the singers who they think must have those needs too, and they sit imagining they're letting their urges to shriek come out with the people who really are doing that, so they feel better."

Another student, Sophie, said with a grin, "And the psychologist could say something like that about people who like heavy metal music too; he could invent a theory that they're all very angry people who don't feel as if they can shout and yell at people as much as they'd like to so they listen to that as a substitute, and if they put it on loud, they can shout and yell about how they feel to it, and no one will know because they won't hear them over it."

A student called Tim said, "I bet a lot of people think something like that already."

They all smiled, as if they thought it was probably true.

Becky may have been intellectually advanced enough to be in a class with people who were eighteen or nineteen years old, but she still loved playing like an ordinary child of her age sometimes . . . But it turned out that everyone else must have loved playing too, because they loved the idea she came out with next, and did what she suggested immediately when she said:

"Hey, let's play a game. Imagine if the psychologist who invented that theory about people who like opera and heavy metal music felt sorry for opera lovers and heavy metal lovers and decided to help them all overcome their problems, but he didn't tell them what he was going to do, because he just thought he knew best, and felt sure they'd think he was doing them a favour in the end, even if they didn't like it at the time; and he employed some police and some staff from psychiatric hospitals who were good at restraining people, and one night they all walked into theatres where there were operas, and stadiums where heavy metal concerts were going on, and dragged everyone out. Imagine if they tied them all up and took them to big halls together that they'd hired to put them all in, where the psychologist said they could feel free to let out all their supposedly repressed emotions without worrying about it, and then ask for therapy if they wanted.

"Imagine if the audience members yelled and shouted and shrieked at the people dragging them off when they were tied up, but those people interpreted it as evidence that they were unleashing their repressed emotions and just praised them, saying the treatment must be working.

"Let's pretend we're those people, doing those things for real!"

Becky wanted to play the game right there and then, so she said, "Dave and Tim can be the arresting officers and staff from psychiatric hospitals with me, and everyone else can be the people watching opera and heavy metal concerts who are yelling in protest when we pretend to tie them up and drag them off and put them in the big hall where they're supposed to feel free to yell and shriek all they like."

The others liked the idea and cheered and laughed. As if they'd simply forgotten they were supposed to be in a lesson, they put all the chairs and tables around the edges of the room so they could do the dragging off scenes without furniture getting in the way. Becky, Dave and Tim went outside the door. Sophie pretended to be an opera singer in full flow, and the rest pretended to be watching.

Suddenly, Becky, Dave and Tim burst in and pretended to drag the others off. There was a lot of shouting and yelling in protest as the others pretended to be furious that they were being dragged off, and scared they were being attacked by criminals. Becky, Dave and Tim shouted things like, "Good! Well done! You're unleashing your repressed feelings! Very good; you can be very pleased with yourself!" All the while they were trying to drag them right outside the door.

Sophie pretended to be trying to rescue the audience who were all being dragged off, and shrieked and shouted in protest as loudly as the rest.

The students pretending to be the opera lovers pretended to fight back, and Becky and the other make-believe police and psychiatric workers told them they were being naughty now and would have to be tied up to stop them fighting against what was good for them. They pretended to tie them up, and then pretended to drag them along again, in reality being helped by the pretend opera lovers who were moving themselves along the floor to make it easy for them, till they were all outside the classroom door, still all shouting, cursing and shrieking.

After the make-believe opera lovers were tied up in the game, they yelled things like, "Help! Someone help!" But Becky and the other pretend police and hospital staff still shouted back as they were pulling them out the door, "Well done! You're doing a good job there! Carry on releasing your pent-up feelings; you'll see it's good for you."

The curses and yells grew louder and louder. Some of the students had been pulled along the corridor to make way for the others being pulled out the door and were outside other classrooms, still shouting.

Then, they spotted the tutor coming along the corridor. Not only him, but also other tutors who were coming out of their classrooms to find out what the noise was, thinking there must be a real fight going on – or opening their doors only to find there were students on the floor in the way so they couldn't get out.

Their tutor shouted, "Hey, what are you all doing?"

They all stopped, looking a bit shame-faced.

Becky thought that perhaps she'd better own up that it was her idea, and said, giggling, "Sorry, that was just a bit of psychology drama. We were just acting out what would happen if psychologists got to do anything they wanted whether the public liked it or not."

Their tutor said, "There aren't many psychologists who like to make their clients scream and yell, and drag them around . . . although I can think of a possible few. Alright, get back in your places please so we can have the lesson."

They put the tables and chairs back where they were supposed to be again and sat down. The other tutors went back to their classes, wondering what on earth had really been going on.

As the tutor began the seminar, he said, "Please don't do that again! Remember this is supposed to be a university classroom."

They mumbled apologies. Then they just had the lesson as normal, doing their best to stifle grins whenever they thought about what they'd done.

Becky didn't normally have outbursts of bad behaviour the way she did that day. Most of the time she was well-behaved, and the tutors thought she was a good student.

Chapter 2

Interesting, Amusing and Inappropriate Conversation Over the Longest Ever Lunch Break

One day not long after a psychology lecture, Becky and a group of other students on the course went for lunch to one of the university cafes together, and some of them bought burgers, while others bought some of the other things on offer. They went to eat their food somewhere quiet so they could all hear each other talk.

The Students Chat About False Rumours

When they sat down, Becky said, "I heard a rumour that one of our tutors is leaving soon … Or maybe it was just wishful thinking."

The others asked Becky who she meant.

She said, "Alan Jones. Someone said he might leave after he gave that lecture where he said he liked the idea of going to work in America ... Actually, I didn't hear the whole conversation, so maybe the person who said he might leave was just speculating ... Yeah OK, ignore what I said. I probably don't know what I'm talking about really ... I suppose that might be one way rumours get started though – someone gives an opinion or speculates about something, or what they say gets only half heard by someone who gets the wrong impression of it because of that, and then what they said gets passed on, sounding like fact."

A student called Dave – the Dave who'd helped Becky pretend to manhandle other students during the game they'd played in the psychology department when the tutor was late – said, "If you want a rumour, that's nothing! Someone once told me McDonald's puts cow eyeballs in its burgers."

A few of the students were shocked, but some didn't believe it could be true. One, Colin, joked, "That's not a problem! I put cow eyeballs in my coffee in the morning!"

Dave didn't believe that for a moment and said, "Yeah, but really, that's what I heard about McDonald's."

"What?" said another student, Mya, in mock horror, trying to suppress a grin. "You heard McDonald's puts cow eyeballs in its coffee as well? Oh! And there was me thinking those eyeball thingies were just exotic sugar lumps that don't melt very well!"

"No," said Dave. "I mean I just heard McDonald's puts cow eyeballs in its burgers."

A few students grinned mischievously, thinking of making up gruesome stories about other things they could say went into food that they might be able to scare Dave with for fun. But another student, James, said sarcastically with a chuckle and then a grimace, "Thanks for that, Dave! That was just what I wanted to hear, having just taken a mouthful of fish burger!"

Another one of the group, Kirsty, joked, "Well, as long as it's not a fancy newly-discovered fish called cowfish, that the people who make the food they sell around here think is similar enough to cow that it'll be OK to put cow eyeballs in burgers made of that too, I wouldn't worry if I were you."

One student, Suzy, said, "Actually, I've heard there really is a fish called cowfish. It's got horns, and that's why they call it that."

"Yikes!" said another student, Catherine, with feeling. "Imagine being surrounded by a pack of fish like that, especially if you were swimming in the sea in just your swimming costume!"

Another one, Stuart, was genuinely horrified to hear about eyeballs in food, and said, "What were you saying though, Dave, you really heard McDonald's puts cow eyeballs in its dinners?"

Dave said, "Yeah. I didn't feel like going to McDonald's for a while after I heard it, but then someone emailed me a link to a website all about the kinds of stories that get passed around to loads of people by email, where the owners investigate whether they're true or not. It said McDonald's doesn't really do that at all."

"Oh why did you tell us about it then?" said another student, Jackie, with a pained grin, having just been put right off her food, and still not sure she fancied eating it even after hearing that the story wasn't true. If she had regained her appetite for it, she would have been put off it again immediately afterwards though, when another student, Emma, said,

"I've had emails telling me McDonald's puts feathers in some of its drinks. I thought it was hard to believe, so I looked for information about it in Google, and found websites saying the rumour's rubbish."

"Why do people invent stuff like that?" asked Mya with morbid curiosity.

Kirsty said, "Maybe it's mums trying to scare their children off eating junk food, because they want them to eat healthily, and they can't think of any other way of persuading them to. Maybe the kids who believe their mums tell other kids, and the story gets spread around."

One of the students, Heather, said, "Or maybe it's one of these things where the wording of something gets changed as it's passed on; I mean, maybe the thing about eyeballs started when someone was trying a burger and really didn't like it, and they said as a joke that they bet it had cow's eyeballs in it. Then someone who heard them say it might have told their friend later that the first person reckoned the burgers have cow eyeballs in them, but said it seriously so their friend thought they meant it for real. Then maybe that person passed it on, saying someone thinks McDonald's burgers contain cow eyeballs, and the next person repeated it to others as if it was a definite fact, and so on. I think that's one way rumours get started.

"Something a bit like that happened to me. I remember day-dreaming one day, and I said to my brother in a dreamy wishful thinking voice, 'Wouldn't it be nice if there was a swimming pool in our garden!' I only meant it in a day-dreamy way, not for real, but later I overheard him telling my parents I thought it would be nice if there was a swimming pool in the garden, and they laughed, and said things in scornful voices like, 'Does she think we're made of money?' But I never meant it seriously like they thought I meant it; I was just day-dreaming."

One of the Group, Anne, Starts Talking About an Aggravating Experience She Had

A student called Anne said with a note of irritation, "Oh I know what you mean! Something a bit like that happened to me.

"When I was younger, my mum used to take me with her to visit friends of hers sometimes in the afternoons during the holidays when I wasn't at school. That was probably just as well when I was little, but it lasted till I was a teenager. She insisted I go with her, because she said I spent too much time on my own and that it would be healthier for me to socialise; and also she'd never liked me playing or hanging around outside when she wasn't within supervising distance, because we didn't have a garden and there were busy roads around us, and she'd always been worried about me being safe, especially with the horrible stuff in the news about kids being abducted. She didn't even like me sitting or playing in the park on my own. Maybe she'd have worried less if I'd had older brothers and sisters I could have spent time with instead of being an only child.

"I think she was worrying more than she needed to; after all, child abduction's rare in this country, and I wouldn't have been spending much time in the road, but still. I think she's always been a bit over-anxious. I'd have preferred to spend my time on my own sitting in the park reading a book or using the play equipment there than to sit indoors on warm afternoons with people who were much older than me. At other times I used to spend a lot of time doing my own thing in my room. But my mum insisted it wasn't good for me to spend so much time alone. I didn't agree. She thinks socialising's a lot more important than I do.

"When I was about thirteen, she made a new group of friends, who would all meet up at the house of one of them, Mary. That summer, my mum took me with her when she spent the afternoons chatting to them. There were half a dozen women there besides her. They were all way older than me. My mum was about the youngest, but she was about fifty.

"At first it was nice there, because the women told me interesting stories about their lives. They used to pet me and give me little cakes they'd made sometimes. And there were a few times when they made me laugh. Some afternoons were quite enjoyable, at least at first. But it came to a bad end for me. I'll tell you about it.

"After several visits, I began to get a bit restless, because although the women were often nice, it was warm and sunny outside, and I preferred to be having fun with a couple of friends I had and doing energetic things, like most young people probably would, or doing things on my own on my computer that got my brain into gear so I got a bit of an adrenaline buzz, or else where I felt as if I was making progress achieving something.

"And as nice and interesting as the women could be sometimes, there were quite a few times when I ended up feeling a bit down, at least till I got home and started getting on with something else. I think it was partly because most of them were way past retirement age, and they didn't really have any hope of achieving much to speak of in the future, but instead, one in particular would talk about her increasing health problems, and I was sympathetic, but I kind of captured the mood that was there sometimes, and started spending moments afterwards feeling as if spending a long time there meant my chance of playing lively games for hours was slipping away from me, and that there would come a time when I myself would go into decline and it would be too late; and that got me down a bit – not much, but for a few moments after I went there sometimes.

"Actually, there are quite a few things I want to do in life, and occasionally, I even wonder now whether I'll manage to achieve them before I can't any more because my health has got so bad, or I've died."

Some Humour Lightens the Mood for a Little While

Another student, Matthew, said sarcastically, "That's a cheerful thought!"

Then he said, "Come on, you could have decades and decades of good health to come yet before anything like that happens! Just be thankful you're not a mayfly. I think some species of those only have a life span of a few hours!"

Anne chuckled and said, "Wow! But somehow I think that if I was a mayfly, I wouldn't be daft enough to even have the ambition to be a psychotherapist, or to create a psychology website, or to do some other things I'd like to do. Actually, I don't suppose I'd even have any idea what computers and websites and things are even for!"

Mya grinned and joked, "Are you sure about that? Are you sure that if you could listen in on a mayfly's thoughts, you wouldn't hear them thinking, 'Oh if only I had the time to create a website, and play video games, and become a psychotherapist helping people with anxiety and drink problems before I die!'?"

Anne laughed and said, "I'm pretty sure I wouldn't hear them thinking that!"

Jackie asked, "Wow, if some mayflies only live a few hours, how long is it between the time when they're born and the time they get to adulthood and start having babies of their own?"

Emma said, "Actually, I don't think it's quite as drastic as that; I think it's just that when they get to be adults they only last a day or so, but they live for longer than that in other forms when they're younger, you know, a bit like the way ordinary flies aren't always flies, but they're maggots when they're younger.

"I think there are some things in nature that would seem weird to us! I actually heard that some species of mayfly don't even eat anything, at least when they're in their adult form. So I definitely wouldn't want to be one of those! I heard that they've got primitive digestive systems, but they're just filled with air and never used! I'm not sure if that's really true, but that's what I heard! I think the fact that they don't eat is why they die so quickly."

Colin grinned and said, "Who did you hear that from, your biology teacher? Just imagine if someone kept saying to their biology teacher who was trying to teach them things they needed to know for their exams, 'Is this really true, or are you just joking around with us?' "

They chuckled.

Emma grinned and said, "Yeah, that would be a bit disruptive! Anyway, I think it's probably true about their digestive systems. And I heard that they like to live in water when they're still growing up, in places like rotting vegetation. Lovely!"

The others giggled.

Then Becky joked, "You see, Anne, things could have been a lot worse for you. At least your mum took you to be with humans in the afternoons. Just imagine if she'd had some kind of weird obsession for taking you to be with strange creatures that lived in rotting vegetation, that had digestive systems filled with air, that you couldn't even communicate with!"

Dave grinned and joked, "But you don't communicate with a creature's digestive system anyway."

Becky said, "Cringe cringe! Come on, you know what I mean! I don't mean just their digestive systems. And you wouldn't have got any cakes out of them, Anne, that's for sure! Or if you did, you might not have wanted to eat them if you were being put off by sitting in a wad of rotting vegetation with them in a river!"

Anne Gets Back to Telling More of her Story

Anne giggled and said, "That's true!"

But then she got serious and said, "Anyway, to carry on with my story, if you're wondering why my mum wanted to be with the other women quite a bit, even though most of them were older than her, well, she liked their company. She had me when she was nearly forty, so it isn't as if there was a really massive age gap between them.

"Anyway, yes, I know I was better off than I would have been if I'd been sitting on a heap of rotting vegetation in a river with a load of crawling insects, but I still used to end up feeling a little bit depressed when I was with them. One reason was that one or two of the women in the group could repeat themselves quite a bit – I think their memories were going a bit because they were old; and also they quite often talked about depressing things in the news for a while, sometimes the same old things, so I ended up feeling a bit down because of that too, at least for a few minutes after each visit. Not that long, but long enough for me to start wishing my mum didn't keep wanting me to go there.

"Also I think just sitting around doing nothing for ages can make you feel less alert, and your metabolism probably slows down so you don't feel so lively, especially if you're not taking much part in the conversation; and it can be a bit of effort to motivate yourself to shift gears and get livelier and into thinking mode again afterwards; so I'm pretty sure that was contributing to my slight depressed feeling at the end of some of the chats, especially when they were long, even when I enjoyed them at the time. I couldn't tell I was going to feel like that at the end while they were happening most of the time.

"It's funny, I know someone who said her little sister seems a bit depressed after she's been watching the television for quite a while, even when the programmes have been cheerful. She reckons it's for a similar reason, since she said that when her sister gets called in to dinner and starts chatting with everyone else, she cheers up."

Dave smiled and said, "Well who wouldn't cheer up when they start eating food . . . provided it's nice food, of course! . . . And I suppose the company might have helped as well."

The others grinned.

The students wondered just where Anne's story could be leading. It didn't seem to be about rumours, the thing she'd given the impression she was going to talk about when she started. Mya made a fairly accurate guess in her mind as to where it would go. One or two others wondered if Anne had forgotten what she'd said she was going to tell them and had started psychoanalysing herself out loud, perhaps because she was maybe obsessed with work, and thought she may as well use the lunch time to practise in preparation for learning to do that to others in her career. They were going to have to wait longer before discovering where the story was going, because it didn't show any signs of getting there soon, as Anne continued, depressing some of the listeners:

"Anyway, as well as those reasons why I sometimes felt a bit depressed after being with my mum's friends, there was another one: As nice as they could be sometimes, sometimes they could have discussions that sounded bigoted and heartless to me, or at least a few of them did, such as one day a teenage boy who'd been on drugs died of an overdose of them, and it was in the news, and a couple of them were saying he was stupid to have got into drugs, and that dying served him right. I thought, 'Hang on, what if he got into drugs because he was fed up of life or really stressed a lot of the time, maybe because he had big problems? Or what if he was easily led by others he'd thought of as friends, so he was persuaded to get into drugs after they got into them themselves and told him they enjoyed it? Anyway he was so young, didn't he deserve another chance at life?'

"It was as if they just didn't see any complexities in situations sometimes, but just thought they could make quick simple heartless blanket judgments, as if all cases could be judged as if they were just the same as each other – you know, like saying a boy who gets into drugs deserves to die, the same as they might say a drug dealer who's ruined loads of people's lives might; and I didn't like that.

"I mean, to give another example, some of them often said things with feeling like, 'We shouldn't let any immigrants into this country, and there are far too many here! They shouldn't be allowed to be here.' To a certain extent, I could understand them feeling that way; after all, I think a lot of immigration does cause problems, although I don't actually know that much about the effects of it, so I can't really say. but they were lumping immigrants all in together, as if they could all be judged the same way. But I thought that wasn't fair, since after all, some immigrants come from war zones or places where they've suffered other hardships; and should those people be sent back into places where they might be killed or injured or suffer badly in other ways? I don't think anyone should think it's easy to decide they should be.

"Besides, there are lots of immigrants who benefit people here in some ways. I mean, some have shops that stay open longer than most shops do, and a lot of the dirtiest and most boring and unpleasant jobs in this country are often done by immigrants – jobs no one here seems to want to do. At least, we're told people here don't seem to want to do them; how true it is, I'm not quite sure. But if there were no immigrants here, would the people complaining have been willing to do those jobs themselves, or would they have liked their children to have done them? Probably not."

One of the women who served the students food was walking past just then, and heard the end of what Anne was saying. A mischievous grin flashed across her face, and she joked, "When I'm in government, I'm going to make students do all the dirtiest jobs in the country at weekends . . . That's until my kids grow up and go to university, and then I'll scrap that law."

She waited long enough to see the indignant looks of some of the students, and then walked off, laughing to herself, just before they would have managed to protest. Some of the others realised she was joking though, and chuckled.

Anne carried on with her story as if nothing had happened, saying, "Or one or two of the women would say things like, 'I don't think fat people should be given any treatment from the health service for problems brought on by them being overweight if they still eat a lot of fatty or sugary food after a doctor's told them they need to cut down on it, since it'll be their own fault they've got the problems.'

"I wondered, 'Just how far would you go with that? If one of the fat people who'd been refused heart medication because they wouldn't give up unhealthy food had a heart attack that was brought on by eating too much fatty and sugary food, would you say they should just be left to die? If so, how would that work? How do you think health workers could sort deserving people from undeserving ones quickly? I mean, every time someone phoned an ambulance or came to the emergency department of a hospital, would someone have to sort through a massive list, to find out whether they were one of those people who didn't deserve treatment because they hadn't made any effort to get slimmer after a doctor warned them they had to? Imagine how much time that might take! What if a lot of supposedly deserving people died while health workers were looking through a list to find out whether they were deserving or undeserving?

" 'Or would you just say fat people who don't lose weight shouldn't receive medication for heart disease, but they should be treated if something that could quickly kill them happens to their health? If you would, what if one of the people who'd been denied medication then had a heart attack, when they wouldn't have done if they'd been able to take it? If you wouldn't want them to be left to die, would you take pity on them and allow them to have treatment then, when they might be in intensive care for ages, taking up a bed that someone else who badly needed it could have had if the fat person had been prevented from having a heart attack by being given medication before? They'd be getting treatment in hospital that would cost much much more than their heart disease tablets would have done! Would you still say they shouldn't have been given the tablets? What would have been the point in refusing to let them have them?' Some of the women didn't seem to think through what they were saying sometimes. That put me off wanting to spend time with them."

One Student Tells an Uplifting Story About Someone They Know Who Lost Lots of Weight, and Then the Students Start Joking About Fat

Anne paused for breath, and Kirsty changed the topic of conversation a bit, saying, "You know, I know someone who lost ten stone in about six years, mostly just by eating smaller portions of dinner. She said that when her oldest daughter was little, someone told her she was giving her too much food, and bought her a child's plate with a cartoon character on it to use for her, that was smaller than a normal dinner plate. When her daughter got older, the mum decided to lose weight, so she started eating off it herself. She went to the gym sometimes, but not all that often; she mainly just lost weight by eating her dinner off the child's plate. She must have lost an average of about twenty-three pounds a year! Not loads of weight at once, but over that six years, she went from being grossly overweight to actually being underweight."

The students were impressed. But then Matthew smiled and said, "Hey imagine if every overweight person in the world was given liposuction, and all their fat was shipped out and put in the same place. I wonder how much room it would take up."

More than one student who'd been in the process of raising junk food to their mouths put it down again for a little while, grossed out by the thought of all their fat being piled up with that of other people somewhere.

But Suzy laughed and said, "Just think! It might make a massive lake of fat! Wow, imagine people swimming in it!"

Becky grinned and said, "What if it started going solid while someone was in there! It might stick to them, and they might come out with more fat on the outside of them than they had on the inside. Imagine them phoning a friend and saying, 'I've just been for a really energetic swim! It was really good exercise, but I've found out that while I was in there, I put on four stone! Not in a place where you'd expect it to be though.' "

Mya said, "Imagine if scientists discovered it's possible to use fat as fuel. It would be in demand then!"

Colin laughed and said, "If there was a massive lake of fat, they'd probably get enough fuel to power a rocket ship to Mars!"

The Students Joke About Going to Mars

The students smiled. Then James got more serious and said, "They're thinking of trying to colonise Mars, aren't they? It might come in handy soon, since I've heard the Earth's population's growing really fast. We might need another planet soon to put a lot of the people on."

"Who would volunteer to go, I wonder," said Jackie thoughtfully.

"People who hate the human race and want to escape from it, perhaps," said Matthew with a mischievous grin. "Imagine loads and loads of people who hated other people all flocking to Mars! They'd all hate each other, so they'd probably start fighting each other and cause mass destruction to the planet within hours! Or sooner! All that time and effort NASA and other organisations would have spent trying to make it habitable for humans, only for it to be destroyed in minutes!"

Anne Talks More About People Making Unfair Judgments About Things

Most of the students laughed. Anne wasn't feeling so happy though. It seemed she wanted to carry on depressing them with her depressing reminiscences, for some reason. Or more likely, she didn't realise they were depressing. She started talking again, and continued to tell her story as the rest of her lunch went cold. One or two students hoped she didn't mind cold lunch, since her story went on for a while, and her food was bound to get colder the longer the story carried on.

She said, "Talking about too many people being in the world reminds me of another example of the kind of thing the people I was with used to say: One of the women once said with feeling, 'I heard about someone who's got a house by the seaside they only use in the summer for holidays. The law should be changed so people are only allowed one house; we need to stop the housing shortage, without having to build more and more so we destroy more of our woodlands by building more houses on them.'

"Well that might have sounded fair enough, but I thought, 'Surely there can only be a tiny number of people who have houses that don't get used a lot of the time, so surely going to all the trouble of making a new law to stop them having them won't achieve much at all, whereas there are probably much more major causes of the housing shortage, and if those were the ones being given attention and sorted out, it would make much more of a difference!' I mean, for one thing, there was a television programme about how lots of houses are left empty for ages by councils after tenants move out because they're not in very good condition, that would make perfectly good homes if a bit of work was done to them and then they were given to people on the housing waiting list. I bet there are a lot more of those than rich people's second homes that hardly get used, but nothing else got a mention by this person who seemed to have such a strong opinion about solving the housing shortage.

"And what about the reasons why people are selling places as holiday homes rather than permanent ones anyway? What if it's because quite a lot of them aren't sturdy enough to be real homes, like if they don't have the insulation to protect them from getting freezing in winter when there are high winds coming in from the sea, or if no one seems to want to buy them to live in permanently because people don't want to live in a lot of the areas where they are? Like in the north of Scotland, where it's all cold most of the year round, but some people might want to go up there for the pretty scenery in the summer? Stopping people using them as holiday homes won't solve the housing problem then, will it!

"I mean, maybe when rich people buy little houses as holiday homes in some areas, it does sometimes cause problems for locals, like shortages of housing there, because they could have bought the houses to live in if the rich people hadn't snapped them up – I don't know enough about it to really be sure; but this person seemed to think it was causing problems for people all over the country, although she didn't seem to know nearly enough about it to justify the amount of feeling she was putting into criticising people who buy holiday homes. People really ought to think more before they come out with opinions! I mean, if you're going to declare that a whole new law ought to be brought in that's going to change some people's lives in ways they won't like, you ought to at least try to make sure it's going to have the effect you want it to have first, and look into whether something less drastic would work better!"

Maybe Anne had been longing for a sympathetic ear or two for some time, and had decided to tell the other students about her experience of having to put up with hearing things she objected to after finally feeling sure she'd found some – after all, they were all psychology students, and perhaps she assumed – wrongly – that they were all hoping to go into careers where they were helping people with psychological problems so they were all sympathetic beings. But she would have been a bit disillusioned if she'd been able to read the thoughts of some of them. Though some found what she was saying interesting, one or two had begun to feel a bit uneasy, thinking they'd better be careful about what they said while she was around, in case she went back to the old people she was grumbling about and complained, "I've just been with some students, and I was a bit depressed because they talked such rubbish," and then listed several things she thought they'd said that were wrong.

Actually Anne was being much more talkative than usual; it might have been to do with the fact that she had a class discussion that afternoon with a tutor she didn't like, talking about a subject she didn't see the point in discussing; and she anticipated it being so unbearably dull, judging by the way it had been in the previous few weeks, that she'd resorted to drinking a few shots of whisky (mixed with a bit of ginger ale to slightly improve the flavour) to try to dull her senses a bit, in the hope it wouldn't bother her so much after that; not the ideal way of dealing with it, she knew, but the only one she could think of at the time.

It had had a different effect than the one she'd intended though, although she did also tend to get more talkative when she was feeling provoked, or felt strongly about something. If it meant she was going to tell the tutor just what she thought of his discussion class that afternoon, the way she was insisting on telling the other students just what she thought of the opinions of her mum's friends, she was going to find herself in a bit of trouble!

Oblivious to the thoughts of the students who wondered what uncomplimentary things she might tell other people about their own conversations, and ruining any enjoyment any of them might have had while eating any food they had left, she continued,

"There was one day when I thought the conversation got especially depressing, when one person announced that she didn't think a certain celebrity on trial for child abuse was guilty; her reason: People have accused innocent celebrities of abusing them just because they were after the compensation money that victims of serious crime can get if they take someone to court and they get convicted of it. That seemed to be it! There were actually dozens of people accusing him, but instead of actually looking at the evidence, it seems that all she thought needed to happen to decide his innocence or guilt was to think about what she'd heard some people had done in the past. They might not even have been the majority of people who'd taken celebrities to court!

"I mean, can you imagine a judge thinking like that, standing up in court and saying, 'Members of the jury, I submit to you that you must find this man not guilty, because, well, after all, everyone knows some people accuse people of serious crimes just to get the compensation money available to victims.' You'd expect a stricter standard of evidence from a drudge – I mean a judge, wouldn't you; – sorry, I don't know why I just said drudge. Anyway, you'd expect a stricter standard of evidence from a judge, so why wouldn't you want to judge by good evidence when you're just talking about it in ordinary life? The person who brought it up was just dismissing dozens of women as liars, just like that. I thought it was offensive and depressing, and I'd like to have just got up and walked out. I could have argued with her, but I didn't want the hassle; I'd been hoping for a relaxing time."

James said, "Yes, it doesn't sound fair to judge people without looking at the evidence; but still, I've heard that quite a few people have been falsely accused of crimes like that by people wanting the compensation money on offer. I don't mean just celebrities being accused of crimes, but ordinary people. I think the system should be changed so instead of compensation money, victims of things like sexual abuse who take their abusers to court get the best-quality counselling around, to help them get over the effects of the crimes that were committed against them. I heard about a country that changed the rules like that, and accusations went down quite a bit the next year, which seems to prove that some people really do just make serious accusations against other people just for what they can get."

The Students Talk and Joke About Misleading Statistics and the False Conclusions People Who Believe Them Can Make

Becky said, "It might prove that, especially if the numbers went down a lot. But don't forget that the figures would vary from year to year anyway. It would be strange if they were always the same. And some years there might be things going on that make them vary a lot from average levels, such as if one year, police cracked a big crime ring and lots of people got prosecuted, which would mean that the next year the figures would be almost certain to go down; they might be going down to levels that were a lot more like the normal levels, if the crime ring hadn't been in operation for that long before it was busted; but anyone who just looked at the figures for those two years wouldn't know that; it would just look to them as if there had been a big drop in the crime figures. So other things would have to be ruled out before anyone could be absolutely sure the cause of the drop was one thing or another.

"I'm not saying anything like what I'm about to talk about is happening here – in fact, if I had to guess, I'd say it almost certainly isn't; but I've read that sometimes, people who want to convince people to believe something they want them to believe will trick them by using statistics in certain ways. An example I read about is that a person who doesn't believe in global warming, who wants to convince other people that it's just a hoax, or that people are mistaken to believe in it, might look at information about how warm it's been each year for the last few decades, and pick a year when it was much hotter than usual, and without telling people it was a lot hotter than average, they might tell them that since that year, temperatures have gone down quite a lot, making it look as if the Earth's cooling instead of warming. If they'd picked the year just before the one they chose, it might have been a much cooler year than the one they chose, so to anyone who looked at both years together, it would look as if warming definitely is happening.

"But someone who wanted to prove that the Earth is getting warmer might choose two years when the second one was hotter than the first one deliberately, so they could tell everyone what the temperature difference was between the two years, and say it proved global warming's happening, when if they'd told them what the average temperature was the year after those two, the statistics might not have looked nearly so convincing, because the temperature might have gone down again, and the person might have had to admit that it was just chance, not global warming, that had made it look as if temperatures were going up in those two years. In reality, the average temperature over the decades they were looking at might not have moved up or down much at all most of the time.

"That's one kind of trick people like politicians can use when they're making claims to supposedly prove their policies are right, or that the opposition's policies are bad for the country or the world, in their speeches and interviews and things."

Becky took a swig of her drink, and then continued, "And I've heard of people making bad decisions because they thought one thing was causing another one when it wasn't, and they read too much significance into some statistics.

"One example is that I read about some air force officers in Israel who were training a group of pilots, who noticed that whenever they praised them for doing an especially good job, the next time they went out, they didn't do such a good one, whereas whenever they told them off for doing a bad job, they did a better one the next time. The officers wondered whether that meant they should stop praising the trainee pilots and do more criticising. But the variations in performance might not have been caused by the praise or criticism at all. Really, it's very unlikely that anyone will perform at their best or their worst all the time; most of the time, they'll likely be about average; so there's actually a really high probability that anyone who does really well won't do so well the next time, or that someone who does worse than usual won't do so badly next time. So that was probably what was really happening with the pilots.

"I've read that it's quite a common mistake for people to think one thing might be causing something, when really it's just happening at the same time as it, or else for them to think one thing's causing another, when in reality it's the other way around – that the second thing's causing the first.

"I mean, for instance, imagine if it was found that every week when cheese sales went up one year, certain football teams won their matches, but every time sales of it went down, they lost their matches. It might just be a coincidence. But some people who noticed that might start developing theories about how cheese must boost footballers' performance, and about how those teams must be eating a lot of cheese when they won games. If reporters on the radio or television started believing that, they might ask members of those football teams if they ate more cheese when they were winning games, and not believe them if they said no. There might be newspaper articles about how there might be secret cheese eating among sportsmen, and how there might be a conspiracy in some teams to keep it quiet, in case other teams started doing the same so they wouldn't have an advantage over them any more."

"That would be funny!" said Suzy. "Especially since cheese is fattening and high in salt, so it's probably not all that good for you . . . at least in high doses . . . if it's appropriate to talk about doses of cheese! Mind you, it would be even funnier if it was sales of something like perfume that went up every time a team won and went down whenever they lost. Reporters might start trying to sniff footballers while they were interviewing them, hoping none of them would notice, just to see if they were wearing perfume."

"Yeah," said Dave with a chuckle. "Or just imagine if it was garlic sales. Reporters might start interviewing footballers from a great distance, shouting their questions from some way away, just in case the footballers had been eating loads of garlic and belched garlic fumes all over them!"

The students laughed. Then Mya said, "Hey imagine if it was found that sales of lemonade went up whenever sales of televisions went up, and went down whenever they went down. It might just be a coincidence, but imagine if there were reports in the papers saying it seemed that drinking lemonade was somehow making people want to buy televisions, or that watching television seemed to be giving people a thirst for lemonade."

The students grinned. But Becky said, "Or to give a serious example I heard about, say if there's a high rate of crime and a high rate of homelessness in an area, some people might think that a lot of the crime must be being caused by the homeless people; and other people might assume it was the other way around – that some of the crime must be making people homeless, thinking that it might be things like arson, or other kinds of criminal damage to homes.

"But in reality, the cause of most of the crime and most of the homelessness might be something completely different; for example, a lot of people might be becoming drug users at school, and it might lead some people to start committing burglaries and muggings and things to finance their habit, so most of the crimes in the area might be that kind of thing; and other people might not be able to keep up with their rents because they feel the need to spend all their money on their drug habits, or they might steal from their families to pay for their drugs, till they end up being thrown out of their homes; so drugs could be the cause of most of the homelessness as well as the cause of most of the crime."

"Don't forget that the drug use itself would be classified as a crime, so that in itself would be causing an increase in the crime statistics too," remarked Matthew.

Becky said, "That's true!"

"I was listening to the radio the other day," said heather. "There was a phone-in show on, and they were talking about drugs. The presenter said that since the police cracked down harshly on drugs years ago, drug use has actually increased a lot. It was tempting to wonder what it was about cracking down harshly on drug use that could have led to it increasing so much. But thinking about it, there are probably completely different reasons why it's gone up so much. I mean, maybe some sections of the community have become more disadvantaged in that time, so some people who are affected by that are more likely to want to take drugs; or maybe drugs have become much more easy to get hold of because there are a lot more around, regardless of the crackdown, or something."

Becky said, "Yeah. Mind you, it would still be worth wondering if the increase in drug use could have had something to do with the crackdown in some way; and it would certainly be worth wondering why the crackdown has been so ineffective, if it's really true that drug use has gone up a lot since then."

Kirsty smiled and said, "Hey Imagine if drug use went up at the same time as lots of new radio stations came on air that played classical music. Some people might start developing theories that a lot of people must find listening to classical music stressful, and that the stress of listening to it must be making people turn to drugs, who maybe couldn't get off them again because they were so addicted, so even if they stopped listening to the stressful classical music, they still had to stay on the drugs.

"Or imagine if the sale of cakes went up whenever the average temperatures around the world went up, and went down whenever temperatures went down. Some people might start thinking that making or eating cakes was causing global warming, when really it was just a coincidence."

Emma said, "Cake sales go up at Christmas though, when it gets colder. Imagine if politicians started thinking eating cakes must be the cause of the drop in temperature, and an item came on the news one day that said, 'People are advised to eat more cakes, since it seems it's an antidote to global warming.'"

The Group Discusses Immigration, and Some Humour Breaks Out

Anne brightened up for a second or two, before getting back to her melancholy story. She clapped her hands once or twice with glee and said, "Oh I wish the people I'd been with had talked about things like that! It would have been interesting to learn new things like that stuff about confusing the cause of a thing with the effect of it, so as to think one thing caused another when it was really the other way around, and about how people can assume things that just happen coincidentally have more to do with each other than they really do. I'd have wanted to be with those people a lot if they'd talked about things like that. But they seemed to want to talk about things they were unhappy with all the time. It didn't even matter what was going on at the time.

"I mean, one day one of the oldest ones of them had a birthday, her 82nd, and they had a little tea-party, where they gave her presents and got in some party food. But they didn't think to try and get a party mood going! The conversation was all about people dying, and then a few of them got worked up and started talking about how outraged they were about immigrants coming here and claiming benefits. Some party!

"The woman who was getting the angriest seemed to think there are loads of people who come to this country just to play the system, by not bothering to work but just scrounging benefits. But I don't know if she really had the facts! I mean, she said she'd seen a few immigrants on television boasting about playing the system; but I wonder if she had any idea what percentage of the benefits budget is spent on people like that. What if it's just a tiny one, so it can't really be called a burden on the tax payer? And I wonder if she had any idea what percentage of immigrants come here just to scrounge benefits. Again, what if it's a tiny one? The amount of publicity people get doesn't necessarily correspond to how many of them there are, does it! So if there were a couple of people boasting about playing the system on television, it doesn't mean there must be loads of those people out there doing it. I mean, there might be, for all I know; but you at least ought to wait till you're sure of that before you become convinced it's a serious problem for the country!

"So I wonder what actual evidence she had that it's a serious problem! Somehow I doubt she had much. Without evidence, you could be getting far more angry than you need to, for all you know. And what if she went to the country where a lot of the immigrants on benefits came from, and found that a lot of people there live in mud huts with no sanitation and no electricity or something; I wonder if she'd be just as angry about them coming here then.

"I don't know the answers to any of these things. I just think people ought to make sure they've got good evidence before they condemn whole groups of people as if they're all doing something wrong."

Becky said, "Yeah. Maybe some people think immigration's bad for the country when it isn't really, at least immigration from some parts of the world.

"I used to take it for granted that immigration was just bound to reduce wages for people working in the kinds of low-skilled jobs that a lot of new immigrants try to get work in, since after all, if there are more people who want to work in them, and a lot of those are pretty desperate for jobs to make a bit of money so they'll take anything even if the wages are pretty low, employers who employ people like that will be able to put wages down, because they'll be able to employ people who'll be willing to work for lower wages, knowing that if some people don't want to work for them, others will, and that they won't have to increase wages or keep them decently high to attract people who wouldn't want to work doing their jobs if wages were lower. So I thought there must be something in the complaints of some people that immigrants take jobs locals could have because they're willing to work for lower wages than people here would.

"But it turns out that there are studies that have found that wages don't go down all that much at all when immigration rises. Maybe even a lot of immigrants who really need work still won't work in a place that pays wages that are too low to let them make a decent living."

Anne said, "Maybe. Anyway, at the end of this so-called party, the woman who'd been getting the angriest asked me if I'd enjoyed it, as if she thought getting angry and sounding miserable was a whole heap of fun, and that she expected everyone else to feel the same way!"

The mood had been turning a bit gloomy up until Anne's last sentence, and Dave, thinking the lunch break was becoming way too depressing for his liking, decided to lighten it by making a joke. He said, "Imagine if there was a foreign restaurant where the owners decided to at least have a bit of fun with the idea of people getting angry about immigrants coming here, so they decided to create a new range of meals, starting with, 'There are 47 benefit scroungers in my family soup', followed by, 'We'll always be in front of you in the housing queue turkey and mushroom stroganoff', and then, 'We're taking your jobs meringue', topped off with a nice cup of hot 'Us immigrants are over-running your country coffee'. Customers could be given a couple of complimentary 'If you read the tabloids you might assume the worst and be very angry after-dinner mints'."

Several of the students grinned, but Catherine was offended. "Don't mock!" she said. "Immigration's a serious problem! I mean, for one thing, it must be very difficult for some kids from this country going to school, when there are a whole load of kids in their class who can't even speak English! Surely either the local kids won't learn nearly so fast, because their teachers will have to give lots of their attention to the pupils who need most help, like the kids who need to learn English before they can do anything else, or else the kids who aren't good at English won't get the attention they need, because the teachers are helping the other kids most."

"That might be a problem, but the solution doesn't necessarily have to be to stop people coming here altogether," said Dave. "I mean, maybe foreign families who need it could be sent to classes where they could learn English, before their kids go into ordinary classes. Anyway, I don't know that much about it; but I agree with Anne that people should make sure they really know the facts before criticising."

Anne was pleased someone agreed with her, but a bit dismayed that she thought she'd just been talking about how she didn't like opinionated conversations about immigration, and lo and behold, one had immediately started. It stopped being serious fairly soon though.

Stuart said, "I don't think people should be allowed into this country unless they can speak English."

Emma replied, "Why not? You couldn't speak it when you first arrived here."

"Yes I could!" said Stuart heatedly. "I'm English! . . . Well alright, I'm half-Scottish; but I've lived here since I was really little."

Emma said with a grin, "What I'm saying is that when you first arrived in this country, you were a tiny baby, who couldn't say a thing. It took you a few years to learn English. So why can't foreigners have the same chance to learn, just because they're older when they come here?

"I personally think people who aren't good at English, or who can speak it but they have an accent that makes it hard to understand them, shouldn't be allowed to work in jobs where communication's important to people's well-being, at least till their English improves. I'm thinking of jobs like doctors who have to tell people what to do, or care workers who need to understand what people who are ill and have a lot of needs want from them, at a time when those people have got enough to cope with without worrying about not being able to communicate well with the person looking after them; But banning people who can't speak English from the country altogether sounds a bit harsh, especially since people can take classes here. And just think of all the jobs their presence here could create for teachers of English as a second language!

"I've heard that governments think immigration's actually good for the economy, especially because when it's legal, immigrants with jobs will be paying taxes, so governments will get more money. And they'll spend part of it on the health service and education and things, so that'll be good for us.

I even heard someone say that young healthy single immigrants with no children who come here to work are less of a burden on the country than native people who live here, because they don't need to use the schools, and barely need to use the health service, and most of them will probably leave before they get old and in need of care."

Dave joked, "Gosh, don't say that too loud, or you'll have governments wanting to encourage more healthy young immigrants to come here, and trying to kick all the people who are native to this country out! . . . Or trying to encourage them to emigrate to other countries before they get old!"

They giggled.

Then James said with a grin, "I heard a couple of cats screeching outside my window the other night, and later I'm sure I heard a fox, disturbing my sleep. I wish those were all illegal immigrants, from places called Catland and Foxland and things, and they could all be sent back there!"

Jackie said, "Someone gave me a nice big cake the other day, and I took it out of its packet to cut a bit off, and found it hard to get it back in the packet again at first. I said to it, 'Get back where you came from!' wanting it to get back in the packet. If someone had overheard me from outside the door, they might have thought I sounded like an angry person insulting an immigrant, and come in all ready to have a go at me. Imagine if all cakes came from a country called Cake Country, and no one ever had any cake except if they travelled there. But then imagine if some cakes came here and claimed political asylum, and marched into a benefits office to claim benefits."

"There would be a simple solution if people didn't like that!" said Colin, chuckling. "All the people who objected to cake immigrants claiming benefits could just eat them!"

"But imagine what civil liberties groups would have to say about that!" said Mya with a grin. "You'd hear them on the radio declaring, 'Cakes have the right not to be eaten!'"

Suzy said, "Maybe the cakes would give people permission to eat them. Just think! They might be huge big things, on massive cake legs, with great big cake arms! A bit like life-sized jelly babies or gingerbread men! But their arms might be made of cream sponge cake, twice as thick as human arms, and some of their heads might be covered in marzipan and icing! Some of them might have icing all over them!"

The students thought that sounded yummy. Dave said, "Imagine eating a whole cake head at once! Wouldn't that be nice!"

"I think you might be sick for a few days afterwards if you ate something that big!" laughed Kirsty. "Still, you wouldn't feel as bad as you would if you tried to eat an entire life-size cake body!"

The Conversation Turns to Discussion of How Depressing the News Is and How It's Fun to Talk About Things Like Scientific Discoveries Instead

The students chuckled. But that was the end of the jokes for a little while; Anne wanted to continue her depressing tale to the end, and said,

"I wish the women I've been talking about had joked around like that instead of wanting to talk about depressing things in the news so much! I don't know why people want to do that; I mean, there's nothing we can do about the problems we hear about on the news, so I don't see the point of hearing about them again from ordinary members of the public."

One student, Sarah, said, "My mum gets depressed about bad news and things like that nowadays; she never used to much. She used to be interested in documentaries about problems in the world and tragedies in history, and that kind of thing, but she says she can't watch them now without feeling down afterwards. If we're watching one and she's in the room, she'll walk out. She thinks it might be to do with the menopause making her feel more moody or something. Or one day she said she wondered if it was just old age creeping up on her, and she just didn't have the resilience she used to have to be able to tolerate hearing about things like that without feeling depressed."

Some of the students looked at Anne, as if scrutinising her for signs of ageing. She must have realised what they were thinking, because she said, "Well I get depressed about that kind of thing, and I'm only 18!"

Some of the other students started feeling a bit depressed, as she carried on talking about what her mum's friends had said.

Then Heather asked, "Why do some people like talking about the horrible things in the news so much? I mean, just think! If those women Anne was with had read popular scientific magazines instead of newspapers, then instead of filling their minds with gruesome stories about crime and things, they could have been filling them with information about the latest medical advances, and useful new gadgets that were being invented, and the latest in space exploration, and other discoveries! They could have talked about those things instead! That would have been interesting! I mean, some medical advances might help paralysed people walk again soon, and there might even be driverless cars one day, and all kinds of other things are going on!"

Matthew said, "There are some spoof newspapers on the Internet with science sections, reporting on pretend scientific discoveries. It would have been fun if your mum's friends had all read that kind of thing, and told each other what they'd read, Anne! There was an article the other day in one that said scientists have discovered that regular cannabis smoking improves the part of the brain that's there to help people make excuses when they're trying to avoid having to take responsibility for things they've done wrong; if they smoke the strongest kind every day, it said they become 84 % better at inventing excuses; and they're not convincing excuses, but people like them anyway because they're creative. Like, someone who didn't pay his council tax might say he was going to, but just then a massive fierce wild boar somehow seemed to come out of nowhere and jumped into his garden, and he spent all day trying to chase it out."

The Students Start Telling Each Other Funny News Stories

Suzy grinned and said, "It's not just spoof news that can be funny. I found a real news publication online that's got a funny news section. One story was about a Belgian man who got sent a speeding ticket for supposedly driving his mini at over two thousand miles an hour, which is three times the speed of sound! The police apologised for issuing it later, and said there had been a mistake.

"And there was a story about a newspaper advert, where a woman advertised her brother for sale. The advert was put in the miscellaneous items section for things being sold for under fifty dollars. She got lots of phone calls, one even asking if she could lower the price. It turned out that she'd told the newspaper she wanted to sell her Brother sewing machine, and the paper had left the last detail out.

"And one story was about an Italian man who stole an ambulance from outside a hospital, parked it outside his girlfriend's house, turned the siren on, and started singing love songs to her. Neighbours called the police to complain about the noise, and when they came, he told them he couldn't play a musical instrument, and had wanted some musical accompaniment while he sang to serenade her."

Becky said, "I've read some funny news stories. One was about a man who got a gas bill for over two trillion three hundred billion pounds. It said it was a final demand and the bill had to be paid in full immediately or he'd be taken to court. The man tried phoning the gas company up to protest, but he couldn't get to speak to anyone, and he eventually thought of going to court and offering to pay the whole bill at the rate of a penny a week. But after the media got involved, the company admitted it was a mistake, and said it had been caused by a computer error.

"And I read about a pensioner who once called the police in the middle of the night and complained about loud music that was keeping her awake. She thought one of her neighbours must be causing a nuisance. But when the police arrived, they found the noise was coming from her own radio, that she'd put in the back garden during the day; she'd gone inside and left it playing at full volume, and then forgotten about it. One of her neighbours said she was often playing her music as loud as that and disturbing them, so it was good that she'd been woken up by it, since it would teach her what it was like for other people to have to hear it when they didn't want to.

"And then there were neighbours who called the police thinking they could hear screaming from a house next door, only for the police to find it was a pensioner practising for a yodelling exam. The police said that either the neighbours couldn't be used to the sound of the songs she was yodelling, or she wasn't very good at it!

"And one story I read was about a cat called Thomas who must have been put on some kind of mailing list as a joke once, because he kept getting credit card offers, offers of free Internet surfing time, and other things, addressed to Thomas Cat. One was an 18 inch tube with an advert for a local gym inside, including a poster of a musclebound human body, headed with the words, 'Thomas, this is what we'll do for you this year'. Once the cat even got an offer of a 250 thousand pound loan."

Anne Talks More About Conversations She Really Didn't Like Listening To and Explains Just Why

Anne's face lit up with delight at the thought of the women she'd been with having talked about articles like that every time she was with them, instead of depressing things. She laughed and said, "Oh it would have been so much fun if my mum's friends had talked about things like that all the time instead of about bad news!"

But quickly she became very serious again, looked a bit irritated, and continued her gloomy tale, as if a powerful magnet was drawing her irresistibly into misery mode and attracting her to the story. She said:

"Anyway, it wasn't just gruesome stuff in the news that those women seemed to like talking about their opinions of. They said other things that sounded a bit heartless sometimes. One thing that bugged me was when one day, someone talked about a friend of hers who'd got breast cancer, and she said the friend hadn't gone for screening tests like mammograms, and she said, 'So she's only got herself to blame for it'. I mean, the person who said it was a bit upset about her friend being ill, I think, but still, why would anyone say a thing like that? I mean, the only way her friend would have been to blame for her cancer is if she'd deliberately swigged a bottle of cancer-causing toxic chemical!"

Colin had just picked his drink up to swig it had it almost to his mouth, but put it down again at that without tasting it. He picked it up again later when the conversation was a bit more light-hearted, when all that the students were talking about was companies putting crushed beetles in certain food products or something.

Dave said, "It might be in bad taste to mention this now, but that reminds me of a comedy sketch I heard, where two men were ordering drinks that would make them look tough, trying to outdo each other. I can't remember quite what they said, but it went something like this:

"One said, 'A pint of whisky please!' and the other one said, 'Just whisky? You wimp! A pint of bleach please'. And the other one said, 'Oh you wimp! A pint of petrol please'. The other one said, 'Only petrol? You big weak-kneed wimp! A pint of liquefied ear wax please.' The other one said, 'What? You wimp! A pint of chilli peppers please!' And the other one said, 'You're the real wimp round here! A pint of squashed maggots please!' The other one said, 'That's pathetic, you wimp! A pint of rat poison please!' The other one said, 'You massive wimp! A pint of nerve gas please!' And the other one said, 'Oh, you wimp! A pint of cancer please!' The other one said, 'What? You wimp! A pint of nuclear fuel please!' And it went on and on like that … Sorry Anne. Carry on."

Oblivious to the fact that she'd just put Colin off his drink, and smiling briefly at what Dave had just said, but then looking serious again, Anne continued, "What I was saying is that it isn't fair to blame people for getting cancer because they didn't go for cancer screening, and that kind of thing, like the woman I'm talking about did.

"For one thing, her friend might not have gone for screening for what she thought was a good reason, like because she thought she was in a low-risk group, for whatever reason, or she was scared of being diagnosed wrongly, or knew that some people get given major cancer treatment when they don't really need it, because what's showing up in the screening is a cancer that's so slow-growing that the person will likely be dead before it can do them any harm, but it's indistinguishable from something major so it gets the same treatment – apparently that happens sometimes; or she might have worried that the test would be painful, or she was really busy, or she didn't go for screening for some other reason. And it wasn't as if not going was a direct cause of the cancer! So it wasn't fair to blame her for getting it!

"So I'm saying that some of those people my mum wanted me to socialise with, who seemed nice and friendly at first, turned out to have some pretty chilling attitudes when you got to know them a bit better! And when they were talking about things in the news, I wouldn't have minded if they'd just talked without really thinking about what they were saying just a few times, but it was quite often. The ones who used to talk like that didn't seem to think of finding out more, or investigating more than one side of things before making up their minds a lot of the time. The fact that they didn't seem to know much about a subject or can't have thought it through that well didn't stop them forming a strong opinion about it and talking about it a lot! Probably because they didn't realise how few things they really knew about it, and that it would have been a good idea to have found out more before forming an opinion. I mean, isn't there a saying that goes something like, 'The more I find out, the more I realise I don't know'?"

It occurred to Jackie, who didn't understand why Anne wanted to tell them all that, that there might also be a saying that went, "The more I find out, the more I know that I wish I didn't know", and that that could probably be applied to what Anne was telling them.

Just then, Dave accidentally dropped a bit of paper his lunch had been wrapped in on the floor. He seemed to be taking quite a long time to pick it up, head under the table; and Jackie wondered if he felt the same way as she did, and was trying to hide from whatever other information they might be about to hear. She smiled at the idea that it would be funny if all the students suddenly jumped up and ran off to hide from what Anne was saying; she wondered what Anne would think when she found herself suddenly alone without warning! Still, she kept her thoughts to herself, as Anne continued:

"And just in case anyone's wondering why I didn't take the initiative to start conversations about nicer things instead, so they wouldn't have had so much chance to talk about things I didn't like hearing, or why I didn't dispute what they were saying to try to change their minds, I never really wanted to get into discussions with them about their opinions on things in the news, partly because it would have been difficult to get a word in edgeways because some of them were very talkative, but partly because I often hoped to enjoy myself when I went there, and didn't want to join in conversations about subjects like that, which would have maybe caused arguments. Anyway I prefer to listen to the whole of what someone's got to say about something, rather than assuming there isn't any more to their opinion than they've just said and chiming in quickly to disagree with them. But that meant I would listen till they changed the subject, so it would have been too late to say something even if I'd wanted to."

Actually, no one had been wondering why Anne hadn't spoken up more. She'd mentioned it because she was used to being questioned like that by her family if ever she said she hadn't liked a conversation, and she expected the same again; but actually, Colin was wondering why it felt as if he had a stone in his shoe when he hadn't been walking anywhere stony, Stuart was thinking he wasn't looking forward to getting down to writing an essay that evening, Suzy was laughing at a student she'd spotted on the other side of the room trying to chew a bit of his lunch that had been way too big to have fitted into his mouth all at once, Becky had just started wondering what would happen if she took the bag her lunch had come in into her next lecture, made a paper plane out of it and hurled it towards the tutor in the middle of a boring bit, and several of the students were sympathising with her – Anne, that is.

Far more talkative than usual, Anne continued, "But having said all that, I wouldn't want anyone to think being with them was all bad, because it certainly wasn't; they could be nice and kind sometimes, and there were times when I did enjoy their company. It was just that I felt a bit down when I left them sometimes because of the things I've mentioned. I liked it much better when they were talking about their own personal experiences than I did when they were getting annoyed and making judgments about things in the news. They could be interesting when they talked about things that happened to them in the past.

"In fact it's a shame: I've often thought that older people must be full of stories about interesting things that have happened to them over the years; and when they die, the stories in them are all lost, and it's a pity; so it's nice if you can get them to tell you all about them before they die. I wish I'd spoken to my grandparents more before they died.

"Actually, I heard someone say the other day that old people have probably accumulated quite a bit of wisdom over the years, and it can be good if they can have a think about it all and pass on the lessons they've learned before they go. I wish the women I'd been with had thought of doing that, and I wish I'd asked them about it. I mean, a few of them might have had some pretty unwise opinions about some of the things in the news they talked about, but they might still have had worthwhile things to say about other things. It makes me sad to think I could have learned some decent things from them but didn't."

Though some of the students were interested in what Anne was saying, one or two of the less sensitive ones began to think it was beginning to sound like a whinge, or an essay, or some kind of miserable reminiscence about the bad old days from someone who must have turned old and bitter before her time; or they thought maybe she was someone who'd forgotten it was supposed to be a light-hearted lunch, and imagined she was in a counselling session and they were all her counsellors, who she thought were helping her come to terms with her past.

Poor Anne; she'd have been better off confiding her story to a close friend over a private cup of tea than burdening a dozen or so people with it who she had no evidence wanted to hear it; and if she'd been entirely sober, she'd have realised that. Normally, she wouldn't have dreamed of telling them all that.

As it was, though most were sympathetic, a few students wondered if in reality, she was just as judgmental as the people she was condemning for judgmentalism were, considering all the criticisms she was making of them. They'd thought the conversation was supposed to be about eyeballs anyway, the first topic that had been brought up over lunch. They hoped she wasn't about to get to that bit, like perhaps complaining that one day, all the women's eyeballs had come flying out when they sneezed, or rolled out because the women were falling to bits with age or something. Those students began to accidentally put themselves off their food with the thoughts that flickered through their minds.

Anne Finally Gets to the End of Her Sad Story

They soon found out that the end of the story wasn't quite that gruesome though. Anne said, "Anyway, after I started feeling a little bit depressed and restless after listening in on my mum's friends' conversations most afternoons for a few weeks,

I decided it would be nicer being with one of my friends, so I asked one if I could go to her house every afternoon for a while, and she said I could.

"So one day, I mentioned to the woman whose house my mum and her friends and I met in after the others had gone that I wasn't going to go there for a couple of weeks because I'd arranged to go to a friend's house. She said something like, 'Oh, you'd prefer being with your friend than being with us, would you? Don't you like being with us?' I was foolish enough to mention a bit of what I've just told you – not much, just a little bit; I was put on the spot, and thought I ought to answer the question and explain things, but I wasn't thinking about how to word things as carefully as I could so as not to offend her, or about how I could balance anything critical I said with positive things, like you're supposed to if you criticise someone, so they can at least be happy with some of the things you say. I didn't even know that's what people are supposed to do then. And I didn't even realise she'd be offended by what I said.

"All I really said was that I sometimes felt a little bit depressed straight after being there just for a little while, because I preferred conversations where my brain was getting a workout to ones about upsetting things in the news, and I'd prefer to be doing something that gave me a sense of achievement than chatting. I didn't expect her to be offended by what I said, since it was just the truth about the way I felt; I said it in an unguarded moment, thinking she'd understand. She didn't ask me any questions that would help her understand better; she just said they wouldn't want me to feel down, so if I wanted to go I should go.

"But a couple of weeks later when I went back with my mum, I ended up in an argument, because a couple of the women, who she'd obviously told, as well as telling them good-ness knows what else that she'd read into what I said, said they didn't think it was nice of me to have said they weren't good enough for me and that I'd prefer brainier company, and that they got me down. That wasn't really what I'd meant at all when I said what I'd said. I hadn't even said or even thought that me feeling a bit down sometimes was anyone's fault!

"And I didn't think it was very nice that instead of caring that I'd said I'd got a little bit depressed sometimes, they seemed to think it was an insult, and got offended by it. I don't know why; I mean, for one thing, they would talk about things in the news like murders and wars and child abuse sometimes, and I wonder what kind of person wouldn't get depressed by conversations about that kind of stuff! I don't understand why anyone actually wants to talk about it. But one or two seemed to actually enjoy mentioning things about crime in the papers, and having a chinwag with the others about how shocking it was! For whatever reason, one or two would sit with news-papers in front of them, and actually announce tragic news as they came across it. How they kept cheerful, I've no idea! I don't know why anyone wants to do that. I'd find it too upset-ting to actually seek that stuff out and read it every day, let alone repeat it!"

Kirsty voiced a question that a couple of them were think-ing, saying, "Um, do you really think you're going into the right career? I mean, if you end up as a therapist, you might have people telling you depressing things all day!"

Anne replied, "Yes, but at least you're trying to change things for the better if you're a therapist, so you've got hope that things are improving. Anyway, I don't want to go into the kind of therapy where the therapist encourages the client to dredge up everything that upset them in the past for hours; I want to do the kind of therapy where you hardly ask them any questions about their past, but they only tell you what they choose to tell you, and most of the therapy session's about talking through things to do to try to change things for the better in future."

Anne continued to do what one or two students thought sounded like dredging up things from her own past, saying, "Anyway, the group of people I was with never asked why I'd said I got a bit depressed sometimes; they just resented me for having said it, it seems – or at least I think a few of them did.

"It just shows you how careful you've got to be sometimes with what you say, and how things you say can be twisted, and turn into unpleasant rumours! I was a bit upset, because it must have looked as if after they'd been kind to me, I'd kind of just thrown it back in their faces, insulting them and saying they weren't as good as me. I decided to always say as little as I could get away with to the woman who'd told them I said those things after that, in case anything else I said got twisted like that.

"And one woman who'd been kind to me stopped going there soon afterwards, and someone told me the first time she wasn't there when I was that she'd been upset by what I'd said, as if that was the reason why she'd stayed away; and then the woman got seriously ill and never came back; so I worried that she'd left the group because of what I'd said, and that the last impression she'd got of me was that I'd said bad things about her after she'd been kind to me; and I thought she might never come back, so I wouldn't be able to make things up with her; so I was a bit unhappy about that. Actually, she was one of the ones who didn't talk much about depressing things in the news. I thought for a while after she stopped coming that she'd probably come back again soon and I could make things up with her then. But she didn't. And a few months later, she died, without me ever seeing her again."

The students sympathised with Anne for a moment. Even when Matthew had a sudden craving for chocolate fudge, he didn't say anything, because he thought interrupting the sympathetic silence to tell everyone that or announce he was going to get some would sound insensitive. So thoughts of chocolate fudge went around and around in his brain, till he thought the conversation had become less serious again and he could get away with it without disapproval.

He wasn't the only one at risk of sounding insensitive though. Emma risked being thought so by saying to Anne, "You say all this happened about five years ago. I'm wondering why you're still upset about it all this time later?"

Anne thought for a minute, and then said, "I'm not really upset any more, although I still get annoyed when I think about it sometimes, or regret what happened. Maybe it never really got out of my system because I didn't have anyone to confide in about it at the time – I'm sure my mum wouldn't have approved of me telling her what I thought about her friends, and a lot of my classmates at school were interested in completely different things than me, like fashion and celebrities and boys, so I don't think they'd have been interested in taking the time to listen; and I would have felt bad talking about it anyway, because it would have felt as if I was betraying those women in a way, since after all, they were mostly nice to me.

"So I never got my feelings off my chest. Actually, maybe I would have got them off it if I 'd written about them, not for anyone to read, but just to let off steam, for my own benefit. But I didn't think to do that, so they always just stayed around in the back of my mind, I suppose, just coming back to annoy me every once in a while when something reminds me of them, like it did today. It just bothers me that just a bit of badmouthing and misunderstanding can ruin some relationships forever!"

The Conversation Turns to Talk of Unfortunate Misunderstandings and Funny Ideas

Some of the students became thoughtful. But Becky said, "I've heard about misunderstandings that lead to arguments. I've read that sometimes it can happen especially often when people come from different cultures, so some people use expressions that people from the other cultures don't know they have, which means that some phrases can mean things they don't know they mean.

"I found a website once where someone said she was in a marriage break-up with her Arabic husband – I think her own parents had been immigrants from Morocco or somewhere, and Arabic was a second language for her, but she wasn't familiar with all the slang and everyday usage it's got – and she said that one day, she sighed to her husband, 'I wish I had a magic fairy wand that really works', and it started a three-day argument. She said something like, 'Only him and the heavens will ever know what kind of rude meaning that translated to in Arabic in his mind!'

"And there was a little story on the page that showed just how different the expressions that people often use can be in different countries; it said one Lebanese Arabic phrase is 'Don't get a mind', which means don't worry about it; but if anyone said that to someone in this country, they might think they were being insulted by someone who thought they didn't have a brain, and that if they did, they'd be dangerous or something, so it was better that they didn't. But then we do use a very similar phrase, 'Never mind'."

Catherine said, "Yes, but when people use it that way, mind means worry or care, like if you said, 'I hope you don't mind me slurping when I drink.' "

All the students looked at Becky, thinking, "Does she slurp when she drinks?"

Becky replied to Catherine, "That's true. Maybe the word's got the same double meaning in Arabic as it has in English, so it means both the mind and to care about."

Heather said, "Actually, I don't think it's really a double meaning; I think the word 'mind', when it's used like that, is short for 'be mindful of', which means having thoughts of it going through your mind."

"I don't know," said Becky. "What about child minders? They're not there just to sit there thinking about the babies and children they're supposed to be looking after."

Several students laughed, and thought the subject was interesting.

Colin said, "I once heard a diplomat or politician talking on the radio, saying that once he was talking in the European Parliament to an Italian politician who didn't know English well, so his words were being translated through an interpreter. The conversation wasn't going well, and the man on the radio telling the story said he'd tried to tell the Italian politician that he didn't think it made good sense for the Italian government to wash its dirty laundry in public. Anyone in Britain would instantly know that meant that things it would be better to keep private shouldn't be aired in public. But perhaps they don't have that saying in Italy. When the Italian politician heard the interpretation, he erupted in rage! It turned out that the interpretation of the phrase he was given said the Italian government was being compared to a public laundry that washed people's dirty underwear."

The students laughed.

Then Dave said, "I've made one or two daft mistakes by accident sometimes, once in an exam. I meant to say Catherine the Great ruled Russia, but I looked over my paper after I'd finished, and realised I'd written, 'Catherine the Grape rules Russia'. I don't know what I could have been thinking when I wrote that, except that I had called her that in fun sometimes in lessons. It both changed her name, and said she still rules today! That must be the longest reign ever in that case, considering she was born in 1729! It was a good thing I spotted the mistake so I could correct it!"

Kirsty said, "That reminds me of an email I got from someone once, where someone said she was sorry she hadn't spoken to me much when we'd last met, but she was tied up with a fiend. She'd accidentally left the R out of friend. I wrote back and said being tied up with a fiend must have been a terrible experience, and how did she get loose? I'm not sure she quite got the joke. She might not have noticed that the R was missing from the word 'friend'. I think people see what they expect to see when they read things sometimes, so even proof-readers can miss things. I read about one Hamlet play script that said, 'To be or to be', instead of what Hamlet was supposed to say, 'To be or not to be', and apparently six professional proof-readers missed it!"

Suzy said, "That reminds me of how just one bit of punctuation missing or in the wrong place can completely change the meaning of a sentence. I know someone who bought a t-shirt for their mum's mum, and at the top it said, 'Let's eat Grandma!' Underneath that, it said, 'Let's eat, Grandma', with a comma after the word 'eat'. And below that, it said, 'Commas save lives.'"

They laughed.

Mya said, "I read that in some countries there's a World Teachers' Day every year. One year, someone wrote to a newspaper saying, 'Ways to celebrate World Teachers' Day include balloons broadcasting the names of teachers sent aloft by students.' It sounds as if the person meant some teachers had been sent flying into the sky. A comma halfway through the sentence after it said 'teachers' for the second time would have made it clearer they were talking about the balloons being sent aloft . . . Well, I presume they were anyway. Maybe not."

They laughed again.

Then one of Becky's good friends, Charlotte, who'd been quiet up till then, changed the subject slightly by saying, "That was a horrible storm we had last night, wasn't it! It probably knocked my old headmistress's hat off again if she was out in it. She told us about the first time that happened in assembly once. I hope she wasn't expecting us to feel sorry for her, because we all laughed instead, especially when she said she had to go chasing it down the road . . . Actually, she was smiling when she told us, so I don't think she can have minded us laughing.

"Oh well, it was at least just as well the wind wasn't a hurricane, otherwise it might not have just been her hat that went flying! It would have been funny if we'd all been sitting in assembly at school one day when she came sailing in through the window! One of the teachers might have said, 'You didn't want to use your normal method of transport to come in to school today then?' "

Becky giggled. She said, "That would have been a funny sight to see! Imagine if all the kids got blown into school too though! Imagine if someone was walking past the school, and they saw loads of kids flying across the playground, and neatly flying into the school! They might think that either they'd suddenly gone mad and started seeing things, or that the children in the school must all have magical powers!"

Charlotte grinned and said, "Well, either that or they'd guess it was the wind making them fly!"

Becky grinned and said, "Yeah, that's quite possible actually; but just imagine if it was a strange weather phenomenon that hardly ever happened, where the hurricane was only happening inside the playground and nowhere else, and even just outside it, there was hardly any wind at all!"

Charlotte said, "Wouldn't that be weird! . . . Actually though, aren't tornadoes a bit like that, only doing damage to a small area?

"Hey you know they give hurricanes human names? Well imagine if they named a hurricane Gail. So the weather forecasters would call it Hurricane Gail, and some people might be a bit confused about which of those it was going to be."

Becky and the other students chuckled. But then Becky said, "I read that in America, where they give hurricanes names, they've found that more people get injured when a storm's got a girl's name than when it's got a boy's name. When I first heard that, I thought, 'What kind of freaky thing would cause that!'

"But then the next sentence I heard said that the reason is that some people take fewer safety precautions when the hurricane's got a girl's name, because they don't expect it to be as threatening as it sounds if it's got a boy's name. I don't know why they don't start giving them all boys' names in that case.

"I actually heard someone on the telly once, who lived somewhere where a lot of people had just suffered because of a nasty hurricane, saying that you just don't expect a storm with a girl's name, like Cathy or something, to be this really strong wind that does a whole lot of damage.

"Mind you, I think some of the worst storms on record have happened to have girls' names, so the number of injuries is probably partly to do with that too."

Dave joked, "I don't see why hurricanes have to be named after humans at all. Why not name them after, say, animals, like Hurricane Tiger. Or Hurricane Cockroach. They could have Hurricane Vicious Squirrel. Hurricane Aggressive Rabbit. Hurricane Angry Kangaroo. Hurricane Toxic Frog.

"Or maybe they could be named after fruit. So they could have Hurricane Nectarine. Hurricane Raspberry. Hurricane Raisin. Hurricane Orange. Hurricane Banana. Or maybe they could be named after household objects, like Hurricane Microwave. Hurricane Computer. Hurricane Desk. Hurricane Carpet. Hurricane Hairbrush."

Becky laughed and said, "I think a lot more people would have trouble taking them seriously then! Maybe they could be named after horrible human conditions, like Hurricane Anxiety, Hurricane Brutal, Hurricane Crisis, Hurricane Despair, Hurricane Evil, Hurricane Frightening, Hurricane Grotesque, Hurricane Hideous, Hurricane Infuriating, and so on."

Charlotte smiled and said, "It might be fun for the weather people to think up names like that! Maybe lots of other people would want to join in suggesting them for fun too!

"Hey you know, I was walking back to my room in the beginnings of that horrid storm we had last night, and it was starting to rain. When I got in, I remembered I had some bits of paper with things on in my pocket, and I hoped they hadn't got wet. They hadn't, thankfully. But while I was checking, I just imagined how it would be if I'd been absent-mindedly walking back with my pocket as wide open as it could get, and the rain went in it, but it didn't drain out again, so when I got back in my room, I discovered I had a pocket full of rain!"

Becky grinned and said, "Wow! And if frogs or little fish came down in the rain, they might be swimming around in your pocket! Imagine if you had a pet cat. You might sit down to relax, and it would come and drink the water out of your pocket, and eat the fish while it was doing it."

Charlotte grinned and said, "Yikes! And imagine if the fish had some kind of electrical magnetic connection to the sky, so they were drawn there by it somehow, and that's how they got up there in the first place, and they only got pushed down to Earth by the pressure of the rain, but when the pressure of it on them stopped, they were always going to go back up there; so when the cat swallowed them, they started rising up to the sky again, and they took the cat with them! Imagine if the cat went higher and higher into the sky, and then it was carried along by the wind, and everyone who was around at the time felt sure they saw a flying cat! Maybe they'd think it must be a brand new species of animal, that scientists would probably name a cat-bird!"

Becky chuckled and said, "I get the impression you don't like cats, thinking it would be funny to see them flying like that!"

Charlotte smiled and said, "Well I get the impression you don't like fish, joking about a cat eating them like you did!"

Becky said, "Actually I'm not keen on fish. Hey do you know, if I'm remembering rightly, the French word for fish is spelled in a very similar way to our word for poison. I think it's just got another S. Imagine if you got a job as a waitress in a restaurant, and everything on the menu was in French, just to make it sound more exotic, because the owners hoped that would mean people would be willing to pay more for things if they sounded exotic; and someone was taking a while making up their mind what to have, so you thought you'd try recommending something to them, and the only thing you thought you could pronounce was the word for fish, because you hadn't been trained to pronounce things properly, so you pronounced it wrongly and said, 'Would you like a plate of poison, sir?' "

Charlotte laughed. She said, "I don't think I'd have that job for very long, somehow!"

Becky smiled and said, "No! Mind you, at least you wouldn't be offering them real poison . . . well, hopefully not! I suppose in some restaurants, you can never quite be sure, what with bad hygiene practices!"

Charlotte agreed. She said, "Ugh! That's not very nice to think about!"

Colin said, "I've heard some funny stories about some British people abroad trying to speak the languages of the countries they were in. There was one who accidentally asked for a caesarean section in a restaurant, thinking she was asking for cheese on toast, since the words are very similar. And another person got angry with a man and shouted at him that she insisted he give her a recipe, because she thought the word she used meant receipt, because it was very similar to our word for receipt."

James said, "I heard about a tourist who went on holiday to Denmark, and saw some chocolate mice in a sweet shop that were called Scum; but I met a Danish person, and I asked if she'd heard of them, and she said she hadn't. I suppose they might have just been pronounced a bit differently."

Catherine said, "You know, it's not just wording and things like that where misunderstandings and other embarrassing things can happen; they can be caused because of different customs, such as one where making a lot of eye contact while you're talking is considered friendly in some cultures and rude in others. It seems to me that if anyone wants to go to another country, not only should they learn the language, but they should learn a bit about the country's culture and customs, and what they think is polite and bad manners and things like that over there, so they're prepared. Mind you, even that won't protect people against all misunderstandings.

"You know there used to be a feature on Radio one called Embarrassing Stories, where people would send in stories about funny things that had happened to them, and one would be read out every weekday in the early afternoon? I heard one by a Dutch woman who said that when she was younger, she spent some time in England, and when she first got here, she was feeling a bit down one day because it was an unfamiliar environment with so many new things to get used to, and she was having dinner in this canteen or somewhere, and she got her dinner, and she saw something that looked nice and brightly-coloured, so she thought she'd put it on her dinner to cheer herself up. She was told a bit later it was custard!"

Some of the students giggled, and then Catherine continued, "And I heard about an immigrant to America from Malaysia who stayed with an American family when she first went there. When she first tried to have a good wash, she made a mistake, because she'd never seen some of the things people in the West use in bathrooms. In Malaysia when people wanted a wash, she said they just used to tip water over themselves outside. That's alright in a tropical country, where you won't freeze half to death if you stand in your garden and just pour water over yourself!

"But she went into an American bathroom, and wondered where the drain holes were in the floor, since she assumed Americans just tipped water over themselves too, only indoors. She couldn't find any holes, but thought Americans must just use a higher technology that would get rid of the water without them. So she scooped water out of the sink, and poured it over herself onto the floor, time after time. But after a while, someone knocked on the door and said water was coming out underneath it. She opened the door and explained what had happened, and they cleaned it up together."

Most of the students had finished eating, but they didn't want to get up, as they were enjoying the conversation. So it carried on. In fact, it went on for so long that several of the ones who'd bought big lunches when they first came in decided it would be nice to buy more food.

One Student Tells the Rest About a Cultural Tradition That Might Have Been Started For Good Reasons But Which Has Unfortunate Effects

The students were interested in what Catherine was saying. She'd expected they would be. She was a talkative student, seemingly sure people were bound to want to know what she had to say, which they often did, since she could be interesting to listen to. But they didn't always feel so interested, especially when she'd been talking for a while, and because she would talk for just as long about trivial things, or specialised subjects that could only be of interest to people with unusual hobbies, as about things that would be of more widespread interest.

She was sometimes invited to social gatherings because the people organising them had heard her talk for some time about a subject they found interesting, and decided she must be a good conversationalist who people were bound to want to listen to so they'd enjoy being there more. Sometimes she did make the gatherings more interesting. But things didn't always go as planned. One evening, a man told her he was a bit late because his train had been delayed, just looking for a bit of sympathy. Half an hour later, as she continued to explain the relative merits and failings of train operators all across Europe, which she'd been doing all that time, he nodded off to sleep and dropped his drink in his lap. Some people would probably have found the topic very interesting. But all he'd been interested in throughout all the time she'd been talking was what food was going to be on offer that evening, because he felt as if he was in need of refreshment after his frustrating train journey.

Catherine had made some good friends at university. Sadly, her attempts to talk to other groups of friends hadn't gone so well. While if she got onto an interesting subject she was entertaining, unfortunately for her, she talked a lot whether she was being interesting or not, and she'd often been known to clear a small room of people, because some tended to jump up and leave quickly when she came in, perhaps because of their dislike of her habit of immediately grabbing the conversation as she approached and holding onto it for all it was worth, hogging it for a long long time, regardless of how deep in conversation the others had been and what they'd been talking about when she came in.

She didn't do that all the time, but she did it often enough that people would worry she was about to do it and take evasive action, even people who would invite her to social gatherings, while they were having matey conversations with close friends and didn't want to have them interrupted by her. It was a pity she didn't realise her conversation-hogging habit was off-putting, but everyone was too polite to tell her.

So she concluded they just didn't like her, and told Becky she was becoming a bit of a recluse in her spare time because people didn't like her for some reason she didn't understand, but she supposed her face simply didn't fit. Becky thought that it was probably just her mouth that didn't fit, but she kept her thoughts to herself.

Still, Catherine's talent for talking non-stop for ages like a radio – a strange one that was switched on by asking it a question or saying something else to it – came in handy when she was talking about something people wanted to hear, especially if they were quiet types themselves who didn't often have much to say, so there probably wouldn't have been much conversation if she hadn't been around.

She sensed the interest of the students right then, and misunderstanding the reason for it, not realising they would have preferred to listen to something amusing, she continued talking, as her food went cold, and a few others were put off theirs, saying:

"But I know misunderstandings can happen in more serious situations. I heard that in China, like in a lot of Asian countries, the idea of honour is very important, though it might not have quite such an ominous meaning there as in some other Asian countries, where there's a culture of families having very strict honour codes, and family members can be physically harmed or even killed for breaking them even in trivial ways, such as if a young woman strikes up a friendship with a man and her parents are angry because they think it brings shame on the family because some people might suspect her of flirting with someone other than the man she's been arranged to be married to.

"But I've heard that if someone's criticised in front of others in China, they consider it to be much more serious than people do in the West, because although in the West it might be seen as humiliating and it might cause resentment, in China, at least among the older generation and those who haven't adopted Western attitudes, it's considered a really serious breach of good manners, and people have gone out to get revenge because of what they've learned to think of as their loss of face sometimes after they've been publicly criticised.

"It doesn't even have to be criticism, but anything which – however unintentionally – might make a person feel shown up. I've heard that bosses have even punished workers for doing something that turned out to make the workers look better than them, or even just because a worker's had a better idea than them, and things like that.

"People have to be careful of what they say at work in some companies, it seems, because even making a suggestion at a meeting about how the boss could do things better could be seen as a loss of face for the boss, so they won't like it, whereas in the West, if the suggestion's good, a lot of bosses would be pleased, although not all of them. Honesty tends to be appreciated in the West, even if it means other people's bad ideas and decisions are criticised publicly; but that would be frowned on in China, because, if I understand correctly, it tends to be thought that the most important thing is that people get along with each other with no problems, at least in public, and it's thought of as important for nothing to disrupt a hierarchical structure, even in small ways, such as by a boss's policies being criticised by a worker in front of him.

"It's possible that those rules came in in the first place, however many hundreds or thousands of years ago they did, to try to stop bullying in the workplace, and to help make for a more friendly atmosphere, by discouraging conflict. But things can go over-the-top nowadays."

Some of the students were interested in what Catherine was saying. But one or two thought it sounded as if she was reciting an essay she'd written. Stuart decided to make fun of her, and said,

"You know, I'm wondering if anyone would prefer to hear about the biological structures of the finer points of the toenails of the greater whiskered newt, as compared to the exquisite points of the claws on the hind legs of the lesser spotted odorous dwarf rat, than they would to hear about this?"

A few of the students giggled. But no one said anything.

Then Anne and a few of the others got up to go to the class they had. All the others had their discussion classes at other times. They were lessons where the students, who'd been split into fairly small groups for discussions at the beginning of the term, would go to the room of the tutor they'd been assigned to, or to a classroom, and discuss what they'd recently been learning with them.

As Anne left, she joked, "I'm off to my appointment with boredom now – I mean, my class with Mr Rubbishman."

That wasn't really the tutor's name, naturally. It was just Anne's nickname for him, because she thought his class was pointless. Normally, she would have kept it to herself; but the few drinks she'd had had loosened her tongue. The others in the class felt the same way as her though.

(Part of the psychology degree was split into little sub-courses that were called modules. Everyone had to do what were considered to be the most important psychology topics, and an introductory overview of psychology as a whole, but then students had to do a certain number of modules on different aspects of psychology, such as the history of psychology, or psychology in business; and they could choose which ones they did, provided they did the number they were supposed to; and some of the modules turned out to be more interesting than others.)

Most of the rest of the students had no classes for the rest of the afternoon, so they carried on chatting.

Catherine wasn't to be deterred by the joke that had been made just before Anne and a few of the others got up to go about whether it would be more interesting to hear about newt's toenails – if they actually have such things – than what she was saying; and she wasn't deterred by the fact that it might have looked as if a few students had just got up and walked out because they didn't want to hear any more of what she had to say. She carried on:

"Anyway, the rules about honour in China probably differ according to where a person is in a hierarchy; it probably isn't seen as nearly so bad for a boss to criticise workers in public, or for a teacher to criticise a class of children in front of each other, as it is for it to be the other way around. But if people in authority think they're being made to look bad, it can be the worse for the person supposedly bringing dishonour on them, even if they're not doing it on purpose. That doesn't just go for criticism, but even doing better at them at something, or doing better than the authority figure forecast they would at something.

"So for example, someone told me that one year, a vice-mayor responsible for parks and recreation was ordered by authorities to get drownings in swimming pools in his area down from about 45 a year to 25. He started a big campaign where he recruited lots of life guards and did other things, and got drownings down to under fifteen. In the West, he'd have been praised, but he actually lost his job, because the authorities in China thought of it as making them lose face, because they thought it made things look as if the vice-mayor knew more about how to do the job than they did, because their prediction of the amount drowning could be reduced was an underestimate."

Mya said, "It's very difficult to believe things could really be as bad as that! Where did you hear this stuff?"

Catherine said, "I heard it from someone who lived in China for years. I took him to be a reliable source of information about their culture, but I suppose it's possible he got some things wrong. If you're wondering about what I'm saying, look up words like 'culture losing face China' on the Internet, and see if you find information similar to what I've been saying."

Catherine didn't wait for a response, but continued,

"According to what that man who lived in China said, people aren't brought up with a sense of how they shouldn't do bad things because they're plain wrong, or because they'll harm people or cause problems and that's not nice, but instead the morality they're taught is all about not doing things that could be publicly seen to reflect badly on them or others in some way, so as not to risk bringing shame on them or their families or communities by having others look down on them. In private it doesn't matter so much, so some take that as meaning they can do what they like, as long as people whose opinions they value don't find out, or as long as those around them – who after all might sometimes be a gang of criminals – don't disapprove. It's sad really. At least that's what I've heard."

A melancholy atmosphere began to come over the students. Charlotte started dreaming of eating a chocolate bar as comfort food. She decided to get one when there was a pause in the conversation and she could get up without looking rude. Then her mind wandered and she started imagining having such a giant chocolate bar that she was still eating it all the way through a talk by an outside speaker who'd been invited to give a lecture at the university that she was planning to go to the next evening, imagining she still hadn't finished it when she went back to her room afterwards.

But unconscious of the affect she was having, Catherine the talkative student continued:

"This kind of thing has meant Chinese companies have suffered in the past, and employees haven't been as creative as they could have been, because when they've been told to do something by their boss, they haven't wanted to upset him by coming up with ideas about how to do it better than they've been told to do it, or by asking for help if they couldn't do it, since not being able to do the job as well as expected would make them look incompetent and they'd lose face themselves, or if the boss didn't know how to do what he'd asked his employees to do so he couldn't help them when they asked for assistance, it would make him think he'd lost face himself.

If they haven't known how to do the job well, they've often thought the best thing to do was to do the job badly but say nothing about it, all the while giving the boss a lot of praise and flattery, since good relations have been seen as better than good performance, especially since the government's subsidised companies in the past, so they'd make money whether they did well or badly.

"So when people do business in China, it's worth them remembering that if they have any criticisms, or ideas that might make them look better than a Chinese boss, they should at least mention them in private, so the boss doesn't feel as if he's being made to look bad in front of others. That's good manners when it comes to criticism anyway, since people in the West don't like being criticised in public either. And after all, there can be jealousies in the West, so if, say, a boss who wasn't very nice took someone under his wing but then found they were performing better than him, he might feel jealous, and try to engineer their downfall in some way. But that kind of thing would be frowned on here, whereas it's more of a cultural norm in China."

Suzy said with a note of protest, "I've got a Chinese friend and she doesn't get all offended when someone disagrees with her, and she doesn't seem the type of person who'd think she could do something bad as long as she didn't think she'd be found out! She's a caring person!"

Catherine replied, "I'm not saying everyone from China's like that. I'm just saying there's a tradition of people being brought up with attitudes like that. But actually, I think a lot of the younger generation have more Westernised attitudes."

Colin said, "China's a powerhouse of industry. Things can't be all that bad, or they couldn't be as successful as they are."

Catherine said, "It's possible that things have improved a lot recently; and in any case, a lot of bosses and workers were likely to have always been good at their jobs."

The Students Start Having Fun Talking About Funny Stories and Misheard Song Lyrics

Dave said, "I heard about a Chinese man who must have thought he'd lost a lot of face; but he wasn't concerned about the face of the bosses of a company he'd bought something from, so I wonder how common that kind of thing really is; he sued a shop where he'd bought a very expensive belt, because it came undone twice during a business meeting he had with a female senior manager from a company in Canada, who was interviewing people in China, trying to find someone to help run some kind of immigration agency there. If he'd got the job, his company would have got loads of money. He'd actually been told that it was virtually certain he'd get the job, but when he shook hands with the manager, his belt suddenly came undone. The manager looked away in embarrassment. He apologised, and went to the bathroom to do it up again. He came out, and was in the middle of a conversation with her when his belt sprang undone again.

"He didn't get the job. He obviously wasn't all that concerned about preserving the reputation of the shop the belt came from; now he's suing them for the equivalent of £15000."

The students sniggered. Catherine was about to reply when James looked thoughtful and asked, "China's a dictatorship, isn't it?"

A few of them said they thought so, and then James said, "I heard about a dictator from some African country in the 1970s who had a mistress called Cecilia. There was a song around at the time called *Cecilia*, by Simon and Garfunkel, I think. It was about a relationship breaking up and then the two of them getting together again. I reckon the dictator must have been a bit paranoid, because he got annoyed because he thought the song was about his mistress, and that it made fun of their relationship. I mean, why would an American pop group be singing about the mistress of a dictator in some obscure African country?"

The students giggled, and Kirsty said with a grin, "Who knows! Actually I think I heard that song once. I seem to remember it does have a tropical vibe about it. Do you think that could be a bit suspicious?"

They laughed.

Then Dave said, "I was sauntering out to a lecture the other day when I walked past someone's window and heard a song they were playing, and there was a chorus where a line was repeated over and over again, and from where I was, it sounded a lot like it kept saying, 'Freed from mayo', as if it was talking about being freed from mayonnaise, you know, as if it was saying, 'I'm so happy! I've finally been freed from the evil clutches of mayonnaise!'

"Or it sounded as if it just might have said, 'dreams of mayo'. What kind of dreams would you have of mayonnaise? It was such a cheerful-sounding song that maybe the singer was dreaming of having a massive tankard of the stuff in front of him and piling it into his mouth by the spoonful, or just glugging it down like a drink, enjoying every minute of it. I can't say that's my idea of fun! No way!"

The students laughed, and some said things like, "Oh yuck!"

Then Emma said, "I misheard something myself the other day. It wasn't a song lyric, but just something someone said. I'd asked if she had any pets, and she said her family had a pond full of fish. We were in a cafe full of people all talking, so I couldn't hear what she was saying as clearly as I would have done otherwise, and at first I thought she said her family's got a pond full of pigs!"

They giggled.

The Students Joke About the Weather, Time Zones, Misheard Words and Other Things

Just then, someone came in, walked up to someone near the group of students and said loudly, "It's pouring with rain out there!"

Heather said in dismay, "Oh no! I hope it's stopped by the time we leave here!"

Jackie smiled and said, "It probably will have. After all, we're chatting so much, it might be late into the evening when we go!"

Becky grinned and joked, "The rain doesn't work to the clock like that, you know. I mean, it's not as if when it gets towards evening it thinks, 'Right, I've done my lot for one day! Time to clock off!' And then it stops."

Jackie chuckled and said, "Come on, you know what I mean! I was just thinking it might be some time before we leave, and the rain might only be a shower."

Charlotte smiled and said, "It would be good if the rain started and stopped punctually at certain times of day, so you could actually tell what the time was by it! But then if you walked into a different time zone, in countries where there are more than one, it might suddenly start raining on you again after it had just stopped doing that, and you might think, 'Oh no, there must be a bug in the rain that's making it behave abnormally!', before you realised you'd just gone into a different time zone, so it hadn't got late enough for it to stop there yet, or it was time for it to start again."

Stuart grinned and joked, "I bet there are lots of bugs out in the rain right now! But I doubt there are any with the capability to make it misbehave!"

Charlotte joked, "I meant a software bug. You know, the kind of thing that makes the rain soft.

"Anyway, I was thinking about time zones the other day. Like in America, I think there are several. I was wondering how that worked, like whether the time lines could go through the middle of houses, so it might, say, be midnight in one part of the house, but only 11 PM in another part of it, or whether someone could be in bed, and it would be midnight where their head was, but 1 o'clock in the morning where their feet were. Imagine it being one time when you were in your hall, and then you stepped into the kitchen and it was suddenly another time, a whole hour later, as if a single step had taken you an entire hour to do! Or imagine a mum going into the sitting-room where her kids were playing and telling them it was time for bed, and they said, 'Oh Mum! It's way too early to go to bed!', and she said, 'Go into your bedroom, and then you'll discover it's an hour later than you think.'

"And I wondered if some schools might be half in one time zone and half in another, so half the pupils would go home at one time, and half at another. And if the playground was in one time zone while their classes were in another, it might feel to them as if they were travelling back or forward in time every time they went out to play.

"But then I found out that the time zones change at the borders of states.

"But imagine what that must be like! Maybe it's possible to run several metres, and when you start it could be 4 o'clock, but where you finish up it could be 3 o'clock, so it's as if you ran so fast you went back in time!

"And in some places there surely have to be very thin lines where the time zone changes from one time to another, so you could stand on one of them with one foot in one time zone and one in another, or where it's even officially day-time where one of your feet is and night-time where the other one is.

"It would be interesting if you could have it dark on one side of a thin line and bright and sunny on the other one, because it was an hour earlier on the other side. It would be even more interesting if you could have season zones, so it could be winter on one side, and summer on the other, so you could stand on the line with your back freezing cold and getting snow on it, while your front got really hot in the bright sun and your face got sunburned. Maybe if you stayed there, your back would even get hypothermia and your front could get too hot!"

Becky grinned and said, "I think I prefer the world the way it is! Mind you, wouldn't it be good if when sunshine came into a house, it stayed there, so it was still nice and sunny there when it got dark outside, and to get rid of it, you'd have to open the window and let it out . . . Well, it wouldn't be so good in the winter, I suppose.

"Mind you, if the sun could get in without the window open, I suppose it would be able to get out with it shut too. It would at least be good if it was possible to capture some, like if we could put a big box up to the window and sunshine would go in it, and then we could shut the box and it would stay there, and then later when it was going dark, we could shut the curtains so it wouldn't just go out the window, and then we could open the box and have a load of sunshine wafting up out of it into the room.

"Or imagine if sometimes sundrops would fall out of the sky, that were a bit like raindrops, but when they fell on the ground, they'd burst apart, and sunshine would start shining up from the ground. So if it had been raining, you might hear what sounded like rain outside and think it must be still raining, but then you might discover it was really sundrops."

Charlotte said, "I heard big raindrops splattering against my window the other day, and then they stopped, and I thought, 'Oh, someone's just turned the rain off!' But then they started again. Then I remembered it isn't possible for people to just turn the rain off. Pity! . . . Well, I didn't really forget that; it's just that it seemed to stop so suddenly that that's what it sounded like."

Kirsty said, "Imagine if there were recommendations for things to do on some websites that have weather forecasts on them, and one day in the middle of March, there was one that said, 'It'll be a nice sunny day today, with a cold wind that'll make it feel delightfully bracing. Just the right conditions to go to the seaside and have a swim in the sea. It'll make you feel all sentimentally nostalgic, reminding you of those good old days when you were a child and you used to go to the beach with your parents, and you would say, "I'm cold! I don't fancy a swim!", and your kindly mother would say in irritation, "Stop moaning!" You must miss those days! So go on, bring back memories of the good old days by going for a swim today if you can!'"

Colin chuckled and said, " 'The good old days!' I know weather forecasts can be nuts sometimes, like when they say it's going to be cloudy all day and then there's lots of sunshine, or when they say it's going to be rainy and then it's totally dry; but I don't think weather forecasters would ever do anything that nutty!"

They giggled.

Then Charlotte said, "The other day I wondered how my dad would react if I suddenly died of something, and someone phoned him up and told him the news. I can't imagine him caring that much. But I was imagining how it would be if he was a bit shocked, and all the colour drained out of his face. Then I imagined him suddenly feeling lighter and thinner, and telling someone, 'I had a bit of a shock a few minutes ago and all the colour drained out of my face. I think it must have drained out of the rest of me too, because I suddenly felt lighter, and my stomach seemed smaller; and I went and weighed myself, and I'd suddenly lost a stone! Colour must be really heavy! I hope it hasn't all come back again!' "

Mya grinned and said, "Last Easter when I was at home, one day I heard a child outside, sounding as if they were saying something about being sick. But then immediately after they said it, a seagull started squawking – or whatever the noise they make is called. It seemed to blend in seamlessly with the child's voice, as if the child was speaking when some mysterious force suddenly turned them into a seagull, so they had to say the rest of what they wanted to say in seagull language."

Heather smiled and said, "Have you ever completely misheard something someone's said? The other day I put the radio on, and I heard someone say something about a multi-storey car park, but at first I thought they said 'naughty story car park'. I wonder what one of those could be!

"And then just recently I heard someone say something like, 'Execs are weighing up the pros and cons of investing in industrial hemp', and at first I thought they said insects instead of execs. I thought, 'Wow, those must be sophisticated insects!' "

They chuckled. Then Suzy said, "I heard someone say the word 'sprinters' the other day, and thought they were saying 'sprinklers'. Can you imagine if an athletics commentator said, 'The race is about to begin. All the sprinklers are lined up at the start.' You'd wonder why on earth the race organisers thought the athletes might need a drenching! Maybe you'd wonder if every one of them had a sprinkler trained on them from behind, in case they ran so fast they over-heated or even caught fire, so water might be needed to put the fire out or cool them down."

Kirsty said, "I heard the word 'sulking' the other day, and thought the person said 'soaking'. Can you imagine if you thought your mum said to you, 'Are you just going to sit there soaking in your room? Why not come out for a walk with us?' "

They grinned, and Colin said, "Imagine if it was raining at the time. Maybe you'd want to say, 'I don't know what strange illusion's making you think I'm soaking in here; but for some weird reason, you seem to be saying you'd prefer it if I did it outside!' "

The students chuckled.

The Student Who Decided to Tell the Others About the Cultural Tradition She'd Heard About Finishes What She Wanted to Say

But then they all became serious, as Catherine cleared her throat and said, "Can I finish what I was saying before, please?"

She'd at least been patient. The students apologised and fell silent. She carried on from where she'd left off before:

"Well, back to the conversation about the way culture's different in Chinese society: All I really want to say now is that Chinese workers working for Western companies can have the same old attitudes as they would if they had Chinese bosses, because they don't realise things are different here so they don't have to worry about asking for help with anything they can't do, or about speaking up if they've got good ideas. They can be misunderstood by Western bosses who can think they're lazy, or that they haven't got any initiative, or that they're bad workers, if the job isn't straightforward and they're having difficulties doing it, and not trying to get help with it or think of solutions. That's a shame, because they'll often be behaving the way they are just because they think they're expected to behave in the same way towards them that they'd behave in their old Chinese companies, being scared to speak up, because they think the same rules about not causing someone to lose face by saying things that might turn out to make them look less competent apply.

"They can easily be helped to understand that a different style of behaving is expected though, with just a bit of explanation. If they're asked to do something, they'll tend to say yes whether they can do it or not, because that's what they'll have learned to do for the sake of supposedly keeping the peace in China, by not causing either themselves or their boss to lose face, either by supposedly showing up their boss as someone who asks them to do things they can't do, or showing themselves up as not being able to do something. But if they're asked a lot of questions about just how they'll manage to do what they've been asked to do, then any difficulties should come to light, because it might turn out that there are things they don't know how to do, and then a more honest discussion can take place, especially if they're encouraged and told it's OK to say what they think."

Colin grinned and said, "You make it sound as if Chinese workers have a whole lot of difficulties doing their jobs; but a lot of them can't have any, because just think about the amount of goods Chinese factories turn out! Loads of the things we buy seem to be made in China!"

Catherine blushed slightly and said a little indignantly, "I'm not saying all Chinese workers will have the difficulties I'm talking about! I'm just saying that the way they'll have often learned to behave if they've worked in China can cause problems for some of them if they're doing difficult jobs!"

The students were surprised to hear that things can be so different in other cultures. They didn't really need to know what Catherine had just told them, since none of them were employers with a workforce that included Chinese employees. It would have been surprising if they'd been employers of anyone, since most of them were only 18 years old. Still, they thought it was quite interesting.

One Student Tells the Others About a Time in History When World War Three Nearly Broke Out

James pondered out loud, "I wonder if any wars have been started between countries because of misunderstandings that came from cultural differences, or when leaders from one country have offended others' cultural sensitivities, maybe ones they didn't even know they had, by maybe doing things that would just annoy politicians in this country, like criticising them in public, but which leaders from some other countries would think of as such a serious loss of face for them, because their reputation might be being damaged in front of their people, that it was considered an offence that just needed to be punished!"

Mya said, "It wouldn't surprise me! Mind you, some war-mongering leaders who don't like criticism might just use their culture as an excuse for aggressively retaliating against their critics, as if they imagine they have a macho culture where it's acceptable to do a lot of harm by inflicting violence against enemies, but God forbid that anyone should even just say something bad about them! How convenient!"

The students tittered, and Kirsty said with a grin, "Yeah, it would be like if a parent was to lock a child of theirs in their room for a week for just dropping a sweet wrapper on the floor. 'What, so dropping a sweet wrapper is a terrible thing to do, but locking your child away for a week is perfectly reasonable and acceptable?' "

They giggled.

Then Sarah said, "It's not just politicians in other people's cultures who can behave as if their reputations are far more important than things that are far more harmful in reality though. Lots of politicians in all cultures probably can, I wouldn't be surprised. Case in point: I read a depressing story about something President Kennedy did. From what I read, he nearly caused World War Three to break out, all because he was worried that if he didn't, his reputation would be damaged, because he thought lots of the people who voted for him would think he was weak, so he was worried they might not vote for him in the next election."

The students burst out laughing, and Colin said, "Don't be daft! I'm sure not even the daftest politician would be silly enough to do something that illogical!"

Sarah said seriously, "Well I know it sounds a bit far-fetched, but that's basically what I've read, anyway. Maybe people make drastic decisions for all kinds of daft reasons sometimes. But I'll tell you the story if you like."

Some of the group expressed interest in it, so Sarah said:

"Well, it seems that President Kennedy's thought of as a hero by lots of people, partly because he could come across as charming, and he made speeches about wanting to change things for the better. And from what I read, the press was misled, and some of his fellow politicians distorted the truth, so as to give the public the image of him that he wanted them to see. Another reason he's apparently thought of as a great man is because he was assassinated before he really had the chance to foul things up in such an obvious way that everyone would know about it, like a lot of politicians who are in power for longer probably do. Well, he did nearly manage to foul things up so catastrophically that all his voters might have got killed, but he and his regime managed to lie about what happened and conceal the incriminating things they'd done to provoke what happened so convincingly that no one realised, according to what I've read."

Heather grinned and joked, "The art of keeping catastrophic foul-ups secret! What a pity he isn't alive today to give us all advice on how to achieve that one!"

They laughed.

Sarah said, "Yeah, I suppose it could have come in handy, if all he was permitted to do was to advise university students on how to keep their mistakes from becoming well enough known to cause them some public shame or something, instead of being involved in politics now! But anyway, this is serious. Another reason why people don't realise what President Kennedy was really like was that most of his misdeeds went on in private, I think, so the press never got to find out about them at the time when he was alive.

"To tell you the story about how he could have caused World War III though, from what I read, when he first came to power in about 1960, he ordered more nuclear missiles to be put in countries around the world than were already there, to be aimed at Russia, including ones in Turkey, which is right next door to Russia. He also tried to get rid of a Russian ally, Fidel Castro, the new leader of Cuba, by trying to get him assassinated, and trying to have the place invaded, and then trying to get him assassinated again, and things like that. He carried on wanting to get rid of him after he failed the first time, and the second time, and time and time again after that, it seems."

James asked, "Why did he want to get rid of him so much?"

Sarah said, "Well, it was something to do with Castro taking over Cuba in a revolution a few years before, and then taking over loads and loads of businesses that had been run by Americans there, declaring that from then on, they'd be run by the Cuban state, supposedly for the benefit of all the people, instead of for the benefit of the American bosses who'd made big profits from them before. So he introduced reforms that gave ordinary Cubans a guaranteed job for life or something, even if they didn't do it very well. But they weren't paid well. And he did other things like that. I read that the Cuban state didn't do a good job of running the businesses, although I don't suppose making them less efficient can have been part of the plan. It wouldn't go down well in a party manifesto, would it! Or whatever dictators have instead."

The students grinned. Then Sarah continued, "I read that Fidel Castro did introduce free healthcare and free education for people, so they were at least better educated and healthier than a lot of people in other developing countries where the governments wouldn't provide things like that. Apparently, he did promise to pay the American business owners some kind of compensation for taking their businesses away, or to give them guarantees that they would be paid something at some later date or other, but I think they rejected the deal.

"Actually, there's a whole lot about it I've realised I don't really know. I watched a television documentary about the revolution in Cuba once, about how a murderous extreme right-wing dictatorship that the Americans had supported till not long before was replaced by a repressive extreme left-wing one that they opposed, and what the Americans did to punish Cuba afterwards, by ordering American companies not to trade with Cuban ones or something; and then I thought I'd learned what went on there. But then I read some more about it, and realised it was more complicated than I thought. And the more I read about it, the more I realised I didn't know, because the more questions I ended up with, and the more I realised there was to it.

"So it's funny how you can think you understand a thing, only to realise you understand it a lot less than you think you did, after you read more information about it! Maybe it's that way with a lot of things."

The others chuckled.

Then Sarah continued, "Anyway, according to what I read, The Russians didn't like the fact that their country was being surrounded by nuclear weapons that were aimed at them, such as the ones in Turkey, and they didn't like the fact that their ally Fidel Castro was being threatened; so they decided to try to even up the nuclear balance a bit, and protect their ally Fidel Castro, by putting nuclear missiles in Cuba, to try to deter the Americans from trying to get rid of him again, and to try and show them what it felt like to have nuclear missiles aimed at them from a country really near them.

"The Kennedy leadership didn't like that though, and decided they were going to make the Russian leaders back down. The conversations that went on between Kennedy and his advisers and fellow politicians were recorded on tapes, which were kept secret for years, but then declassified in the late 1990s.

"Historians who've listened to them since have found out that the leaders and advisers didn't really think the missiles in Cuba were really much of a threat, because they knew Russia was just trying to even up the balance of missiles a bit, in a point-scoring kind of way, and that if Russia wanted to nuke them, it wouldn't make much difference whether they nuked them from Cuba or from Russia. And since the nukes in Cuba would have taken some time to be prepared for launch, American satellites would have detected the activity in time for them to have tried to destroy the missiles if the Russians did ever try to launch them. There are actual recordings of the politicians and military advisers talking about how the missiles didn't increase the threat to America really at all.

"But what did worry President Kennedy and the others, it seems, was that he and his party didn't want the American voters who'd voted him in at the last election to think he looked weak. If an article I read about the crisis is to be believed, The politicians thought it would just be terrible for their reputations and vote count to suffer the embarrassment of not threatening military action to try to make Russia remove their missiles from Cuba and possibly causing a conflict that could actually have led to a nuclear war. As strange as it sounds, they seem to have really believed that the voters would admire them far more for risking a conflict with Russia over the missiles that could have led to everyone in the country being killed than they would if they just tolerated the nukes being in Cuba, and supposedly looked shamefully weak.

"Of course, they didn't let the people believe that that was the way things really were. According to what I read, they lied, announcing to the press that Russia had dangerously and unfairly provoked America by putting the missiles in Cuba, and that the missiles were a terrible threat to the whole of America, and that the Kennedy regime was doing some heroic things to make the Russians back down.

"Apparently, President Kennedy thought he'd won the previous election partly by promising that he'd be tough on the spread of communism, and that he'd be tough on Cuba too, which had recently become communist. He'd criticised the opposition party in America for allowing Russia to get more nuclear missiles, implying that his opponents were putting America at risk, when actually, it was an unfair criticism, and America had a lot more nukes than Russia did, and he knew it. And he'd unfairly criticised the opposition for not being tough enough to stop Cuba becoming a Communist country under Fidel Castro, promising to do better than them. So he thought he'd lose credibility, and that might lose him votes at the next election, if he did something that made him look soft on Russia, like tolerating them putting nuclear missiles in Cuba without him making a big fuss.

"So he actually provoked a conflict that could have led to nuclear war, by ordering Russia to get rid of the missiles, and sending the military to blockade Cuba to stop Russia putting more missiles there, all for the sake of his reputation, and the votes he wanted at the next election. Pretty stupid really, especially because if his behaviour actually had led to nuclear war, a lot of the voters who might have voted for him would have been killed, and any who were left would almost certainly have changed their minds about who they wanted to vote for next time, if there even was a next time, considering that the candidate they'd voted for last time had behaved in a way that had ended up destroying the country, and killing most of the people in it!

"Apparently, it wasn't just his own credibility that Kennedy was worried about, but he was concerned that America itself might look weak if the government just put up with the nuclear missiles being in Cuba. He thought that maybe no one would ever believe that America was willing to go to war to defend people's freedoms again, if they didn't risk nuclear war unnecessarily by provoking Russia after they'd said before that they wouldn't let Russia get the upper hand. Something like that anyway. It didn't seem to matter to Kennedy that the leaders of the countries whose opinions he was worried about didn't think that at all, but thought his aggressive actions were just stupid.

"Apparently, there's a declassified tape of President Kennedy telling his advisers that the previous month, he'd told the public that the government wasn't going to allow Russia to put missiles in Cuba, but that he realised he should have said they didn't care instead, but that it was a bit late for that, because since he'd said they weren't going to allow it, the government had better not look cowardly by seeming to back down by allowing it. It didn't seem to occur to the government that definitely looking reckless and stupid was actually worse than possibly looking cowardly. It was as if they were trying to send the message to the countries that were America's allies, 'We're willing to provoke another world war, just in case if we don't, you lose confidence in our commitment to protect you from war.' Pretty daft, when you think about it!

"America and Russia did a secret deal in the end, where America removed their missiles from Turkey, in return for Russia removing theirs from Cuba; but the American leaders apparently told the Russian leaders that it had to remain a secret, or the deal would be off, explaining that the American leaders couldn't possibly be seen by their people to be looking as if they'd backed down, because it might lose them votes at the next election.

"mind you, apparently, President Kennedy did learn from his mistakes, and decided that world peace was so important that he'd better start trying to make more agreements about limiting nuclear weapons with the Russians after that. And he at least stood up to some of his advisers during the crisis that could have led to nuclear war, who were telling him to reject a deal with Russia and try to make them back down by force; and he was sensible enough to accept Russia's offer to take the missiles off Cuba in return for America removing theirs from Turkey. So it's at least a good thing that it was him in charge, rather than one of his more warlike advisers!"

Matthew said, "Some advisers! Wow! The things politicians will do for votes! If nuclear war had broken out, I wonder if Kennedy would have said to the Russian leaders, 'OK, I don't suppose there's anything I can do to stop you nuking us now, but could you at least nuke the parts of America where the least people voted for me? Then afterwards, I'll make it worth your while by doing a deal with you that you'll like, about . . . oh I dunno, selling Russia masses of rubble at a bargain price or something!' "

They giggled.

Then Matthew said, "I wonder if President Kennedy would have tried to find some way to protect his voters if nuclear war had broken out. Mind you, I'm not sure there would have been anything he could have done really, short of inviting a select few to share the privilege of joining him in his nuclear bunker.

"I remember hearing an old song by a group called the Dubliners, about a document or pamphlet that I think the government in this country released once to advise people on what to do if a nuclear war starts, called *Protect and Survive*. It makes fun of the pamphlet, as if the people who wrote the song didn't believe the advice could be any good. It advises people to call the police if they see a nuclear explosion, and then says that all the politicians who started the war will rush off to their bunkers when it starts, and when they come out and discover no one's left alive, they'll just have to order each other around and take authority over the rubble instead of having other people to rule over."

The students chuckled.

James asked, "What did that document really advise us to do?"

Matthew said, "I don't know; but if parts of that parody song are to be believed, the advice is about as effective as advice to shut yourself inside a broom cupboard and tape over any cracks between the door and the door frame to stop the radiation getting in. And if you haven't actually got a broom cupboard, you'll maybe just have to make do with trying to dig an entire nuclear shelter in your garden . . . or someone else's if you haven't got one, within the four minutes you get between the time you find out your country's going to be nuked and the time when it happens. I think the song was implying that surely there isn't any point in even having a document advising people about what to do, since after a full-scale nuclear attack, everyone except some politicians and a few other privileged people who've got nuclear bunkers already will all be as dead as the dodo! . . . Or should that be dodos? If there was only ever one of them, no wonder it died out!"

They giggled again, but Kirsty said, "Actually, provided a nuclear war didn't destroy the whole country, it could make sense for a lot of people to shut themselves indoors to protect themselves against radiation, since for anyone who wasn't near enough to the blast zones to be killed instantly or soon afterwards, the radiation blowing their way in the wind would probably be the biggest threat to them. I read that it would be at its worst for the first couple of days, and then it falls to less dangerous levels."

Becky said, "So hiding in a broom cupboard could help after all! Then again, I don't know how likely it would be that an enemy that wanted to nuke us would stop at only destroying part of the country, especially once the war had got going and they'd been nuked in retaliation themselves."

Suzy said, "Well, let's just hope it doesn't happen. On a more cheerful note, talking of broom cupboards and the politicians we have to put up with, I heard that there are some polling stations in weird places at election times. I heard there's one at a train station, and one in a cafe. And there's one in a big broom cupboard under the stairs in the hall of a house that used to be a school. I think it's in a little village where only about seventy people go to vote. The couple who run it supervise the voting from their settee. I don't know if they take their broom out of the cupboard before people go in there and vote."

They laughed.

Then Becky smiled and remarked, "I wonder who President Kennedy thought was going to vote for him if everyone who couldn't escape to his nuclear bunker with him had all been nuked in their broom cupboards!"

Then Kirsty turned the conversation serious again by saying, "My mum's mum once told me that she remembers that on the day President Kennedy was assassinated, she was worried all evening, because no one knew who'd assassinated him at the time, and she wondered if he might have been killed by the Russians, and it might lead to nuclear war. I wonder if lots of people were worried that that's what had happened, not knowing about what Kennedy had done himself that risked nuclear war earlier."

Mya said, "Wow, if nuclear war had broken out then, none of us would have been born!... Mind you, if nuclear war breaks out in our lifetimes, maybe we'll all suffer so much we'll all wish we hadn't been!"

After Some Humour, One Student Talks About Some Reasons Why Some People Get Lower Wages Than Others, Even Though They Work Just as Hard

Then Sarah lightened the mood for a little while, before making it serious again, by saying, "I read that Fidel Castro was born from infidelity, between a Spanish man who'd emigrated to Cuba and his teenage kitchen maid. Why they decided they wanted to call him Fidel after that, who knows, since it sounds as if the name's got something to do with fidelity, which I'm presuming must be the opposite of infidelity, so maybe it would be as if they'd be reminded of their misdeeds every time they said his name . . . Or maybe it means something a bit different in Spanish, or they don't have a word that sounds like 'infidelity' at all in that language, so it's just a coincidence.

"Mind you, imagine if some nasty religious extremist groups had decided to nickname Fidel Castro Infidel Castro because of his decision to be a communist, which they thought must mean he was anti-religious. Imagine if they thought they were being clever and insulting, but he decided it would actually be a good name for him, and he was proud of it, and he officially changed his first name to Infidel, and ordered everyone to call him Infidel Castro from then on!

"I heard that one of the other leaders of the revolution in Cuba was Chee Guevara, who was from Argentina, not Cuba at all, but for some reason he decided he wanted to help start a revolution there. Perhaps he enjoyed starting revolutions or something. I don't know. But I heard that when he wasn't killing people, he was trying to cure them . . . or at least other ones. I think he could be pretty brutal to his opponents. But I heard that before he got involved with the revolution, he'd built up some kind of basic medical knowledge, and he used to go around visiting people as a kind of amateur doctor. Goodness knows whether he was any good or not! But I heard that after the revolution in Cuba had been going for a while, his dad visited him, and during the visit, he said, 'What are you going to do with your medical career now!'

Maybe he was thinking, 'Do you really think starting a revolution is a good use of your time, when you could be doing a proper job like a sensible person, instead of wasting all that studying you've done?' "

The students giggled. But then the mood was turned serious, when Sarah said,

"Actually, I get those kinds of comments from my mum – well, not about whether starting revolutions is a good use of my time, obviously, because I've never had any intention of starting any; but she says things like, 'What are you going to do with your life? Do you really think studying psychology is a good use of your time? Do you really think it's realistic to follow this pipe dream you've got of being some kind of psychologist one day, or whatever you're hoping to do? What if you don't succeed, after all this money we've spent to try to help you through university? Why don't you just go out and get a proper job like your older sister did?'

"My sister got a job straight after leaving school. It sounds like a boring job to me, but she's earning quite good money for it, and she can use some of it to support our family, so my mum puts more value on that than on what I'm doing, which she seems to think is just self-indulgent and probably a waste of time, because I get the impression she thinks it's just some silly dream that might not ever lead anywhere.

"It gets me down a bit when she starts talking like that. But at least now I know it's not just me who gets comments like that; even people who are making history and changing the world get them, it seems!"

Colin said supportively, "I heard that graduates get paid more highly on average than non-graduates do though; so maybe you could say to your mum that you might be taking a few years out to study now, but you might be able to spend more money to support the family than your sister does later."

Sarah replied a bit gloomily, "Possibly. I've heard that statistic about graduates typically getting paid more than non-graduates; but I've read that it doesn't tell the whole story, because averages can be misleading, since there are huge variations. I think medical and law students, for example, can end up being paid a huge amount more money than, say, sociology students, since after all, doctors and lawyers do get paid a lot. And among non-graduates, there'll be a massive difference between the amount that, say, someone who's worked for a business for years and got promotion after promotion might earn, and someone might earn if they've, say, got a job as the office cleaner. High-flying non-graduates might earn a lot more than a lot of graduates do.

"And I heard that people who go to the top universities often get paid more, because people need to get higher grades to get into them than they do to get into places like the one we're at, so employers expect them to be more skilled or brainy or better educated than people who go to ones that haven't got such a good reputation, like this one, so they offer to pay them higher wages to attract them, I think."

Charlotte smiled and said irrelevantly, "Do you think it's fair that lawyers get paid so much? I mean, they haven't got a very good reputation either, have they. Actually, I read a joke that hints at that on the Internet. It goes:

"A man went to a lawyer because he wanted to write a will. He said he was worried that it might be a bit difficult, and the lawyer said, 'Don't worry; just leave it all to me.' The man was a bit taken aback and said, 'Oh, I was hoping to be able to leave at least some to my family!' "

The others grinned.

Then Sarah said, "Yeah, maybe some people get paid a lot more than they really deserve . . . or pay themselves a fair bit more than they really deserve, if they're like company bosses or politicians and can choose or vote on how much they get. But I've had quite a think about the differences in the amounts people get paid since my mum brought the subject up.

"On the face of it, it doesn't really seem fair that some people get paid much more than others at all – I mean, there must be people who get paid really low wages, who work just as hard and are just as tired at the end of the day as the most highly-paid people in the country. And a lot of those jobs are just as valuable – I mean, for example, if no one was willing to do work like labouring on building sites, no houses would ever get built, so humans wouldn't get enough shelter, so we'd all die of cold, and the human race would go extinct. Maybe. So really, you could say builders are just as essential to the health of humanity as doctors, so why shouldn't they be paid the same? And you could say the same for people in lots of other occupations, such as workers in clothing factories, or workers on farms, who are essential to the health of humanity, because we'd all probably freeze or starve without them.

"And all kinds of other people could be included too, like people who help give us a decent standard of living so life's actually worth living, such as people who make computers and music, and all kinds of things like that.

"I think that's the way socialists think; so I think in communist countries, the wages of all kinds of workers are much more similar than they are here, although for people who tend to get paid highly in this country, like doctors, I think that means their pay's a lot lower there. I'm not really sure, but I think everyone's pay's pretty similar, although I think politicians might make an exception for themselves wherever they live, and always pay themselves higher salaries.

"But I studied a bit of economics at school, and we had to read a booklet about the reasons why some people get paid much more than others. It was interesting. From what I remember, it said one reason is that the more skilled a person needs to be to do a job, the more time and intelligence it'll take to learn to do it, and that might mean there are far fewer people who've taken the time to learn to do it than there will be people who can do jobs that don't require so much skill, so there'll be more competition between employers to get the workers who can do the job, because there likely won't be enough people who can do it to go around, so they'll offer to pay a higher salary to try to attract people to work for their own firm instead of for another employer's firm.

"It does seem unfair in a way that so-called low-skilled workers can be paid a lot less, since after all, society might really suffer without them. You know, for instance, if people who wash up in kitchens didn't do that, and people got served food on the same plates that loads of other people had used before them, without them ever being washed up, people would probably all start dropping dead from food poisoning … if anyone actually dared to eat off them!

"Or imagine if no one ever cleaned the streets. We'd all be wading around in mouldy old litter whenever we went outside!"

Emma said, "Yeah. Funnily enough, the other day I was thinking I'd hate to do a job where I just had to clean houses all day, or do some other thing that I'd think was boring or really repetitive and monotonous, or where I had to work outside in the cold, or without using my brain that much, and things like that; but then I thought, 'What would the world be like if everyone thought like that, say if everyone just wanted to study higher mathematics or work doing counselling, or things like that?'

"We'd probably all still be living in the Stone Age, with everyone shivering, doing their best to study higher mathematics or counselling other people, and doing scientific experiments and things, all half-freezing to death, starving in our caves, with no one wanting to get their hands dirty by hunting and preparing food, or slogging away in a boring search for firewood and fruits and vegetables, or cleaning up, or anything like that; so our caves would get dirtier and dirtier, and we'd get hungrier and hungrier and colder and colder, till we all died, all trying to study mathematics or counsel each other to the last!

"Then I thought about how good it is that there are people in the world who are willing to do jobs that I'd think of as boring or yucky. Society couldn't succeed without them! It's a good thing that some people think differently from people like me … I'm not saying I'd want to study higher mathematics, of course; I'd probably quickly die of brainache or something! But you know what I mean. It's a good thing people aren't all the same."

Dave grinned and asked, "If you hate boring work that much, do you ever get round to doing your washing up?"

Emma blushed a bit and smiled and said, "Well, I probably don't do it as often as I should, really. I don't think I've ever left it long enough for mould to start growing on it though … Well, maybe once or twice, thinking about it, but not that often."

Sarah said, "My older sister's got a microwave, and she didn't bother to clean it for ages, but then she got a bit worried because she couldn't feel any air coming out of the air vents, and she wondered if they might be being blocked by old bits of food that had splattered over them when they were being cooked. She read on the Internet that if they really were blocked, then it could cause a fire, because the microwave might over-heat when she was cooking something, because it needs to suck air in and let it out in another place because that cools it down so it doesn't get hotter than it should. So she gave her microwave a good clean after that. But it just shows you that cleaning things might sometimes even save lives. And obviously that's even more true in places like hospitals, where cleaners will be helping to cut down the risk from nasty bacteria by reducing their numbers. So maybe some employers ought to value jobs where people do that more and pay people who work in them more.

"... Not that I really know enough about how much people get paid to make a proper judgment. And there are lots of different reasons why people get paid what they do.

"Another thing I learned at school was that a lot of the work that's thought of as unskilled that might have once been done in this country is being done overseas, like repetitive work in factories, and it's actually cheaper to import products from there than it is to employ people here to do the work to make them sometimes, partly because employers here have to pay workers a fair bit more than they would in some countries, and if there's a big workforce, the costs of wages here can be pretty high! I think some company bosses from this country have even gone abroad to countries where it costs a lot less to pay the workforce, and then they sell what they make back to this country! So there's less demand in this country for some kinds of unskilled workers than there used to be, so people who try to go for some jobs that are called unskilled will find fewer around.

"And it'll be harder for people working in jobs like that to get decent wages than it will be for people in some other jobs, if they want to carry on doing that kind of work, because it'll be harder to just leave a job they're already in and find a better-paying one like it, because there won't be so many around. And employers won't have an incentive to put wages up if a lot more people want the jobs they're offering than there are jobs on offer, since if some people refuse them because the pay's too low, it probably won't be a problem for them, because the chances are that other people will quickly take them.

"But also, employers like that won't be able to put their wages up much, because their companies will need to compete for customers with companies abroad where the cost of living's quite a lot lower, that pay lower wages, so companies there can sell the same products more cheaply, because the lower wage bill makes them cheaper to produce; so if the employers in this country who manufacture the same things put wages up, it might even drive them out of business after a while, because their products would get more expensive, because the money for the increased wages would have to come from the sale of them, so it would really be being paid by the customers buying the products, who wouldn't like paying more, so more people might switch to buying the cheaper products from abroad.

"It seems it's best if people can get lots of skills, so they get to have a higher chance of getting a good job. I've even heard that there are shortages of skilled workers in some careers, such as engineering, so it's worth people taking the time to train for careers like that if they can, if they think they might be into that kind of thing."

Food Comes Up in the Conversation, and it Turns Humorous for a While

Emma grinned and said, "Or people could do really really valuable things, like making home-made cakes! Yum!

"Actually, the other day I came across some cakes in a shop, and it said on the label that they were just like home-made cakes, and that they had the same recipe that the person who thought up the idea of making them used to use to make them in a cosy cottage when she was a milkmaid working on a little farm in the old days, using recipes from her childhood. Then I checked the ingredients, and some of them were things like sunflower seed oil, and a few E numbers. Not quite what you'd expect from supposedly old-fashioned, homely ingredients! Can you imagine someone's mum making cakes with them, saying things like, 'Hey, go to the cupboard and bring me that bottle of yummy E450! Actually, we could do with another dollop of E341 as well! Good old E341! Cakes just wouldn't be the same without it!'

"I think salespeople try to attract customers by making things sound a bit more attractive than they really are sometimes!"

They giggled. But then Heather said, "Actually, I remember making cakes with my mum as a child, and when we followed a recipe from a recipe book, we sometimes put drops of things in them like food colouring and vanilla flavouring. My parents had a little plastic box in the cupboard full of little jars of things like that; and I suppose they must have been E numbers really. So it probably wouldn't really have been all that unusual for people to use E numbers in cakes they made with their parents when they were little.

"Whether they're actually good for you, well, that's another issue! Although if you were concerned about what was good for you, you probably wouldn't eat the cakes anyway! Or make them in the first place! But at least the E numbers will almost certainly be safe to eat. I mean, I think all the E numbers that are actually allowed to be in food are chemicals that have been passed as safe by some European organisation . . . although quite possibly not passed as healthy!

"Hey imagine working in a factory where your job was to make E numbers all day! And I wonder what it would be like to just put your head back and gulp a great big cupful of an E number down! Mind you, they probably all taste different. Imagine if someone had a job producing an E number in a factory all day, and they started drinking some, and they loved it, and even found it addictive, so they started sneaking whole crates of bottles of it out with them and bringing them home, and saying to their family, 'I've got some more of that gorgeous E number today! I'm going to sit in front of the telly guzzling it down all evening with my dinner!' "

The students chuckled. But then Dave said, "Mind you, they might be put off them if they had to work with them all day. I know a man whose parents both worked in a chocolate factory, and neither one of them ever wanted to eat chocolate, and they didn't give him any chocolate when he was a little boy. Whether that was because they were somehow fed up of it after working with the ingredients all day, or whether they never liked chocolate anyway, and that's one reason they thought working in a chocolate factory would suit them, because they thought it wouldn't tempt them to eat loads of chocolate and get massively fat, or whether they were put off chocolate by finding out what went into it or something, I don't know!"

The Conversation Diverges Onto Pesticides, Before Getting Back to Discussion of Wages

Sarah said, "Hopefully nothing that bad goes into it! I'll probably keep eating it anyway though, even if I find it does!

"Mind you, I've heard some bad things about the production of some foods! Well, mainly grains and fruit and vegetables ... Maybe we should all give up eating those and eat chocolate instead ... Or maybe not.

"But getting gloomy for a minute, I've heard that people who work on some farms cultivating fruits and vegetables sometimes have to work with unsafe insecticides and other chemicals, and their health can suffer because of it, especially if too much gets sprayed on the plants. It's not very nice to read about ... Obviously it's much less nice for the people who get the problems! It might not happen anywhere near as much in this country as it does in some parts of the world though. I think it mostly happens in developing countries, where workers maybe aren't given such good protective clothing to wear when they spray them, and where they still use old pesticides that were replaced a while ago by less toxic ones in developed countries.

"Pesticides have done a lot of good in some ways, killing a lot of insects like mosquitos that would otherwise have spread serious diseases, and other insects that would otherwise be eating quite a lot of what was intended to feed humans, which might mean some humans went hungry or even starved. But pesticides can have harmful effects for people who accidentally get exposed to toxic amounts of them.

"I wouldn't fancy a job spraying insecticides! I'm not sure if any of the kinds of workers who are exposed to the risks of working with some of them get extra money to compensate them for taking the risks.

"But talking about that kind of thing, another thing that can make a difference as to how much people are paid, at least in this country and in other developed countries, is if a job's dangerous, so employers might pay higher wages to entice people to do it, or unions can demand that they pay higher wages in compensation for the danger, threatening that their workers will strike if they don't. I think there might still be quite dangerous jobs where the pay's low though, especially in developing countries that haven't got many regulations about workers' rights, or in industries where workers are only taken on as and when they're needed, like some workers on building sites, where more or less people might be taken on depending on what's being built, so a lot of people might not have regular jobs where they'd be encouraged to join strong unions that could campaign for their rights.

"And talking about the reasons for wage differences, I think there are quite a few other reasons why people get paid different amounts too. One is the availability of work in an area: In areas where there aren't many employers around, just a few big ones, so people have less choice about where they work, the employers might be able to get away with paying lower wages, because they know it's going to be harder for employees to leave their jobs if they're unhappy and go to work for other companies who are paying them more, because there aren't so many around. Mind you, where there are powerful unions, they can bargain with employers to get them to put wages up, saying it'll help them prevent strikes.

"And another thing that makes a difference is how high the unemployment rate is, since if it's high, there are going to be loads of people trying to get each job a lot of the time, so employers will know they can likely attract people who really need a job to work for them even if they don't pay them very well, because a lot of people will be finding it hard to get other jobs, while if unemployment's very low, there might be lots of jobs still available – more jobs on offer than there are people to fill them even – so employers will know that if their workers aren't happy, they might easily be able to find other employers who are willing to pay people a bit more as an incentive for them to work for them instead, and leave to go and work for them; so their current employers will likely think it's worth paying them more to keep them.

"Then again, even at times when it's easy to get other jobs, a lot of workers might not be in that much hurry to leave the jobs they've got, because they might like the people where they are, or not want to spend more time travelling to a workplace where they could get higher wages but it's further away, or they might not even know there are other employers paying more, and that kind of thing; so employers might not put wages up till they're sure there's a problem."

Heather asked, "What about this 'gender pay gap'? That must be the cause of some wage differences."

Sarah said, "Partly; but actually, the reasons for that are more complex than men and women just being paid different rates for the same work. I think that can still go on, although I think it's illegal nowadays in this country. But some of the reasons aren't really employers' fault. I heard that one reason is that women who take some time out to have babies might be able to go back to doing the same job they were doing before afterwards; but in the meantime, some of the people who haven't been taking time out will have been working their way towards promotions, and by the time women of the same age who've taken a break get back there, the people they used to work with might be in more senior positions where they're making more money; so those women might end up years behind on the career ladder, spending some time catching up, or never catching up.

"And I think some employers can be reluctant to promote women to more senior positions as well, partly because the people in senior positions have to work for long hours, and they like them to be really committed to the firm, and they think women who have to look after children won't be able to dedicate as much time to the company as they'd like, because of the time they have to take looking after their children, and the time off they might have to take if the children are ill. So naturally since people in more junior positions will almost certainly be paid less than people who've been given promotions, the women who aren't being promoted because of that will be paid less than colleagues they work with who are being promoted instead of them.

"Another thing is that a lot of women choose to work part-time, so they can more easily be around at times when they need to take care of their children; and obviously if you're working fewer hours, you're going to get less money – at least, as a rule. But also, a lot of part-time work is more poorly paid than full-time work, so if most of the people who do it are women, and there's a lot of it around, that's going to mean that a lot of women will be in work that's more poorly-paid than a lot of the work men are more likely to be in.

"But also, a lot of the full-time work that's a lot more likely to be done by women than men is quite low-paid, like caring and nursing, although I think the reasons for that are a bit complicated, and not really to do with the fact that women are doing most of the jobs, such as a lot of those jobs being work for government organisations like the health service and schools, and the government not wanting to put more money into them than they think they have to, because they're worried about becoming unpopular if that means they have to increase taxes to pay for it. Their wage bill's already really expensive, because quite a large percentage of the money that goes into organisations like the health service goes on wages, which isn't that surprising, considering how many people work for organisations like that."

Heather said, "Doctors get paid way more money than a lot of nurses do though, don't they."

Sarah said, "That's true. Maybe that's partly to give doctors an incentive not to leave the NHS to go into private practice, after all the training they've been given over years and years.

"Anyway, all that gives the impression that a lot of the cause of the gender pay gap isn't just outright discrimination. But that doesn't mean things couldn't be done to make things more equal sometimes, or that unfair discrimination doesn't happen."

The Students Discuss Some Experiences of Transsexual Men and Women Who Have Compared Their Lives as Women to Their Lives as Men

Kirsty said, "I read something interesting by a transgender man on an Internet forum I like to go to not long ago. He'd grown up as a woman, and then had a sex change operation, and he was talking about the differences he'd noticed in the way he used to be treated when he was a woman and the way he's treated as a man.

"He said he gets more respect as a man, and it's been really noticeable that it quite often happens that people treat him as if he's more competent in some ways than people used to when he was a woman. He said that other people he knows who've had sex changes have noticed the same thing.

"He said that in places like school or work, when he was female, he would often say something in a discussion, and he got ignored; but then a male would say the exact same thing a few minutes later, and get congratulated for coming up with such a good idea! Or people would ask the males in the group he/she was working with to explain what the projects the group had been working on were about, even though he – when he was a she – had done most of the work on them.

"And he said his teachers and other people at school seemed to assume he couldn't possibly be as good at maths, science and computer programming as the male pupils. There was one time when they were soon going to leave school, when they were asked what they wanted to do afterwards, and when the boys said they wanted to study computer science it was just accepted; but when he – or she, as she was then, said she wanted to study it, people were skeptical, and asked if she was sure, and whether she even knew the basics of it, which they didn't do with the boys at all, even though she actually knew more than some of them did.

"And he said they had a physics teacher who paid special attention to the boys in the class and was convinced that boys were better at physics than girls, even though he – or she – and a female friend of hers were actually top of the class.

"And he said that female him used to play football, and was so good she got to play for her city in tournaments; but a lot of people seemed to assume that boys would naturally be able to play better than her even if they didn't play football.

"And he said that when he was playing online games with people, when they didn't know what gender he was, they thought he was good, but when he said he was female, people didn't take his gaming skills so seriously, because there's often an assumption that female gamers won't be any good.

"But he said that since he's had surgery to become male, now everyone he meets assumes he's a man, he gets treated as if he's more qualified to answer questions about science and technology, and people pay his ideas and opinions more attention. And they assume he'll be good at video games too. He said the change has been really noticeable.

"I don't know what the reasons are why that kind of thing happens. Maybe it's partly that some men are used to women staying at home to care for kids and do the housework, so they just assume women can't possibly know much about the world outside or something, although that wouldn't apply to people at school or doing university degrees. Who knows what the real reasons are!

"Anyway, he said he knows people who used to be men who've had sex changes to become women, who've been really surprised when the opposite things have happened to them.

"The reason he was talking about that kind of thing was because someone else put a link on the forum to an article where some other people who'd had sex change operations were talking about the differences between the way they were treated as women and men, and then asked questions about whether anyone on the forum had had similar experiences.

"The article was about the experiences of some people who'd grown up as women before becoming men, and they were interviewed about the different ways they were treated before and ever since their sex change operations, when people just started assuming they were ordinary men.

"One talked about having the same kinds of experiences that the person on the forum said he'd had, saying that since he'd become a man, he'd noticed that people at work would just assume he knew a lot about things and was the spokesman for his team of mostly women, and they would ask him about things in preference to asking women on their team who were actually more senior than him. And there was one day when there was a meeting of several teams working on things, and he got praised for his team's work, but there was a woman team leader next to him whose team he thought had done even more successful work than his, who didn't get a mention. He said it had made him feel uncomfortable, and brought back feelings of when he'd been a woman and hadn't been given credit for work.

"He said that when he was a woman, people would give him vague answers when he asked questions at work, but now people assumed he was a man, they'd put more effort into answering, even if it meant they had to do some research before they could give him a clear answer.

"And the article where the transgender men were interviewed started by saying there was a neuroscientist who isn't alive any more, but he had a sex change a while ago to become a man when he used to be a woman, and he had said he was surprised that after he became a man, he got treated with more respect by other scientists, who took his work more seriously than scientists had before. He said he could actually speak without being interrupted by a man, which he'd found difficult to do before. And he said a scientist who assumed he'd always been a man and that he must be the brother of the woman he'd actually been before praised his work as being much better than his sister's.

"I suppose it's possible that his work really was better than it had been earlier, but that it was increasing knowledge and experience over time that had made the difference, nothing to do with gender. But then, who knows; I've heard that people doing school exams are given numbers to identify them when their exams are being marked nowadays instead of their names being shown, because it was discovered that a lot of people marking exams had a bias where they'd give boys higher marks for the same-quality work as the girls did, for some reason. So numbers started being used to identify people, so graders wouldn't know whether they were marking the work of a male or a female.

"But anyway, I decided to find out a bit more information about that transgender neuroscientist, and I found out about more sexism he'd experienced. It seems he'd studied at some of the top universities in America when he was a woman, and there was one time when he, or maybe I should say she, solved a really hard maths problem that a lot of the males in the class couldn't work out, and the tutor was convinced her boyfriend had solved it for her. And she was top of her class, but found it hard to get a supervisor for research projects. She was in a scientific competition with a man once, and the university dean was convinced she'd win, saying her work was a lot better than the man's, but the man won, only to drop out of science a year later!"

Emma said, "I heard someone who was born a man but was in the process of transitioning into a woman, but still had a man's voice, telling a story about how she loves a particular video game, and she likes to go to tournaments where people compete against other people playing it. She said almost all the people there are men; there are only a tiny tiny minority of women there. She used to go to those tournaments a lot when she was a man too.

"She said she went to one when she was only just beginning to transition into a woman, but she was dressed as one, so people assumed she was one. She was playing against this man, and he started explaining all kinds of basic things that realistically, she was bound to know if she'd played the game enough to be in a game tournament. She realised he was mansplaining things to her, assuming that a woman would likely not know them. She decided to get her own back on him by doing her best to beat him at the game, and she did.

"Then she noticed the man had a look of shame on his face, and it brought back memories to her of how men would get mocked by other men if they lost to a woman, and it would be as if their status was lowered, and they would even be thought of as less manly for it. She realised that was a stupid attitude.

"When the tournament finished, they all went to the pub, and partway through the evening, a man who'd actually known her for some time, so he knew she used to be male, and now thought of herself as a lesbian, put his hand on her leg. She said a small part of her was delighted, but a bigger part of her was confused, and part of her felt scared and violated. And it reminded her of times when she was a man, when she – or should I say he – was a bit drunk, and his hormones would stir a bit, and he would sometimes put his own hand on a woman's leg, even though he knew the woman was already in a relationship, or not interested in having a sexual relationship with him, or she was just a friend. She realised she'd had an ignorant entitled attitude in those days, and felt ashamed of herself.

"And it occurred to her that disrespect of women was likely to be a far bigger problem for her in future than transphobia!"

Kirsty said, "That's interesting. It seems there are advantages and disadvantages to transitioning each way though. The people interviewed for the article I was talking about that was linked to on the forum where the person was asking about the experiences of transgender people said that in some ways, it was harder for them as men than it had been for them as women, especially because some of them were black in America, and they said they got stopped by the police and treated with suspicion a whole lot more than they had been before. One said he now got pulled over by the police a lot and asked if he had weapons in his car, whereas before, he, or maybe I should say she, could commit a speeding offence, and usually be let off, sometimes even getting into a fun conversation with the policeman who'd stopped her."

The Topic of Petty Crime in the Workplace Comes Up, Before There's a Bit More Joking

Colin said, "Wow. I wonder if it's more common for policemen to let women get away with petty crimes, or at least speeding, than it is for them to let men off them then."

James said, "I don't know; but it probably isn't worth anyone taking the risk of doing something illegal like that and hoping for the best.

"Mind you, some authority figures would probably even collaborate with people who commit certain offences. I've read about petty offences carried out in the workplace that are actually encouraged by employers, because they're committed against customers, not the employers themselves, and the employers benefit from them, like in some pubs, when some people ask for a gin and tonic, they'll be given hardly any gin in their tonic at all; or there have been times in some supermarkets where checkout staff have been encouraged to keep little items with them that they keep putting through the till along with the shopping of the customers, so it comes to more money, and they'll just apologise to any customers who notice, and say it was a mistake, and that they didn't realise the item wasn't theirs. I read about those things in an interesting book about cheating in the workplace called *Cheats at Work* by Gerald Mars, and I was surprised about how many things can go on, both against employers and against customers!"

Emma said, "I've got a relative who got the sack from a job she had. She was working as a waitress in a restaurant, and when it was closed for the night, she and some of the other people who worked there used to stay behind and chat, and they started drinking. They got into the habit of pouring themselves whisky from the bottles behind the bar and not paying for it, and putting water in the bottles with the whisky that was left, thinking that then no one would realise anything had been taken out of them. But one day, their employer told them an inspector was coming round to check that everything was the way it should be; and the quality of the drinks was checked, and it was found out that they'd been watered down, and the people who'd been doing it were found out and got the sack.

"Mind you, it didn't damage her long-term career; she's actually a teacher now!"

Dave grinned and joked, "Wow, imagine if one morning she said to a group of eight year-olds she was teaching, 'I know you're supposed to be learning French, but today I want to teach you all about what you can do if you want to be more like me when you grow up. Think of it as a public service to you. I've heard that some children think a teacher is a good role model to have, and that they should learn from their example and try to be more like them as they grow up. Well today, I'm going to tell you all how you can do that. The first thing to do when you grow up, if you want to be more like me, is to get a job in a restaurant or bar, and stay behind after it closes with your friendly work colleagues, and steal drinks from behind the bar with the others, partying into the early hours of the morning, till you're found out and get the sack!' "

Becky laughed and said, "Yeah. Just imagine what the parents would think of that! Imagine a horde of angry parents marching up to the school gates, shouting about how they weren't going to tolerate the school teaching their children they ought to get jobs as waiters and waitresses in places that sold alcohol and then stay behind after all the customers had gone and steal the whisky!"

They all giggled.

The Person Talking About Wages Explains More About the Reasons for Wage Differences

Then Sarah said, "I think any kids who absorbed that lesson might find themselves unexpectedly getting the sack a lot from jobs later in life!

"Actually, talking of getting fired from jobs, you know I was talking about the reasons for wage differences earlier? Well another reason why a lot of people get low wages is because part-time workers haven't got the same rights as full-time workers have got, and they're less likely to be unionised, so it might be easier to sack them and employ other ones if they become pests to the employers by complaining a lot about their wages being low, so employers can feel freer to pay their workers less because of that, as well as because they probably don't legally have to pay them as much. And another thing about part-time work is that if people's employment contracts say the employers can choose how many hours to employ them for in any given week, the employees will be quite likely to get lower wages, since in some weeks they might not work many hours at all.

"Another thing is that if you're working for a company that makes a lot of profit, you might get paid more highly than if you work for an organisation that doesn't make much money, or one that has to get given it from money that comes from taxes. Well, sometimes anyway, although it partly depends how much money the bosses of companies that make a lot of profit want to keep for themselves, or want to invest in expanding their businesses and so on.

"As for people who work for organisations that are run or financed by the government, where people get their wages partly or wholly paid out of taxes, one thing is that if the government decides it needs to make spending cuts, for whatever reason, the wages of some of the people who get jobs with organisations that partly or wholly get their money from government funding might get lower, or at least they might not be put up, such as those of – I think – some of the people who go into the homes of people who are finding it difficult to look after themselves because they're getting older and frail or ill and so on, so as to wash and dress them and give them something to eat, and things like that.

"And the problem might get worse in the future as more people get old and need care, if there ends up being less money to go around because there are fewer tax payers, because there are fewer people of working age, which might well happen because people have fewer children nowadays, so fewer people might be around to become adults and get jobs in replacement for the people who stop paying tax when they retire. It might mean the amount of money companies are paid to send people in to care for old people won't increase as much as the number of old people who need care does, so they'll be providing more of it on a tighter budget, so they'll pay their employees less, or else their employees will have to provide care that isn't so good, because they have to see more people in one day so they have to spend less time with each person. That's unless the immigration of people of working age who pay tax makes up for the drop in tax payers who are native to this country.

"Still, I don't really know; and I think there's a lot of variation in the amount of money carers are paid."

The Conversation Becomes Briefly More Depressing, Before Some Dark Humour Breaks Out

Heather said thoughtfully, "I'm really not looking forward to getting old!"

Dave smiled and said, "Don't worry, it might never happen!"

Heather said, "Yes, I suppose I might die before I get old. I wonder which would be worse, dying before my health could deteriorate with age, but knowing it would still have been nice to have been around my family for a while longer, or having to stay alive after I'd stopped enjoying life because my health was getting too bad. I suppose the ideal thing would be to die just before your health got too bad to tolerate or something."

Dave said, "Actually, I wasn't thinking that just you might die young; I was thinking that maybe the world might end, say in a nuclear war, and then none of us will get old!"

Matthew said, "Well, that's apart from the politicians, who'll probably all be hiding in their bunkers when the bombs drop! Hey, imagine if the only people to survive were politicians, and they all lived together for about thirty years, till they got so old they needed people to care for them, like getting them dressed in the mornings and getting their meals and so on, but all the people who could have been their carers had been killed long ago in the nuclear war. Maybe when they started needing to be cared for, they'd begin saying things to each other like, 'You know, I'm just beginning to think that that nuclear war we started thirty years ago was a mistake!' "

The students giggled.

Then Suzy grinned and said, "Actually, they'd probably have decided it was a mistake long before that, when they couldn't get hold of their favourite foods, because all the people who worked to produce them had been killed, and all the places where their ingredients once grew had been turned into toxic wastelands!"

Sarah said, "Let's hope that by some miracle, politicians think of that kind of thing before they even start a nuclear war!

Maybe if we thought they might start one, reminding them how much they must like their food might be a more effective way of stopping them than pleading with them to change their minds or suggesting strategies they could use to turn things more peaceful.

"I suppose getting a low wage working to produce food has to be better than dying in a nuclear war and never being able to eat food again! . . . Well, presumably you'd never be able to eat food again. Imagine if there was just a little nuclear war that didn't kill most people, and then scientists discovered that radiation had this really spooky property that enabled some dead bodies to get up and search for food, and then eat it! But scientists were sure they were really dead, because they didn't have a heartbeat, and they weren't breathing or anything.

"If they could work as well, I wonder if they'd demand wages . . . and end up being paid them, if there were employers still around! Just imagine one employer saying to another one, 'I've got five zombie-like people working for me. They make fantastic workers. It's a pity they're beginning to decompose now! I might have to sack them soon!'

"And then imagine the other employer thinking he was talking about ordinary people, and one of them joking, 'I think I've got a few zombies working for me too. No signs of decomposing though, more's the pity; that would be one way of getting rid of them! They just seem to sleep for half the day!' "

Kirsty laughed and said, "You've been watching too much television!"

Between a Few More Darkly Humorous Comments, the Student Talking About Wage Differences Gives the Others a Final Bit of Information About Them

Sarah said, "No, I just dreamed that idea up myself.

"Anyway, there's just a little bit more information I can remember about why some people get paid more than others – not that the information's going to do any of us any good if we all get nuked soon, but still, maybe we won't, so it might be worth me passing it on, just in case it somehow turns out to be worthwhile knowing about it one day:

"Another thing is that among people in jobs where it's normal for people to actually be lucky enough to get as much training as they really need, a person who an employer has spent more time training will probably get paid more than people who've just started doing work for them, since if you put a lot of money and time into training someone, you're going to want to entice them to stay in your company if they're good at the job, instead of risking having them go off and use the skills you've taught them in a job working for someone else. And you might want to tell them you're going to offer them higher pay when they've been trained, before they are, to entice them to bother to make the effort to be trained to get more skilful in the first place, as well as to entice them to stay on.

"And it's a bit like that for people who study for years and years at university to get qualified to do certain jobs, such as work as doctors – people who do that will have to make a sacrifice to do it, because they could be out in the world earning money if they weren't studying instead, so if there weren't employers willing to pay them higher salaries after they qualify than they'd be able to get if they didn't bother with higher education and went out to work when they were younger , then a lot more people might not make the effort to get more educated before getting a job. So I think paying them higher salaries is partly done to attract enough people to stay on and get qualified enough to do the jobs the employers want them to do, so as to make them decide it's worth the sacrifice of living on much less money than a lot of people around them do for years till they're properly qualified.

"I can understand that. I'm not sure it'll apply to me, because I don't know if I'll ever be in a job where I get paid more than I'd get paid if I'd started working when I left school instead of coming here.

"But I mean, imagine a family that isn't making much money, and they've got a child who's the age where they've got a choice between going to university or medical school and trying to get a job. If the child will have to do years of studying before they can get the kind of highly-skilled job they'd quite like to do, only to be paid the same for it as they would be if they went out and got a job right then, they'd probably think it was less worthwhile making all the effort, unless they were absolutely sure it was what they wanted to do and they thought it was going to be really worth it. And it might be more difficult for them to convince their parents it would be worth it, if their parents were telling them they wanted them to give up their education and get a job to help support the family; it would be easier if their parents could hope that after all their studying, their child might earn a lot more money than they would have done otherwise so they could support the family even better, unless they needed money right then.

"So some of the reasons for wage differences make sense really. I mean, obviously it's not fair when businesses exploit workers by paying them wages it's hard to live on, while the bosses are living in luxury because they're paying themselves loads of money, because the businesses are making masses of profit. But maybe it's a good thing that there are at least some differences in wage levels.

"Anyway, before I started going on about this, I was talking about the Cuban Missile Crisis, wasn't I . . . Of course, if it had led to the world being destroyed in a massive nuclear war, nobody would be here to talk about wage differences . . . or anything else! . . . Well, I suppose there might be politicians in nuclear bunkers offering to fish some old money out of their pockets and pay other ones to go and clear some of the rubble away from the outside of the bunkers so they could go and look around outside without having to break a sweat or get their hands dirty, and they might be discussing whether a politician who has a job clearing rubble away should be paid the same amount as a politician would have been in the old days, or whether they wouldn't deserve as much money as a politician who had the power to just spend all day ordering people around, or something like that. But that might be all."

James said, "Hey, imagine if politicians were paid higher or lower salaries according to their performance, so if they did things that improved the quality of life for people in their countries, they were allowed to pay themselves more, but if they did things like made stupid decisions that caused wars, there was some law that said their pay would have to go right down! . . . I can't imagine any of them allowing a law like that to be brought in though!"

The Students Talk About Misunderstandings, War and Scary War Games, and What Makes for Better Peace Negotiations

Then Emma said, "It's not nice to think that just a few people at the top can determine the fate of all the rest of us! When married couples fall out, they can divorce, and their children can end up feeling unhappy for ages. When families fall out, they can stop speaking to each other. But when politicians in different countries fall out, they can start wars where millions get killed!"

Matthew said, "That just isn't fair, is it! I think when politicians disagree that seriously, they should just shut themselves in a room together and fight it out themselves, without dragging their countries into it!"

Some of the students cheered quietly, and everyone grinned and thought that was a great idea!

But Suzy said, "You'd never get them to do that though!"

They all agreed. It made them feel a bit depressed, and they started thinking about war. As they began to talk about it, some started wishing they'd brought lunch boxes they could have tipped the remains of their food into to warm up and eat later, when they could think about nice things instead and really enjoy it. Others began to gobble their own food up faster instead, because they felt like comfort eating.

Heather said, "War can't be Just to do with politicians falling out though . . . or thinking they'd better risk lots of people being killed because they think they might lose face by looking weak if they don't send their countries to war, or for some other daft reason; surely it's normally a bit more complicated than that!"

Kirsty said, "Probably. But maybe not much more complicated. I've heard that one thing that can cause big problems is misinterpretations of other people's intentions. I'll tell you what kind of thing I mean:

"I heard about a war game that senior military strategists in America played with each other, to try to get a better understanding of what might happen if America went to war with some country or other. One team pretended to be America, and the other one pretended to be the leaders of the other country. The teams were in different rooms, and the decisions each team made about their next move were passed to the other team, but they weren't told what reasons the other team had for deciding to do what they did, so they just had to draw their own conclusions about why they'd done it. They'd just discuss what it might mean the others were thinking and planning to do next, and then they'd make a decision about their own next move in response, and the other team would be told about it, and then make a decision about what to do next. And it went on like that.

"After the game, when each team was telling the other about the reasons why they'd made the decisions they had, they realised, worryingly, that each side in the game had kept misunderstanding the other's intentions, and doing aggressive things because they were worried that things the other side did were signs they were planning to do bad things, when really the other side wasn't intending to do those things at all, and they'd done the things the other side interpreted as meaning they were going to do something especially bad because they were trying to defend themselves against what they thought the other side was going to do, because they misinterpreted things they did as meaning they were about to do something really bad.

"So they both provoked each other without really realising they were doing it, because they thought the other side was planning the worst when they weren't; but they did both do worse things in response to each other's aggression, till a mock catastrophe happened.

"The game showed how things really might turn out in real life, where things like that might really happen in a future war."

The students were all silent for a moment, worrying about the possibility of world war 3 breaking out. The silence was broken suddenly when one of them broke wind loudly. Most of them laughed; but a few of them quickly started feeling bad about laughing when they'd just been talking about war, and put their hands over their mouths and tried to stifle their laughter in unison.

Stuart was feeling more light-hearted though; he said, "I read a funny true story on the Internet: A soldier was about to go to war, and his three-year-old son was holding onto his leg, begging and begging him not to go. Then his wife tried to calm the boy down, by saying, 'Let Daddy go, and we'll go and get a pizza.' Immediately the boy let go of his dad's leg, stepped back and calmly said, 'Bye Daddy.' "

The students laughed.

Then Catherine said more seriously, "I heard an interesting story that I think is true, about how an ancient Greek astronomer predicted that there would be an eclipse on a certain day, based on calculations he'd made after watching how the stars and planets and things were moving in the sky. A couple of armies were fighting each other on that day, and the eclipse happened in the middle of a fierce battle, and they both stopped fighting and made peace. I think they might have done that because they thought the gods were angry with them for fighting, thinking the gods had caused the eclipse, to show their anger with them or something. They didn't know about the astronomer's predictions."

James said thoughtfully, "You know, I hate it when I hear that two sides are heading for war, but they refuse to negotiate with each other. If they won't talk to each other, they could be having all kinds of misunderstandings about what the other side wants that make them angrier; and they lose the chance of bringing the other side around to their point of view too.

"Then again, some negotiations can make things worse if the sides just end up arguing. I read that in good negotiations, they won't just haggle over who's willing to give up or compromise on which demands, but they try to understand each other's reasons for making their demands before they start, and then both try to find solutions that'll suit both sides. So each side isn't just trying to make the other one give in to them, and maybe getting more and more hardline themselves the more they think their interests are being threatened and the angrier they get, like I think they can if negotiations are being done badly and they think they might not get nearly as much out of them as the other side might; but the point of view of both sides is fully examined right at the start, and then both sides try to work out how each can get as much of what they want as they can without hurting the other side's interests.

"I suppose that wouldn't work where one country's just invading another one because its psychopathic leaders want to plunder its riches or take it over, and nothing less than that will do for them, or if they lie about what they really want, to disguise their true motives. But it can work where there's a chance that both sides can be persuaded to be reasonable.

"I read that something like that was done during peace talks between Egypt and Israel once; there was a very short war between Israel and some neighbouring Arab states in 1967, where Israel took over the Egyptian Sinai Peninsula. The Egyptians naturally didn't like that, and there were worries that it might lead to some future war, so years later, they have talks to try to sort out the problem. At first, the organisers of the talks tried and tried to get them to compromise, drawing map after map with boundaries in different places, to see if they'd agree to share the place, with each of them having part of it. Israel was willing to give up part of it, but Egypt insisted they had to return the whole lot, and refused to budge from that demand.

"But instead of the negotiations breaking up with angry words, the organisers then had another idea. They might have been better off thinking of it at first, but at least they did think of it after a while:

"They first asked each side for their reasons for taking the positions they did. It turned out that the reason Israel didn't want Egypt to have all of the place was because they were worried they would station tanks there, and that there might be a lot right on the Egypt/Israeli border, and that that could threaten their security; they'd have been worried that Egypt could easily invade. And the reason Egypt was refusing to give up their claim to any of the place was because they were so fed up of having it ruled by foreigners: The ancient Greeks, and then the Romans, had taken it from Egypt ages ago, and then the Turks, and then others, and they'd only recently got it back, only to have it taken away yet again!

"When it was realised that Israel was only refusing to give back all of the place because they were worried about the security of their borders, and Egypt was only upset that they might not get to rule the area, an agreement was easily reached between them: Egypt would rule there from then on, but a lot of the place would be a demilitarised zone, so they wouldn't station tanks, troops or anything that could threaten Israel there. Both sides went away happy."

"Wow, that's great!" said Suzy. "To think things could have been so different if the negotiations hadn't been done so skilfully!"

James said, "Yes. And I once heard about negotiations between two sides that had been fighting a civil war for years in a country in Central America, where the talks carried on for ages without getting anywhere, and then one side came up with a solution that would have benefited both sides, but the other side refused to even think about it, just because it had been thought up by the other side, because there was a lot of hatred between both sides because of all the bad things that had happened. But then the person supervising the negotiations and trying to mediate between the two sides went to them separately and said to both of them that if they came up with ideas that both sides might agree to from then on, it would be better if they didn't mention them in front of the other side, but just told him about them, and then he'd bring them up when the two sides were together, and the other side might just assume he'd thought them up himself, so they wouldn't automatically object to them like they might otherwise.

"They both agreed to do that, and from then on, they came up with good ideas, and did what he advised them to do, and they started making progress, and came to an agreement in the end that stopped the war."

The students thought that was interesting, although they thought it was a pity it took that for the sides to stop fighting.

Then Catherine said, "I was talking about how cultures in different countries can be very different from each other earlier, wasn't I. Well I wonder if sometimes, cultural things can get in the way of negotiations succeeding. I think the more people know about the culture of the people in any country that has a different one to theirs when they start negotiations with them, the more successful they might be. I'm pretty sure that applies to all kinds of negotiations – you know, like business negotiations and other things, not just peace treaties and so on. Some countries, like China, have quite complicated rules about the kinds of etiquette and other things like that that people there expect to be followed.

"I think it's possible that sometimes even simple cultural differences could get in the way of successful negotiations. I'll give you an example. Actually, I think I've briefly mentioned it already: In Western cultures, it's thought of as a sign that a person's listening to you if they're looking you in the eye while you're speaking; but in some Eastern cultures, doing that is interpreted as being very disrespectful, so it can antagonise people.

"Mind you, if people from one of those countries are negotiating with people from a Western country and they know the rules are different there, chances are they'll understand that the people aren't being rude, but they've just got different customs."

Dave smirked and said, "I wonder if groups from different countries go into negotiations sometimes and soon start arguments because they've been offended by each other's behaviour, and they insist they change it, when really, they've both just been doing what people are brought up to do in their cultures; and I wonder if the people doing the supervising or mediation of the negotiations have had to think up solutions to their cultural arguments before they could help them think up solutions to the problems they came to negotiate about."

Most of the group giggled, and Heather said, "It wouldn't surprise me. From what you hear on the news, you get the impression sometimes that some politicians behave more childishly than some children!"

Becky found that especially amusing, while other students nodded in agreement.

But Catherine said, "It's not really that funny. It could be especially important for governments to find out about the cultures of countries where there's some hostility between their one and the other one.

"I mean, to give an example, the government of a country like America might think another country's a bit threatening and decide to try to intimidate them into, say, giving up ambitions to get nuclear weapons or something. They might put sanctions on that country and threaten them with military action if they don't do what America wants, or that kind of thing; but they might find out that it has the opposite effect, just making the other country's government more determined to get nuclear weapons. The government of any country might react defiantly like that; but one from a country with a culture where it's especially important not to lose face might be especially likely to react in the opposite way to the one the American government intended, because they might think that to back down from what they were planning to do after that might seem especially weak to their people.

"So if a government offers to make some kind of deal that benefits both countries, it might sometimes work better, if the other country's government can then say to its people, 'We're able to make these concessions because the other country has agreed to change their ways towards us and give us this, that and the other.' . . . Well, they wouldn't say that exactly, obviously, but you know what I mean."

The students smiled. Some became thoughtful. But then they started talking gloomily about the possibility that wars could have sometimes happened because cultural and other misunderstandings weren't cleared up.

The Students Discuss Problems Caused by Backbiting and Misinterpreting Things People Do and Say

Then Suzy said, "I wonder if the kind of negotiations where both sides try to think up solutions that'll suit both sides instead of trying to compete to get what they want could work in more small-scale conflicts than war, such as family disputes, and arguments between work colleagues, and that kind of thing. I mean, just to give an example of a little thing, say if a family wants to go on a day out at the weekend, and some of its members want to go to the seaside, while others really want to go to the zoo . . ."

Dave interrupted and said, "One of the parents could say, 'You don't need to go to the zoo when you've got your little brother to look at; just pretend he's a zoo animal, which won't be hard, and your craving to gaze at zoo creatures will be partly satisfied. And when we go down to the beach, it'll be like taking a bit of the zoo with us!' "

The students laughed. But Suzy said with a grin, "I don't mean that! I mean both sides could try to come up with solutions that'll please everyone, instead of arguing about which place to go to. You know, so maybe they might end up deciding to go to both places, the seaside first, if the weather's hot at the time, and the zoo a few weeks later, when the weather might be cooler, but it won't matter, because they probably won't want to take so many of their clothes off . . . Hopefully. I suppose they might really have an urge to live like the animals and feel like taking them all off if they're a bit weird. But if they do it would probably cause less of a stir if they did that at home.

"Mind you, there are other kinds of things that cause family disputes that you couldn't use that kind of negotiation style with. I think big fallings-out can happen between people because of just little misunderstandings sometimes. I heard about even just stupid jokes that have caused serious problems, like when some twit sent a Valentine's card to a married woman for a laugh, saying how nice it was to be with her or something, and her husband got really suspicious that she was being unfaithful, and it caused big problems. And I remember once when I was about eleven, I started a rumour just for fun about a maths teacher who'd recently left the school I was at: I told someone the reason he'd gone was because he'd pushed a girl down some stairs and been sacked. I heard that rumour being told to others about four years later! Goodness knows who'd been told it in the meantime! It just shows you what can happen!"

A sense of horror started creeping over some of the students. Stuart, distracted by the conversation, picked up some pepper and sprinkled it all over what was left of his dinner. He'd meant to put more salt on it. He began to sneeze loudly, and wasn't sure he wanted his dinner any more.

James said, "Things could have got worse if staff heard it."

Another loud sneeze, which everyone in the surrounding rooms probably heard, followed immediately. Some of the group sniggered, thinking some of the university staff probably did hear that sneeze. Guessing what they thought was funny, James said, "I mean the rumour."

As Stuart shook as much of the pepper as he could off every bit of his dinner in preparation for mustering up the stamina to try to eat it, Suzy continued,

"I read about a study that showed that a lot of people pass on gossip about other people, but deliberately exaggerate it or add bits, because they're not just trying to pass along information, but they want to entertain people, or look like a good conversationalist, or do something else like that. They can think that if something makes the story more entertaining, it's worth adding even if it isn't true. Or sometimes they forget bits, and make up things to fill in the gaps, so as not to have to suddenly stop their story when they're halfway through it and say they've forgotten bits. Or sometimes they leave out important details, like saying someone lost his temper at work and shouted and swore at the boss, without saying the boss had been bullying him for months before that, and that he'd always put up with it before but just couldn't stand it any more.

"So it's best not to just believe any old thing people say. I think it's usually best to reserve judgment, and to keep an open mind about what people are like and whether what you're being told is true, unless you're being warned about someone who could be a safety risk or something."

Emma said, "Yeah. I think it might be good to reserve judgment quite a lot of the time. but I think that should only be taken so far. I heard someone say they thought reserving judgment too much could put people at risk, because they might ignore signs that a person isn't safe to be around, because they don't think they've got enough information to make a judgment yet, but then one day it might be too late."

Suzy said, "Yeah. I'm not saying people shouldn't be wary if they hear worrying stuff. I just think that quite a lot of the time, people can harm other people's reputations unfairly.

"Mind you, I think that sometimes, people don't give a bad impression of a person they're talking about deliberately, but they might complain about something they've done, maybe just to let off steam if they're a bit annoyed, or maybe even just because they think it's a decent way to pass the time of day or something; and anyone who doesn't know the person being complained about might think they sound like a horrible person, when really, they might do a lot of nice things; it might be just that the thing they've done that the person's complaining about is what's on their mind at the time, so they're only talking about that, not any of the nice things they might just possibly bring up if they felt like it one day; but it'll mean that if someone hearing about it hasn't met that person before, the bad thing might be the first thing they think about if they do meet them, which might not actually be fair.

"You know, they might be thinking something like, 'Oh no, here's that horrible person who did . . .' whatever it was, when they might not even have done everything the person who complained about them said they did."

Heather said, "I don't understand why people tell tales. If I've got something to say about someone, I prefer to say it to their face, because I don't think it's fair to say bad things about people behind their backs unless there's a good reason for it. Mind you, that backfires on me – I've been called a complainer and a troublemaker by people who think I'm the only one who's got problems with things they're doing, because they haven't realised that actually, other people have said much worse things than me; the difference is that they've complained behind their backs. Maybe doing that's more sensible, even if it doesn't seem very fair to me because the person isn't there to defend themselves.

"But I've also heard the very people who've told me I'm rude saying much worse things about other people than I ever have, just behind their backs. And then later one or two of them have sometimes told me they have a lot of respect for those people, saying that makes them annoyed at something I'm supposed to have said to them. It's a strange world! Why would they say bad things about them in front of other people if they have that much respect for them? And then complain if they think someone else has said something bad about them?

"And there's something weird I've noticed. I know someone who told me she's lived in the African jungle without tap water or electricity, having to wash her clothes in rivers, and seeing severe poverty, and living in tough conditions in other parts of the world too. You'd have thought a person like that wouldn't get all worked up about trivial things, because they'd get them in perspective, but it just isn't true! At least not for her, if she really has done those things.

"She's retired now, and living near my parents, and I don't know if it's because she isn't doing much with her days so she hasn't got much to occupy her mind, so little things go around and around in it till they get to seem more important than they really are – that probably happens to everyone sometimes – but if someone makes a little comment she finds insulting, or even if someone just slams their car door instead of shutting it gently a bit more often than she's grudgingly willing to tolerate outside her house when they go on a few evenings out, she can still be angry and complaining about it months later, literally, mainly behind their back, but to their face if she feels provoked, as if she's still as annoyed as she was when it happened! She's done that kind of thing to me, and she's done it to other people.

"Once, she said I must be a 'mean person', all because I'd made a sarcastic comment she didn't like a few months earlier. I was annoyed with her about something she'd done that was inconsiderate at the time when I made it, but she didn't know that. Fancy thinking you can judge a person's entire personality based on just one single comment they make! I'd say that was getting things out of perspective. And the funny thing is that I heard her say to someone not long afterwards, 'I just don't get offended by things now. I used to – I used to get furious, but not nowadays.'"

"Ah, but maybe you've got the psychology of it all wrong," joked Dave with a mischievous grin. "Maybe it's not that she just hasn't got much to do now so she broods on things more than she should; maybe things happened in that jungle that made a quiet suburban life seem intolerably boring by comparison, and she feels as if she needs to stir up some problems and drama to feel properly alive again.

"I mean, who knows, maybe she was chased by a drunken bear, or had screeching monkeys fling bananas on her head every day from the trees, or had swarms of flies rush her from miles around whenever she tried to eat, and the only way she could get away from them was to jump into a cold stream and almost bury herself in it; or maybe she was flung up into the treetops on an elephant's trunk, or she had to chase hyenas out of her house every evening before she could sleep, or she ate hallucinogenic tree bark and was transported into a nightmare world where she was a Viking fighting fierce gods who'd decreed that she had to be thrown in the river if she didn't win in a contest against them, or she sank into a swamp one day and only made it out alive because a lion thought she looked like a tasty morsel and dragged her out, but then decided she was so muddy he didn't fancy eating her after all – maybe that even happened more than once.

"Or maybe she had to scare off crocodiles every week who tried to eat her washing when she put it in the river to wash; or if she wanted her food to taste interesting, maybe she had no other choice than to flavour it with tasty toxic mould that gave her such bad digestive problems she was blown three feet up into the air every time she broke wind; or maybe she had to rebuild her little house every day because rats and giant snails the size of cats with four-inch teeth would gnaw it to bits every night till it fell on her head.

"Maybe all those things happened. And after all that, a life where nothing went wrong and there were no arguments might just seem way way too boring, so she has to make problems for herself!"

The students giggled.

Then the conversation began to get serious again as Catherine said, "I know people who get upset over things I just wouldn't expect anyone to get upset over too."

"Like the blob of tomato sauce on your nose?" asked Mya with a smile.

Catherine blushed and wiped her hand over her nose. Then she carried on, "Well, maybe. But anyway, I hate it when people gossip about you behind your back and you end up being accused of things you haven't done. But I've found out that sometimes even when someone's telling another person the whole truth about something they're upset with you about behind your back, and they're not even intending to gossip, it can be misinterpreted by the person they're talking to, who can then have a go at you because they think it's your fault, even if the person who brought the subject up in the first place hardly said a thing! And then you end up looking bad. I've known it happen."

Becky started feeling a bit fed up that the conversation seemed to be turning a bit depressing again, and sarcastically announced decisively, "I think it's time we all had a cry!"

Some of the students sniggered. Catherine smiled and said, "Come on Becky, it's not going to get that bad! I'm just talking about one way I've learned that misunderstandings can happen.

"Like, say if someone – I may as well call her Sandra – was looking a bit upset, and a friend of hers – let's say she's called Christine – asked why, she might say, 'Janice said she doesn't want to go to Sophie's party with me'; and Christine might immediately assume that the reason that upset Sandra must have been because Janice said it in a hurtful way that sounded like rejection. She might not ask Sandra the reason, but just assume it must be that. So she might get angry, thinking that Sandra's been kind to Janice at times, so it's unfair that Janice should speak to her like that. So she might talk angrily with Janice later, telling her that if she wanted to tell Sandra she didn't want to go to the party, she could have at least done it nicely! But all along, what had upset Sandra might not have been the phrasing Janice had used or her attitude, but the fact that if Janice didn't go to the party, Sandra would have to go alone, and she'd feel awkward and self-conscious, because she hardly knew anyone."

Kirsty started to smirk and said, "Sandra would have to be a bit of a wuss to get all upset about that though, wouldn't she!"

Some of the students sniggered. But Catherine said seriously, "Well maybe, but this is just an example anyway.

"A different possibility is that Sandra herself might have misunderstood Janice's meaning when she said she didn't want to go to the party, and complained to Christine when Christine found her looking a bit upset, because she thought Janice must have been saying it because she didn't like her company, when all along, Janice just wasn't keen on parties."

Charlotte rubbed her head and said with a grin, "I'm not sure I'm going to be able to keep track of this if it goes on much longer. It might give me a headache!"

Catherine said, "Sorry. I'm just saying I reckon it's often best to ask a person you've been told has done something wrong for their version of events before you have a go at them. I mean, I know you wouldn't always get the truth, because sometimes people can lie and make excuses, thinking up supposed reasons for why they said or did things on the spur of the moment when they're asked about them; but I still think people ought to have a chance to explain themselves."

Some of the students were thoughtful. A few, though, felt as if they were being given an extracurricular lesson. They tried to take it in dutifully, but one or two had started nodding off after their lunch. Not for long though.

A Student Tells a Story Involving a Plumber and a Pointless Argument With a Neighbour

Mya said, "This kind of thing bothers me as well. Some people get offended by surprising things; and you can't always predict that someone's going to be offended by something, because often they get offended because they've taken it more personally than it was meant or something; so it doesn't always help just to be more careful what you say."

Emma said, "One of My sisters had a weird problem a bit like that, with someone who seemed to be getting offended for no good reason. She's older than me, and she moved into a flat of her own a few years ago. Then at Christmas time – not last Christmas but the one before – her boiler broke, so she didn't have any heating or hot water. She emailed a relative of ours who lives near her, to see if she could come up with any ideas about what might be wrong. Well, the relative doesn't know anything about boilers, but her husband does. But she didn't reply. I think she was busy at the time, and it turned out that her dog was ill, so maybe that was why.

"But about the day before then, someone had given my sister a big plant for Christmas. She didn't really want it, because she was worried she might kill it by forgetting to water it or something. So she asked this relative if she'd like it and she said she would, since she's fond of plants, although she said she could collect it in a few days, but not before.

"But when she didn't reply about the boiler, my sister decided to ask a neighbour whether she knew anything about boilers instead, after she decided to give her the plant instead, since it was her birthday, and she was a bit wary about keeping it for a while in case she accidentally killed it, and she didn't know when she'd hear from our relative again, although she knew it wasn't that nice giving the plant to someone else after saying our relative could have it. But now she wishes she'd just waited a while longer and given it to our relative, and phoned her up to discuss the boiler so they could have arranged for her husband to come and look at it, since he would probably have known what he was doing, and she knows them both well enough to have been pretty sure they wouldn't have got offended by daft things, like the neighbour did in the story I'm going to tell you. But she didn't know there would be a problem with the neighbour at the time.

"The neighbour, who's in her seventies, I think, was nice to her when she first moved in. She said she'd help her if she needed it, and did things like driving her to the shops so she could buy a freezer and tumble drier, and driving her to the hospital to see our dad after he broke his hip. She seemed friendly. But it turns out it seems she can get upset surprisingly easily, over things a lot of other people wouldn't be bothered about at all, for some reason. It seems a bit strange, since her husband was in the navy for years, and I think he was in some situations where Britain was in conflict with other countries; but it seems that didn't make his wife get smaller things in perspective so as not to get so upset about them.

"What happened was that when my sister told her her boiler was broken and asked if she knew anything about boilers, she said she didn't, but she said it was my sister's lucky day because her brother was coming round later and he did know something about them. Well it turns out he didn't know as much as she thought he did.

"He put the boiler pressure up, which it turns out is often what's needed when it stops working; but he put it up too high, and it seems something broke. We think something else was already broken though, because it took a lot longer than it should have done to go up.

"Neither my sister or me knew anything about boiler pressure before, but we looked online afterwards, and it turns out that boilers need some pressure in them to work, for some reason.

I'm still not much the wiser actually, because I didn't find out everything I wanted to know, or else I did but I've forgotten it; but it's something to do with water expanding a bit when it heats up and putting pressure on the boiler because of that, but how the heating system needs the pressure in it to propel the water around it somehow or something. I don't really know, but it's not that important to know for anyone who doesn't work with boilers for a living, I don't suppose.

"I think the only thing it's necessary for most people with boilers to know is that if the pressure gets too high, the boiler might break, and if it gets too low, it'll stop working, although then it's more easily fixable, because there are a couple of little taps on it that put more water into it when they're turned, and the pressure goes up when that happens, so it starts working again. There's a pressure gauge on a boiler, and it should read somewhere between 1.5 and 2, I think, because that's a healthy level for it to be at.

"But when my sister's neighbour's brother came to look at her boiler, he put it up a fair bit higher than that. I'm not sure if he did it deliberately, not realising it shouldn't be up that high, or whether it kept going up after he turned the taps off, for some reason. But it took way longer than it should have done to go up. Well, I don't know how long it took to just go up to where it was supposed to be, and how much of the time it took was it going up higher than it should have been. But eventually it went up to 3. But then when my sister turned the hot tap on in the sink, it suddenly went up to 4, because it goes up a fair bit when people do that. I think 3's the maximum it should ever go, which is why people shouldn't put it up beyond 2, because it can go up on its own a fair bit for a little while when people put the hot water on.

"Anyway, like I said, I don't really understand it. And my sister didn't realise there would be a problem with the pressure at the time. Her boiler came on again when the pressure was put up, so she thought it must be mended. But then a couple of hours later, it went off again.

"Her neighbour's brother recommended what he thought was a plumber with a respectable-sounding name to come in and fix it, but it turned out to be a plumbing insurance company, so she got no joy there. But then he got in touch with a plumbing company that had done some work for him and my sister's neighbour before, and asked them to come round. My sister was pleased at first.

"A few days later, before the plumber got to come round, we visited my sister – my parents and me, and my brother and my other sister and her husband Mark. My sister who lived there told us about the broken boiler, and Mark went outside and said he could see water leaking near the kitchen window, and told us he thought it was coming from a valve that's designed to open when the boiler pressure gets too high to let some water out of it, and that puts the pressure down, but he said sometimes they get stuck open, and then water keeps on leaking out of them till there's none left in the boiler, and then it'll stop working. So my sister realised that was probably why her boiler had stopped working again so soon after her neighbour's brother had put the pressure up.

"Mark said the valve would need replacing, and that he'd leave a note for the plumber to tell him about it, as well as letting him know about a few other minor things he noticed when he looked at the boiler that he thought might be worth the plumber looking at, such as one of the little taps for turning the pressure up leaking a bit, so water was dripping on the floor in the cupboard the boiler was in. He gave the note to my sister to give to him, but told her to tell him he wasn't an expert, just to make sure he didn't get offended by thinking Mark was trying to tell him what to do. So much for that idea! . . . Well, it wasn't the plumber himself who got offended.

"My sister assumed the plumber might appreciate being told about what seemed to be at least one or two of the problems, because it would mean he could look at those first so it would make his job easier and more quick and efficient, instead of him having to look at goodness knows how many things before he discovered what was wrong, although she knew there might be more things wrong than Mark had found. So she thought giving him the bit of paper would be a good idea.

"But it seems not everyone felt that way! My dad had met the neighbour before, and he wanted to stay on good terms with her, so he went round for what he wanted to be a friendly chat. But the subject of the boiler came up, and she and her husband got a bit edgy about the idea of Mark interfering, saying he should stay out of it since he wasn't an expert. My dad said that he did actually know a fair bit about plumbing, trying to reassure them. Mark's actually installed a boiler himself in his own house, so he must know quite a bit.

"When the plumber came round, my sister's neighbour came in with him. My sister gave the plumber the bit of paper and started explaining what was on it and where it came from, just saying Mark had noticed a couple of things that didn't seem right, but that he wasn't an expert. The neighbour interrupted and told her she thought they ought to just leave the room and let the plumber get on with doing his job. My sister didn't understand why she wanted to hurry her away, but decided to just put up with it, thinking it wouldn't really matter as long as the plumber read what was on the bit of paper himself. She hoped he would.

"The neighbour left soon after that, and my sister went in her lounge and started working on her computer. A bit later the plumber came in and told her the expansion vessel had gone flat. She didn't know what one of those was, but I think he said it's the part of the boiler where the water gets stored. He said he'd inflate it, but that they would often go down again within a month, or even just a day, and then they'd need replacing altogether.

"The plumber inflated it and left, and my sister wondered if it had been the expansion vessel causing the fault all along in that case, not the valve outside. But within a mere couple of hours, the boiler went off again! So she wondered if the plumber might have overlooked the valve and it was still faulty. He hadn't gone outside to investigate the leak. It was the middle of winter, so she really wanted her hot water and heating back!

"It so happened that her loo had started leaking not long before that, and she or her neighbour had asked the plumbing company if someone could come round to fix it. Soon someone did, a different plumber to the one who'd been looking at the boiler, but one from the same company. Her neighbour came in with him again. My sister mentioned that the boiler had broken again and asked if he could leave a note for the other plumber to ask if he could come back and look at the valve that Mark had seen leaking and replace the expansion vessel. The plumber didn't seem to mind her asking, and neither did her neighbour at the time.

"But goodness knows if she went away and stewed over it and worked herself up into a worry or a temper, or what. After the neighbour left, my sister went and did some more work on her computer. But a while later, her neighbour knocked on the door, and came in and started an argument with her! My sister didn't know why. But the neighbour started trying to convince her she shouldn't have told the plumber what Mark had said about the valve being broken, since he wasn't an expert so he couldn't know what he was talking about. My sister said he actually did know quite a bit about plumbing. And considering he'd actually seen water coming out of an overflow pipe near the kitchen window, well, something must have been causing it.

"My sister thought it was odd that her neighbour wanted to turn it into an argument, as if she was thinking my sister thought there was some kind of contest where the plumber was saying one thing was wrong and Mark was saying it was a different thing, so it was a matter of his opinion versus the plumber's, and that my sister was thinking Mark knew better than the plumber did about what was wrong, or that the plumber wasn't doing his job properly. It wasn't like that at all. My sister only asked the plumber fixing the loo to ask the other plumber to look at the valve along with fitting a new expansion vessel because she wondered if he hadn't spotted the problem, and really wanted her heating and hot water back, considering it was the middle of winter! She just wanted the reassurance and the peace of mind of knowing the boiler would be fixed. At least she had an electric heater she was using to warm up the room she was spending most of her time in when she was at home.

"She did also contact the plumbing company to ask them if they could send someone to come round again after that.

"I started wondering whether the real reason the neighbour was making such a fuss about how she thought my sister shouldn't be talking to the plumber about the problem was because her brother had realised he'd turned the boiler pressure up too high so he'd been the one that made the valve open to let water out, so he could possibly be blamed for making it break, and my sister's neighbour was worried my sister might tell the plumber that, so she wanted to shut her up, or discredit Mark in the hope he really was wrong about the valve, so the plumbers wouldn't realise her brother had had something to do with the breakage, since her brother often used those plumbers to fix problems in properties he owned, so she might have thought it was important for them to be on good terms.

"I don't know though. Maybe the neighbour was just working herself up with paranoia in her flat about just what my sister might be saying, and discussing it with her husband who might have been giving her more ideas for what to worry about, till she thought she'd better quickly go and stop my sister from saying whatever she was worried she might be saying.

"Or maybe she's just addicted to being a bit bossy and controlling, and she's got some kind of rigid belief that people shouldn't question tradesmen who know a lot more about the work they're doing than a lot of other people do or something. Who knows! My sister did say she was a bit bossy with her the night her brother came round and put the boiler pressure up, and her husband actually told her off for it.

"My sister says it wouldn't have bothered her if a plumber had looked things over and said there wasn't a problem with the valve after all, as long as the boiler had been fixed properly!

"But she said that during the argument, her neighbour kept saying she should just keep quiet and let the plumber do his job. She didn't like that, because it sounded to her as if her neighbour was trying to restrict her freedom to say what she thought needed to be said, for some unknown reason, and that could have meant she'd be less likely to get the reassurance she needed that the problem was going to be fixed or would be looked into.

"My sister said the neighbour said other things during the argument as well, and she didn't understand why she was saying them, as if she was answering criticisms my sister hadn't even made, like saying the plumber was only trying to save her money by not recommending that the entire boiler be replaced, when it hadn't even entered my sister's mind that the whole boiler should perhaps be replaced.

"My sister had doubts about whether the neighbour was right in what she said about that, but she didn't want to say so in front of the plumber mending the loo, because she didn't want it to sound as if she was questioning whether the boiler plumber really did have those motives or might have other ones, or anything like that. So she wanted to stop the argument, and said she didn't understand why her neighbour had started it and that it was a silly argument. Her neighbour disagreed that it was. My sister didn't want to carry on the argument in front of the plumber, so she told her neighbour to go away. Her neighbour said she would, but that my sister shouldn't expect her to help her in future.

"My sister said, 'Don't then!'

"Then the neighbour left. My sister started chatting in a friendly way to the plumber mending the loo straight afterwards, and he showed her how to put the boiler pressure up if it stopped working again.

"Soon afterwards, the plumbing company told her they always put new valves in when they replace expansion vessels, and sent someone round to do both. Then the boiler at least kept working for quite some time. I don't know why the plumber didn't replace the valve in the first place. I do wonder sometimes whether it could have been because the company knew they'd be called back soon so they could charge more if the valve wasn't replaced there and then so the boiler would stop working again as soon as all the water leaked out of the boiler; but I don't really know.

"Mark reckons the plumber who looked at the boiler might well have been related to the neighbour in some way, which is what could have made her especially sensitive to anything that might have come across as criticism of him; and he thinks she maybe knew he was a bit dodgy, and didn't want my sister to ask him enough questions that she found out. But I don't know about that.

"When the boiler broke again, a few months later, my sister got another plumbing company in, after she looked on the Internet and found one with a lot of good reviews, that was listed on a website with lists of trusted traders on it. That's probably what she should have done in the first place.

"After the argument, my sister decided not to have anything to do with the neighbour any more except in emergencies, since after all, she had said she wouldn't help her, and it wasn't as if they were friends, and she seemed to get offended unpredictably and surprisingly easily. So they didn't talk to each other after that.

"But something weird that happened was that well over a year later, our mum visited my sister, and her neighbour had never seen her before, as far as I know, so I don't know if she knew who she was, but she met her and complained to her about what had happened all that time before, as if she'd been brooding on it ever since it happened so it was still fresh in her mind, and she was still so upset she wanted to pour her heart out to someone about it. But she didn't complain about what really happened, but about some version of events she seems to have made up in her mind. She said she was upset because the brother of my sister and I was shouting at my sister on the phone while the plumber was there, telling her the plumber wasn't doing his job properly, and that made my sister get cross with the plumber, and the neighbour was upset by that, because she'd used the plumbers before and didn't want them to be offended. That never happened!

"Our mum actually knew a bit about what had really happened, and when the neighbour told her our brother had shouted at my sister on the phone, she said, 'Don't you mean brother-in-law? But he doesn't shout.' But the neighbour said my sister had told her it was our brother. In reality our brother hadn't had anything to do with it, and I very much doubt my sister would have told her he had. I don't think he would claim to know anything about plumbing himself.

"The neighbour said it was a very distressing incident for her, and very hurtful, because her family had used those plumbers before, so she was upset that they were being spoken to like that.

"Since her version of events never actually happened, it seems that she was 'very hurt' by a 'very distressing incident' that was mostly manufactured in her own mind somehow! I don't know how she could have got events distorted in her mind like that. I don't know if she somehow misremembered witnessing it. If she didn't, then I don't know how she thought she knew it had even happened, since she wasn't even there when it supposedly did!

"My sister thinks there might have been one point when the plumber mending the loo was there when she did go out of her lounge to just check he remembered she'd asked him if he'd mind leaving a note for the boiler plumber about the boiler breaking again and the leaky valve, just to try to make sure he didn't forget; and her voice might have been a bit raised then, but only because she was in the hall, and she thought she might need to talk a little bit louder than normal because the plumber was in the bathroom with his head down the loo . . . well, not actually down it, but behind it, because that's where the leak was. So it's possible the nosy neighbour was listening outside the door of her flat at the time, and inter-preted that as her being angry – although since the plumber mending the toilet had nothing to do with the boiler, I don't know what she thought the point would have been of my sister getting angry with him!

"And during the argument they had, the neighbour didn't make any accusations at all about her getting cross with the plumber, which you'd have thought she would have done if that was genuinely what was bothering her at the time. It really does seem as if she entirely invented that bit in her mind afterwards. Goodness knows why!

"I wondered if it could be that she was imagining what bad things my sister might have said to the plumber when she went away after the argument, and then her memories of what really happened got a bit hazy over time, and she started mis-taking her imaginings for the truth, or something like that. Or maybe she'd told the story to other people over time, but told it in a way that made her look better, and over time she came to believe her altered version of events. Who knows!"

Charlotte said, "It might not apply in this situation, but I read that some people often have false memories of things, especially people with dementia; but some healthy people can have them too. Some people with dementia can do things like think they've turned the stove off when they haven't really. Maybe they can think about how they ought to do that soon, and when they think back, they misremember that as them actually turning it off. Mind you, that could only be the cause of it till they've got such bad memory loss they can't remember any details at all about anything that happened over the previous ten minutes or so. If they still get false memories like that after that, maybe something different was always causing them, or maybe it was a combination of things before. I don't know.

"I can't remember if what I read said older people whose minds aren't working so well but haven't got dementia are still more likely to have false memories like that. Still, even if that's true, it wouldn't necessarily mean that was what happened with the neighbour."

Becky said, "My uncle Steven seemed to have a false memory not long ago. He's not very old. But he came to visit us recently, and he brought us some food, and he thought he'd brought a loaf of bread, but he couldn't find it. He searched for it in his car, thinking it might have fallen out in there. But it wasn't there. Then he looked at his shopping receipt and it didn't say bread on it. He wondered if it had somehow fallen out of his basket before he got to the till. But I wonder if he'd just thought about how he wanted to get some soon, and then he went to get other things, and then he misremembered him thinking hard about getting some as him actually getting some. Who knows!

"I'm not saying I think the neighbour might have just innocently misremembered things though. Maybe she was deliberately telling a false version of events, for some reason, like if she did know who the mum was, and was worried the sister would tell her something that would incriminate her, or that she already had, so she wanted to make herself look better by trying to make the mum believe her version of events instead. Who knows!"

A Couple of the Group Talk About Experiences of People Being Overly-Defensive

Sarah looked at Emma and said, "When you said that thing about your sister just wanting reassurance and peace of mind that things would be alright when she asked the plumber if he'd leave a note for the other one, it reminded me of something.

"When I was younger, my parents used to get a baby-sitter in to look after me and my younger brother and sister. She was kind and caring, mostly, but some of the things she used to say made me cringe a bit. Before my parents would leave, my mum would say things to her like, 'You won't let the little ones run in the road, will you', and, 'You will give them enough to drink so they don't go thirsty, won't you.' I'm sure she was just saying things like that to get some reassurance, so it would increase her peace of mind about leaving us. But I'm guessing our baby-sitter took offence, thinking, 'Just what kind of person do you think I am?', or something like that, because she used to reply with this trashy unfunny low-grade sarcasm, saying things like, 'Actually, I'm going to let them play in the road till they get run over', and, 'No, I'm not going to give them anything to drink at all so they get dehydrated.'

"I was pretty sure she didn't really mean it, but it still made me wonder if she really cared about us as much as she seemed to, or whether in reality she didn't give a stuff about us, and wouldn't care if something bad happened to us. So I felt less confident about spending time with her than I would've done if she hadn't said those things."

Charlotte said, "It sounds as if maybe her sarcasm was a kind of defensiveness. I think it's funny the way some people get really defensive, thinking they're making themselves look better by doing that, when actually they're making themselves look a lot worse without realising. I've got an aunt who once visited us and used my laptop without asking me, and I caught her looking at my emails. I protested, and she said defensively, 'Well you never said I shouldn't do that! How was I to know you didn't want me to?' Well I didn't think I needed to tell her! Everyone knows it's just polite to ask people if you can use their stuff; and everyone knows it's nosy to look at other people's emails!

"Later I told her she could be overly defensive, and she said, 'I have to stand up for myself.' But she would often look a whole lot better if she just apologised than she does by trying to un-fairly shift the blame for her behaviour onto others, or getting all argumentative at the drop of a hat, turning what should be minor disagreements into extended bicker-fests, like she often does!

"She's got a daughter who's just a bit younger than me, who's developed a few of her habits. Sometimes my aunt asks her to help with the housework, like doing some washing up. The other day she complained to me that her and her husband went out for a while and asked her daughter to do the washing up while she was out. When they came back, she hadn't done it, and when my aunt protested, she said defensively, 'You came back earlier than I expected!', as if it was their fault she hadn't done it. My aunt doesn't like it when she talks to her like that, but I'm sure she doesn't realise she's probably picked up the habit from her."

A Student Tells a Story About an Argument They Had That Could Have Gone a Lot Better

Heather said, "This conversation reminds me of something I experienced when people got all offended: I had this boring summer job not long ago. I was helping in an office, just being a dogsbody-type person, but there wasn't much for me to do. I was making people coffee and running a few errands, and doing a bit of filing, and sorting post that came in and so on. But it wasn't very interesting. It was livened up a bit because I used to get chatting to the people there who used to talk to each other quite a bit, although we had this boss who sometimes came out of his office and made sarcastic bad-tempered remarks if he thought we weren't working hard enough. He would often make them to me, even though there wasn't actually much work for me to do!

"And at first I tended to come in a few minutes late after my lunch break was supposed to end, because I was finishing conversations with people; but I would often stay in the office for a few minutes after my break started, finishing the bit of work I was doing at the time. So it was to do with not wanting to drop things abruptly rather than slacking off. But one day the boss criticised me for coming back a bit late in his sarcastic way, so I thought, 'OK, if you're going to be like that, from now on I'll make sure I come back right on time; but I'm going to go right on time too; I'm not going to stay around finishing work any more before I go!' So that's what I did from then on.

"Anyway, the others in the office invited me out to the pub with them one Friday evening. I went with them, but I didn't have a good time. At first, some of them seemed to be talking a load of old junk, for some reason, just spouting rubbish. Later I got talking to a different one, and I wouldn't normally complain much about people behind their backs, but my boss had been annoying me, and I think I got a bit more drunk than I intended to, and I felt like letting off steam, so I was complaining about the boss to this person for a while.

"As far as I'm aware, what I said didn't get back to him, which was at least one good thing. But a few days later, he had a go at me in front of some of the people there, saying someone had complained to him that I'd said I was brainier than the others in the office. I couldn't remember saying that. Oddly enough, the thought had crossed my mind when they were talking rubbish in the pub, and I actually dreamed I did say it. But I didn't think I'd actually said it. I suppose I could have said it when I was drunk in the pub, and then not remembered the next day. But I didn't think I'd said it. So I denied saying it, and it turned into this brainless argument, where he kept on accusing me of it, and told me all about how unfair it was for me to make judgments like that about people, and I just kept insisting I hadn't said it.

"I asked the boss who'd told him I said it, and he said he wouldn't tell me because it was confidential. There was one person who worked there in particular who was a bit of a troublemaker, who liked to spread rumours and put the worst interpretations on things, but I don't know if it was her. So I thought, 'OK, in that case, since it could have been anyone for

156

all I know, I'll just have to treat everyone here as if they're untrustworthy blabbermouths from now on, and not have anything more to do with anyone than I have to!' So I didn't talk to them much after that.

"If the accusation hadn't come right out of the blue so I wasn't expecting it, maybe I'd have been able to argue a bit more intelligently. I thought about it afterwards, and realised it would have been better if I'd asked the boss questions, like saying, 'OK, I can't remember saying this at all; but if you're sure I did, what was the context? – You know, did I make a pompous pronouncement in front of everyone, saying something like, 'After careful thought, it is my considered conclusion that I'm more brainy than any of you!', or did I say it in a jocular tongue-in-cheek way, like quipping with a smile when someone said something, 'Cor blimey, I reckon I must be more intelligent than you!' Or what?

"And I could have asked him what I was talking about or responding to when I said it, like why it even came up in the conversation.

"If the boss didn't know the answers to those things, I could have asked him how much he really thought he knew about what really happened in that case, like whether he really knew enough to be sure I was being offensive, and how he could be sure I even said it at all if he was so vague on the details.

"And I could have asked, 'So what happened just after I said it? I really can't remember. Were people angry or upset with me? What did they say to me? And what did I say back to them?'

"Again, if he didn't know the answers to those questions, I could have asked him whether he really knew enough about what had happened to be sure what I'd said was as bad as he thought it was. And I could have asked him whether he could be sure I'd really said it at all if he didn't know a thing about what had happened afterwards, since he hardly knew a thing about the supposed incident at all. But if he told a story about what had happened afterwards, I could have either said I had no memory of it and I'd have to ask other people if they remembered it, because it was unclear to me whether the accusation was even true, or I might have said I must have been drunk and not being as thoughtful as I should have been about what I said, and apologised. Or I could have said a mixture of the two things.

"Another thing is that I could have asked him how confident he really was that the person who told him I'd said I thought I was brainier than the rest of them was telling the truth, going by their past record. I could have asked him if he was always confident they were telling the truth when they said things.

"And I could have asked why the person who told him about it didn't want to be identified, asking just what they were afraid of, or whether it was just possible that they didn't want me to confront them about it because they knew full well that they were making something out of nothing, or downright lying.

"And I could have asked how many people heard me say it, like whether it was several people, or whether I just said it to one person, and this other person who supposedly heard it just overheard it said quietly in a crowded room where they could have been mistaken about what they heard.

"And I could have asked why the boss thought no one I'd spoken to since it supposedly happened seemed upset with me, since surely they would be if I'd really said it. He might have said they were probably just being polite or something. But then I could have asked who the people were who heard me say it, saying I'd like to ask them what they really thought. I could have even asked everyone in the office whether they'd heard me say it.

"There are quite a few questions I could have asked, to either reveal the fact that the boss didn't have the right to be as confident about his accusation as he thought he did, because he didn't know as much as he seemed to think he did, or to get to the bottom of things. But – I don't know if it's different for other people – but when I'm put on the spot with someone saying something I didn't expect, I can't immediately think of things like that, especially if it's an accusation that stirs up my emotions a bit, so I'm focusing my attention on them instead of what to say, and the accusation seems to demand an immediate answer, like because I'm worried that if I don't deny it quickly, everyone listening will believe it. You know, you want to stop that happening, because you've started being concerned about what they'll think of you if they do. Not that it really matters if you just deny it, I suppose, since they're not going to automatically believe you just because you do, especially when the other person's insisting they're right.

"But it's easy to think about all kinds of things like this in hindsight. It's not easy to do it right then and there when you're put on the spot. I suppose if someone kept on making similar accusations against someone over time, they could plan for what to say next time they did it, so using those kinds of tactics would probably be easier. I can't be sure how well they would have worked if I'd tried them when I got accused of saying I was more brainy than everyone else though. You can't predict how people are going to respond. And if they respond in a way you didn't expect, you still have to think of how best to reply on the spot!"

One Student Tells the Others About a Joke She Made That Backfired

Kirsty said, "I've upset people without meaning to sometimes, not even realising they were upset till later. Sometimes it was because I said something that was meant to be funny but someone took it seriously. Like once, it was the day after my birthday, and I felt like having a bit of fun to cheer myself up, because I hadn't had much fun on it, and I made up what was supposed to be a joke curse, and printed it out and stuck it on my locker at school, that said something like, 'To all those who didn't wish me a happy birthday, I curse you with this curse.' And then I said things like:

> May your fingers turn into sausages and your
> thumbs to jelly babies!
> May every washing-up sponge you use turn to
> sponge pudding!
> May an oak tree grow in your belly button!
> May you fall desperately in love with a door frame.
> May you develop a fondness for rubbing cream
> cheese all over your hands and face just before
> you have to see someone important.
> May your legs make scary growling and roaring
> sounds every time someone you'd like to im-
> press comes near you.
> May all the trains you travel on take you where you
> want to go via a circuit of the entire country,
> stopping at every station.
> May every one of the songs in your music collection
> be transformed into the sound of a sneeze.

May your nose grow the entire length of your body.

May rain constantly be drizzling on your head when you're outside, keeping up with you no matter how fast you walk, even when it's sunny and dry all around you.

And may you develop the unbreakable habit of saying "Bing bong bung" in a loud sing-song voice every time one of your friends or family members says something to you.

"And I said other stuff like that.

"A couple of days later, someone I didn't know that well told me she'd been upset by it, and said it wasn't fair of me to have cursed everyone, since after all, some people might have been too busy with stressful things to wish me a happy birthday, so they didn't deserve to be cursed. And she complained to one of the teachers about it, who called me over while she was with her and gave me a stern talking to about it. So I had the two of them having a go at me, not willing to believe I'd only been joking, no matter what I said!

"Maybe they'd just been upset by the word 'curse', and didn't look at much of what was on the list of curses, and the ones they did look at, they didn't find funny at all and thought they were meant seriously. But then later they did definitely read it, and this girl still seemed upset, thinking they were deadly serious, even after I'd said I was sorry she'd been upset by them and explained that they were only meant as jokes. She got angry, and said they were as bad as wishing someone would go blind overnight. I didn't understand how anyone could take them seriously, because they're almost all things that could never really happen to anyone, so they'd be pointless curses if they were real ones. I mean, can you imagine someone going around with a hundred foot tall, three foot wide oak tree growing out of their belly button, with the roots spreading for metres and metres all around them? It could never possibly happen, could it!

"Actually, I think the bit of the curse that might have offended her most was one that said, 'May the medical establishment name a disease after you'. That's not at all the same as wishing someone would get a disease, but maybe she thought it was.

"I thought it would be funny to say that, because I've always thought it was amusing and strange that doctors who discover new diseases actually seem to want them named after them. At least, I've always assumed they do, judging by the number of diseases that actually are named after whoever discovered them. I suppose it's possible that there've been doctors who discovered diseases, and other people have decided to name them after them as a tribute, but the doctors were saying, 'No, no, please don't name that horrible thing after me!' but people did anyway. But I can't really imagine diseases being given doctors' names without their permission, at least if they're still alive at the time.

"But you know the kind of thing I mean, there are diseases that I think were named after doctors, or maybe scientists, like Huntington's disease and Parkinson's disease.

"I heard that Tourette's syndrome's named after the person who discovered it. I'm amazed that someone would want a condition where people shout abuse and swear uncontrollably named after them, but it seems the person who first described it did.

"I used to think diseases with people's names in them must be named after patients who had notoriously bad cases of them or something. But then I found out they're named after the doctors or scientists who first recognised them as distinctive diseases.

"Anyway, I know my sister thought the bit of my curse about having a disease named after you was funny at least; she joked that a disease should be named after Her, because she's had aches and pains in various bits of her for years, and most doctors she's been to haven't been able to work out why. But it might be to do with the fact that she's double-jointed; she can bend her thumb right back so it runs the length of her arm . . . Well, I don't mean the whole length; that would make her look scary, wouldn't it! If her arms were hanging down at her sides, her thumbs would be so long they'd dangle down below her knees! It might not be so bad if she could roll them up or fold them up neatly to keep them out of the way. But then, walking around with folded-up giant thumbs could make her look even scarier! Hmmm! If you had massive thumbs, I wonder if they'd get in the way or be a help. But anyway, my sister hasn't really got arm-sized thumbs, just normal-length ones; she can just bend them right back so she can lie them along her arms. That's bad enough!

"Anyway, she said that curse about the disease should specially apply to her. But maybe I should have realised that some people wouldn't think having a disease named after them was amusing.

"This year I felt fed up when my birthday came around, because I knew that my eighteenth birthday meant it would soon be the start of my A levels, and I really wasn't looking forward to them. So I didn't really want to be reminded it was my birthday. Some of my friends wished me a happy birthday. It was nice really. But to cheer myself up, I thought about writing another joke curse to match the first one, but this time saying, 'To everyone who Remembered it's my birthday, I'm furious with you for reminding me of its sorry existence, and I curse you with this curse', putting another string of joke curses up on my school locker. That would have confused them! They might have thought, 'What does she want? One year she curses the people who forgot her birthday, and now she's cursing everyone who remembered it!' But I thought that considering the trouble I got into last time I put a joke curse there, I'd better not.

"When I put that one there, I did think there was a risk that it would upset anyone who didn't read beyond the first couple of lines, so they didn't get to the bits about hoping their fingers turned into sausages and their washing-up sponges turned to sponge pudding, and things like that, but they just read the bit that said I was cursing them; but it just never occurred to me that anyone would still be offended if they read beyond the bit at the very beginning. it just shows you how careful you've got to be sometimes! . . . Well, it shows you something anyway, whatever it is!

"And the person who got all offended about the joke curse might have told other people I'd cursed people, but she wouldn't have said it was funny, because she didn't think it was, and she might not have even told people what my curses were; so They might have thought I'd been nasty. One or two people did stop being so friendly to me around then. I don't know whether it was because of that or something else."

The students sympathised . . . for a few seconds.

The Conversation Turns to Discussion of Misunderstandings and Backbiting Again, Along With a Bit More Joking

Then Matthew said, "That reminds me of a bit of advice I heard once about how people shouldn't make jokes at job interviews, since the interviewer might not share your sense of humour."

Dave said, "Yeah, I suppose they might take something the wrong way, like if they ask someone, 'Where would you want to be in this company in a few years' time', and the interviewee says for a joke, 'I'm hoping I'll have your job'. The interviewer might wonder if they really mean it, and not employ them."

Charlotte grinned and said, "Talking of misunderstandings, the other day I heard an advert on the radio that said, 'Looking for a new job? We have hundreds of job vacancies waiting for you!' I thought, 'How could I be expected to do hundreds of jobs at once?' But then I realised it probably shouldn't be taken quite that literally."

The others laughed.

Then Colin said, "Talking about jokes that could backfire in job interviews though, I suppose another one could be if they ask you how well you think you can do the job, and you sarcastically say you can't do it at all in a moment of madness, and they might think you're being serious. Or it could be a bit subtler than that, like if they asked you to describe yourself, and you said you're always quick to act . . . especially when it's time to rush off for dinner; that would give a bad impression, even if you said it with a smile."

"Oh why would anyone say daft things like that at an interview?" asked Stuart, grinning and then screwing up his face.

"I don't know," said Emma. "Stalling for time while they tried to think of something worthwhile to say, maybe."

James said, "Sometimes you can say things and just not realise how they've been taken till even months afterwards, when someone brings them up! Or maybe sometimes you never will know, and all the while, people might be complaining about you behind your back, or bearing a grudge. Imagine if someone kept joking like that at interviews and never got the jobs they applied for, but never found out it was because they made jokes like that, so they never knew to stop! Wouldn't that be awful!"

Heather said, "But you couldn't expect interviewers to tell all the candidates why they didn't get the job – I mean, sometimes there might be hundreds! If someone keeps failing to get jobs, maybe they should just think through for themselves what might possibly not be working, or change their whole approach, so as to make it more likely that they'll be changing whatever isn't working; or they could maybe get advice from the Internet, or from somewhere else."

James smiled and said, "True, I suppose. But maybe if someone changed the way they went about things in interviews, they'd stop offending the interviewers in one way, only to end up offending them in another way instead.

"But thinking of just people in general, I've found out it's actually possible to upset or offend people without even being there! Miraculously, you can do it when you're hundreds of miles away, and haven't got access to any means of communication, like email or anything. I've done it more than once. Guess how."

Some of the students wondered if James could be talking about some kind of spooky supernatural supposed skill that he might be delusional enough to believe he had. But when no one knew the answer, he said,

"You can've said something a few weeks earlier that gets misunderstood or misremembered, or was misheard in the first place; or in an unguarded moment you can regurgitate some silly thought that popped into your head that you really should have kept to yourself; and then without you knowing it, it gets passed around behind your back, and it might not have even been your exact wording, but some kind of twisted version, with other people's mean-spirited interpretations of it; and then months later, you can be told that 'you' upset people; you can really be getting the blame for what happened afterwards when you weren't even there.

"It's happened to me. I was even told I caused a 'very upsetting incident', when I couldn't think what on earth was upsetting about what I'd said to supposedly spark it off. It turned out that it was conversations people had had afterwards about what I'd said, that I didn't even know they were having, that ended up with someone being supposedly upset, because it seems exaggerated or twisted versions or interpretations of the significance of what I'd said were being passed on!

"I won't say what it was all about. But I got unfairly accused of something, just because people had read way way too much into something they were told I'd said, without being told why I said it, it seems.

"One of the people who stirred things up wanted my help with something not long after that, but I refused, and it turned into a conversation where I told her all about how I was annoyed about what she'd said. She did at least apologise.

"Mind you, I've interpreted things I've been told that someone said in a worse way than they were meant before, or someone else has, and then they've told me an inaccurate version of what the person said, and I've got annoyed with the one who supposedly said it, when it turned out that I shouldn't have done.

"Like there was one time when I'd done some lifting and carrying for someone who was moving house, and later I was told by a certain family member of mine that the person had said they didn't think I'd helped enough. I got annoyed, because it wasn't as if I'd been obligated to help at all! So I had a go at the person I'd done the lifting and carrying for, telling her she was really ungrateful and that she should be thankful I did anything!

"Then she told me she hadn't accused me of not helping enough, and said that what had happened was that the certain family member had asked her if I'd done my fair share of the work. She'd looked doubtful and said, 'I don't know about a "fair" share, but he did quite a bit to help.'

"The person in my family assumed she meant I hadn't done the amount that would qualify as a 'fair' share, but that I had at least done something. So she went back and told me that the person moving hadn't thought I'd done much to help. But what the person told me she'd actually meant was that she didn't think it was a case of doing fair shares, because she didn't think it was as if anyone was duty-bound to help at all, so she thought it was up to them how much they did."

The students were thoughtful.

Then Catherine said, "People can get the wrong impression of things from what people say about themselves as well as from what other people say about them. I don't just mean a bad impression, but often things like the impression that they deserve sympathy when they don't really, or that other people were entirely to blame for something that happened when in reality they themselves were at least partly at fault. Or both in one go.

"I mean, one example is that someone – I'll call him Bob – might complain that he was thrown out of a building for just disagreeing with someone about something and telling them they were wrong and silly when they criticised him. Anyone listening might think it sounds as if it was really unfair that Bob got thrown out of a place just for that. But if they got to hear the point of view of the person who got Bob thrown out, it might turn out that their side of the story is that Bob wasn't just disagreeing, but yelling aggressively, causing people around him to get worried that he might get violent, and that the reason he was thrown out of the building was that he refused to leave after he was told to.

"You know, it might happen if, say, Bob was being interviewed for a job, and he was told that certain things about his behaviour disqualified him from having it, and he refused to accept that he wasn't going to get it, and stayed around arguing because he thought he ought to be given it. I heard about something like that that actually did happen not long ago."

Colin grinned and said sarcastically, "That kind of behaviour's just bound to make an interviewer change their minds and give you the job, isn't it!"

The others chuckled.

But then Mya said, "I heard about a creepy experience someone had, to do with making complaints and being at work – or at least, I thought it sounded a bit creepy myself: She moved to another part of the country because she was hoping to make a new start in life, and she wanted to settle near where her son was living. She moved in with him and his wife for a while while she got things organised for herself.

"A routine started where every morning before her son's wife went to work, she would come into this woman's room and they'd have a friendly chat. But often, in the middle of the day, her son would come and talk to her, saying he'd just been on the phone to his wife, who'd rung up and made quite a few complaints about her; and he'd talk for a few minutes about what he said they were.

"The woman kept wondering what on earth must be going on in her son's wife's mind between the time they had a friendly chat and the time when she phoned her husband to complain about her, to make her change her attitude so much, going from being friendly to deciding there were problems that were bothering her so much that she even needed to phone him to complain right there and then, despite being in the middle of work, instead of waiting till she got home to complain.

"But then one day, the woman found out that it hadn't been the wife complaining at all. What had been happening was that her son had been the one with all the complaints, but instead of telling her he was the one with the problems, he would keep pretending it was his wife who had them and that she'd phoned him up from work to complain about her."

The students were dismayed at the story.

But then Kirsty said with a smile, "I think there might have been a misunderstanding between me and my older sister recently. My family moved house earlier this year, and one Saturday not long before I left school, my older sister, who married and moved away a couple of years ago, phoned up fairly late in the morning and said she was in the area that day, and asked if we were doing anything that day or whether we'd be around if she visited us. We said it would be nice to see her. She spoke to me, and asked me if I was dressed yet. I said no.

I later realised that she probably thought that meant I'd only just got up, when actually I'd been up for a couple of hours; I'd just had breakfast when I first got up while my dad was taking ages in the bathroom, shaving and stinking the place out with hairspray, and doing whatever else he does in there, and then I got absorbed in something on my computer, so I hadn't bothered to get washed and dressed before she phoned.

"Then when we met up and started talking, my sister asked me if I'd been enjoying myself since we'd moved house. I said no. She didn't ask me why, but just asked me if I liked the house my family had moved to better than our old one, and I said no, and that I'd liked the old one quite a bit better. She said, 'Oh well, it's a bit late now!'

"Thinking about it afterwards, I bet she went away with the impression that I'm a grumpy lazybones who would have preferred to have been back living in our old house, and that I wished we hadn't moved. But actually, I was still glad to have moved, even though I'm not so keen on the new house, because I'd met some people I like; and the main reason I wasn't enjoying myself was because I was having to spend so much time revising for exams at the time, and I'd have still had to do that in our old house!"

Sarah joked, "Finding out about all these misunderstandings, I'll get too scared to ever talk again at this rate!"

Suzy said, "You know, if you said that on the Internet with no smilies, some people might think you really meant it!"

"And give you counselling for your anxiety!" chimed in Emma with a smirk.

James said, "Even if you put smilies and things on comments you make on the Internet, people can still misinterpret them. I know someone who often says 'LOL' when he's commenting on things on a forum he posts on, but people have got upset over that, because he said he does it to show he's being light-hearted, but it often looks as if he's laughing At the person he's talking to, so they can think he thinks they've just said something silly and he's making fun of them, like if someone asks him if he's going out that evening, and he says, 'Not with the rain pouring down like this LOL'."

The students began to feel a bit worried about how they might have been misunderstood themselves without knowing, and Heather joked, "Cor blimey, why don't we all take a vow of silence!"

Yet they continued talking.

One Student Talks About Misreading Things in Anger or for Another Reason

Emma said, "It wouldn't necessarily make much difference. I was talking to someone the other day – someone who was quite old, and she said she doesn't like to communicate with people via email, because she's had too many disagreements that have been caused by people misinterpreting things she's said over email. I don't know why that was. I'd hate not to be able to communicate with people by email myself. But I can think of a few reasons why that kind of thing might happen. I've noticed myself that I can read something someone's written to me, and then I can read it again, and notice it says things I didn't take in the first time I read it. That can happen on Internet forums too, and probably when people send ordinary letters, and other things like that. I can't remember all the times when I've noticed that – well, there aren't all that many – it's not as if I'm always doing it … I hope! But I can remember a few times:

"I remember a friend of mine once emailed me and asked if I'd like to go out with her to the seaside for the day in a town near where I live, and she said that after we'd been on the beach, she thought it might be nice to have dinner in a pub. I emailed her back and said we'd have to pick the pub we went to carefully, since there were some in the town that weren't very nice. After I'd sent the email, I read what she'd written again, and realised she'd said she thought it would be nice to go to a pub on the seafront. The few I know of there are all nice. Whoops!

"Mind you, at least that was only a little mistake. Someone else misunderstood something she said the other day. Actually, that was funny! We both post on this Internet forum, and sometimes things get quite argumentative there. This person accused her of something she thought was unfair. She didn't mind much, because she doesn't like that person anyway, and nor do I, because we think she can be obnoxious and insensitive to people who talk about their problems on the forum. So it wasn't as if the person's opinion mattered to her. But my friend was a bit annoyed about what she'd said to her, and she thought she'd hurl a load of pretend insults at her, just to have a laugh and let off steam. I can't remember quite what she said now, but it was something like:

" 'What are you thinking of, saying that to me, you 14-headed 30-horned slime-covered monster! You potato-eyed, lemon-faced, grapefruit-stomached, seaweed-haired, snail-shell-skinned, slug-fingered, worm-tongued, six-legged evil-doer! You who ride on the backs of wolves and urge them on to catch their prey! You who make apples go bad! You who make it rain on people's barbecues! You who caused the whole disgusting genre of rap music to come into being! You who wear necklaces made of live cockroaches for the shock value! You who count the rats in the sewers as some of your best friends! You who caused the ice age all those years ago!

"'You odorous beast, you who enjoy swimming in a pond chock-full of maggots! You who sneak into catering establishments and release cage-loads of mice into their kitchens! You who cause hordes of insects to swoop down and attack crops all over the world! You who lead communist revolutions and would never let people escape over the Berlin Wall! You who make clouds block out the sun! You who cause people's heating to break down in the dead of winter! You whose behaviour led to the Dark Ages! You who invented black holes in space so you could watch things being sucked helplessly in and dragged to their doom and destruction!

"'You metal-chomping, scaly, shark-toothed, elephant-tusked, porcupine-spined, maggot-shedding, baby-eating bog-dwelling alligator-monster fiend! You who bite the heads off rabbits in the night! You who use kittens as cushions! You who have arsenic for bone marrow! You who cause colds to break out in Winter and the sun to burn people in summer! You who eat poisonous berries by the handful as you laugh, just to prove how tough you are! You who throw handfuls of leeches at children for fun! You who carve and eat meat off the cow before it's even been slaughtered! You who crush entire fields of strawberries before people can pick and eat them! You who hurl the roofs off people's houses during storms, knowing they'll think it's wind damage!

"'You have toxic mould for brains, you who whisper in the ears of bankers and tempt them to make decisions that'll bring financial crises hurtling down on everyone's heads! You who put thoughts into politicians' minds about how it would be good to go to war! You who bite the legs off the performing elephants and clowns at circuses! You who steal children's pets and sell them to people making fur coats! You who go around to people's houses when they're not there and hide and move little belongings of theirs to worry and annoy them! You who are single-handedly responsible for all the smut and trash on television! You who walk unannounced onto the stage at children's pantomimes and bite the heads off chickens and stand there for minutes sucking out the blood as if you were drinking a cup of tea! You are so out of order, you who trample people's dreams in the dust with your six feet!'

"My friend assumed everyone would know that was a joke. But one person seemed to be convinced she was being deadly serious, because he said to her, 'Wow, you really believe that person does all that? I think you're insane!' "

The students laughed.

Then Emma said, "Mind you, I've misread the odd thing on that forum so I didn't understand it properly. Not in big ways, I don't think. But you know what I was saying about not picking up on all the details of something you read the first time? Well, I remember I was reading a serious topic on that forum about bullying not long ago. Someone said she'd been publicly bullied at work. She said it happened sometimes in an email dialogue with her boss. I thought, 'Why would you say it was public if it was just going on in emails between the two of you?' Then I read what she'd written again, and I realised she said it was an 'open' email dialogue, so it presumably must have meant the boss was copying their conversations to everyone or something, for some reason! Whether there was a need for him to send them to everyone, or whether he was just being a creepy annoying scumbag or something, who knows!

"But I bet it's not just me who misreads things a bit sometimes. In fact I'm sure it isn't. Not long ago on the forum, someone said someone she knew had declining mental health, and had kept refusing help when she offered it, and recently she'd become impossible to contact. A few people responded by telling her to just keep asking her if she wanted help, since eventually she might agree to it. I thought, 'How's she supposed to do that when she can't even get in contact with her at the moment?' It seems they didn't read her message carefully.

"I don't know why they didn't read it that carefully. But in general, I reckon that sometimes, if there's a lot of detail in a forum message or in an email or something else, or if it says something surprising, and probably for other reasons as well, it might be quite common for people not to take in everything they read the first time, or else to forget some of the details of what they read by the time they've finished it, since after all, when you read one thing and then move straight on to the next thing, there isn't time for your brain to absorb all the details properly and transfer each one to the long-term memory, so they're easier to forget; so if people read it again, they might realise there's more to what was written than they thought there was. Maybe if they read it yet again, they might realise there's even more!

"I've noticed the same thing happening with lectures actually – sometimes I realise I've forgotten most of what the lecturer said by the end! Not that I'd really want to listen to those again and again! But I don't think it's just me who forgets most of them.

"Mind you, I think the opposite thing can happen too, where the people who are actually writing emails and things think they're being clear, but actually they haven't put quite enough detail into what they're saying for it to be fully understandable. I can think of a few times when I've accidentally done that. I remember there was one time just a couple of months ago, when I went away on holiday for a week with my family, and when I came back, I found out that someone had asked me a question on Facebook. I answered her, saying I was sorry I hadn't replied before but I'd been on holiday. Then I realised I should probably have explained that the reason going on holiday meant I couldn't reply was because I didn't have good Internet access there, since I wondered if she might interpret my message as meaning I was having far too nice a time to want to bother contacting the likes of her while I was there! Whoops! But she replied to me, and I'm pretty sure she didn't take what I'd said the wrong way, so that was good.

"And something like it that happened not long ago was that someone posted a message on this forum I've been talking about, where he asked for advice to help him do better at job interviews, since he'd had quite a few, but hadn't managed to get a job. I put a message on the forum with a few ideas for him, saying it might not be to do with anything he was doing wrong, but just that there was a lot of competition for jobs; but I said it might be useful for him to contact his interviewers after he hadn't got a job and ask if they would give him feedback about why he hadn't got it.

"Afterwards I realised that might have sounded a bit daft, since it might have sounded as if I was just saying he could do with finding out what he'd done wrong at those particular interviews, and I thought he might wonder what the point would be of asking for feedback after not getting the jobs he'd already lost the opportunity to get at those places, since he'd have no chance of getting them by then, when I was really thinking that if he got feedback, it might help him work out what to do differently in future at other job interviews. So I wished I'd said that would be the purpose of it, and hoped he didn't take what I'd said the wrong way. But he replied to me, and it turned out he wasn't offended, and understood what I meant, so that was alright.

"But I think maybe people misreading things or not saying what they mean as clearly as they could is one reason why arguments can get as bad as they can on Internet forums. And then when people get angry, they'll be even more likely to misread and misunderstand things, because they'll likely read things in a rush, or not read everything the other person says, especially because they might be so eager to protest about what they're sure the person's saying they won't want to wait till they've read it really carefully. And replying angrily without thinking too deeply's often a whole lot more fun anyway! It probably spoils a good argument to have to think carefully about what the other person's saying, at least if anger's putting the person on the receiving end of it on a kind of high, making them feel more alive, and if thinking carefully about the old rubbish the other person's just said might be a bit boring.

"But it seems it's best, and more considerate anyway, if people can wait a while, till they've cooled down enough to read things more patiently. Mind you, that's easy advice to give, but not easy advice to take, when people really want to protest right then about what the person they're arguing with just said, and don't like the thought that the other person's making them look bad in front of whoever might be reading the conversation, so they want to put the person they're arguing with right as soon as they can.

"But I was on a forum the other day, when I read something someone said to someone else, where they were sympathising with them, saying they didn't think it was fair that certain people kept seeming to think they'd said things they hadn't, which meant they'd argue with them for supposedly having certain points of view they didn't even say they had. Maybe the kind of thing I've been talking about was one reason why it was happening.

"And something similar's happened to me on there. There was once when a discussion started about employers rejecting women as job candidates, because they thought they might get pregnant and then they'd have to pay maternity leave and let them have time off for ages. There were people who were getting angry, saying the employers were all just bigots who should be made to suffer in court.

"I thought that was a bit extreme, and said I could understand things from the employers' point of view, because it can't be nice having to pay people for months when they're not working, and to have to train someone else to do their job, and to have their company's productivity go down a bit while that's happening, because the person doing the training and the one being trained won't be working to produce what the companies are working to produce at the time, because the person doing the training will be taken off their normal work sometimes for a while, and the person being trained will likely need to find out quite a few things before they can substitute for the person on maternity leave, and that kind of thing. Quite a few people just assumed that must mean I supported everything those employers did, and started accusing me of being an uncaring bigot, and things like that.

"But all I was thinking was that if you can understand things from employers' points of view, it might mean it's easier to try and work out solutions that are cheaper and more satisfactory for everyone than just suing them – you know, like maybe coming up with suggestions for arranging things so it's possible for more people to work from home with flexible hours, to make it easier for anyone who would actually like to carry on working after they have a child to do that instead of taking a lot of time off, and things like that.

"I think it would be better if a lot more people asked questions to try to understand the point of view of the person they're arguing with fully before they make a judgment about it, so they're less likely to just get angry with them.

"Another thing is that I've come to think that sometimes, people see what they assume they're going to see when they start reading something, not what's really there, sometimes because they're already convinced they know what it's going to say, so they don't feel the need to check it carefully. And like I said, I think that if they're feeling angry, or in some other state of emotion, that might happen even more, because it'll be harder to concentrate on it properly.

"So if someone says something that looks as if it's critical of something they've said, or expresses an opposing political view or something, maybe some people can start to get annoyed, and think, 'Yuck, this person supports the other side!', or, 'This person's being nasty about me, and I've got to defend myself to save face!', And they don't read what the person's saying carefully, partly because I don't suppose anyone likes criticism, so I don't suppose anyone's going to really want to spend time scrutinising it, especially if they're all worked up with annoyance at the time; so they might just end up with a basic understanding of what it says, that makes them think the person's saying everything they don't want to hear.

"That's one reason why I think it can help to read what someone's saying more than once, whether people like it or not, to get the details of it. And I think if people read it the second time after they've cooled down from any angry feeling that flares up when they read it the first time, it can help. That's unless it really is rubbish, so there's no point in taking it seriously.

"And doing that won't just benefit the person who's written the thing the other person's offended by, who won't then find themselves on the receiving end of something angry in response to it so often; but I think people who feel angry because of something they've just read can benefit themselves if they wait till they've cooled down a bit before they reply, because then they might read it again and realise it doesn't seem as insulting as they thought it did before – I think I've realised that sometimes myself when I've been arguing on forums and re-read things; or they just might not feel like saying such insulting things back after that, whether they misunderstood what the person said the first time they read it or got it right; and that might mean the person they're talking to's more willing to listen to what they themselves say.

"Mind you, like I said, waiting to reply when you're annoyed and you really want to isn't easy!

"But also, if the person on the receiving end of a reply that's been written in anger just feels insulted by what the person who wrote it said, they might just start ignoring them, which will mean the other person loses their opportunity to say anything else that might have influenced them to change their mind about what they think; or else they might reply saying worse things back to them than they said in the first place, because their own anger's flared up because they're offended by what they're reading.

"Mind you, I don't know how much a person who actually likes responding in anger because it gives them a bit of a thrill or something will care about that.

"But anyway, talking of misreading things because people expect them to say one thing when they're really saying another, it's not just in arguments where people can do that. I read a headline the other day; I can't remember what it said, but it was something to do with some statistic or other; let's just imagine it said, '90 % of Americans say they would eat dog food!' It was something as strange as that anyway. But I read the first line of the article, and thought it said pretty much the same thing as the headline. I was surprised about the statistic. Then I read it again, and then I realised it said just the opposite, that 10 % of Americans said they would eat dog food, or whatever it really said, which would mean 90 % wouldn't. There must have been a mistake in the headline – or the article – since the first bit of the article contradicted the headline. But since I didn't expect it to, it seems I misread the first bit of the article the first time, thinking it said what I thought it must be saying."

The Conversation Becomes More Light-Hearted

The students were thoughtful for a few seconds.

Then Jackie grinned and said to the group, "Have you ever had an email conversation with someone where you've started out talking about one thing, and the topic's got onto something else, but you've kept the same subject heading, so your emails say they're about one thing when really they're about something completely different? You know, say if you called an email something like, 'Baked beans', but the conversation changed after a couple of emails so it was all about your favourite music or something, but it still had the subject heading 'Baked beans', so it always looked as if you were going to talk about those?"

James said with a wry smile, "I got an email with the subject heading 'Happy birthday' in the middle of my A-levels, and it started, 'Are you nervous about your next exam? I hope you've been revising hard. I know you've had some difficulty with the subject in the past, so I hope you're getting to grips with it now.'

"Then right at the end, it said, 'Anyway, happy birthday'. Some birthday greeting! It's got to be the most depressing one I've ever had!"

Jackie smiled and said, "Yeah. I'm glad I didn't get one like that. Anyway, I started thinking about emails with inappropriate subject headings the other day when I got an email with the subject, 'Re: Hospital', and it was all about someone being annoyed because they'd got chewing gum stuck on their shoe. The conversation had started off being about a hospital appointment, but then it had got onto completely different topics but had kept the same subject heading.

"Imagine if just for a laugh, you sent an email to someone in the first place where the subject heading was completely different from what you said in the email; so the subject heading might be something like, 'Macaroni', so the person who got it might expect it to say something about that, when the email was really all about how you were late for a train and just missed it. Or you might put the subject heading, 'New car', so they might think you were going to say you'd just got one, when your email was all about how you accidentally made too much porridge for breakfast and you ended up eating it for dinner and tea as well or something; that would confuse them, wouldn't it! They might be puzzling over what on earth what you said had to do with the subject!"

The others giggled, and Becky asked, "Have you ever done that then? I mean cooked some porridge and ended up with so much you ate it all day."

Jackie burped loudly, and then said, "Not quite. I've ended up with a bit more than I intended to before, but never quite that much."

Suzy smiled and said, "That's another thing that could cause arguments really, isn't it. I mean, imagine if there was a family where the person who cooked the family meals kept cooking too much, so the family kept having to eat their tea for the next day's breakfast and dinner, because the parents didn't want to waste it. The mum might keep saying, 'Whoops, Daddy's cooked too much mince yet again!' Maybe one of the older children would be begging to take over the cooking after a while!"

Colin grinned and said, "Well, you hear about parents complaining that their kids don't do enough housework; maybe that's one way they could manipulate them into doing more!"

Sarah smiled and said, "Apart from the fact that a lot of the kids might not beg to take over the cooking, but just criticise the parent making them eat leftovers all the time more and more angrily!"

James said, after enjoying a mouthful of cake, "Talking about having to do things that probably wouldn't be very nice, and eating things, the other day I was listening to something on the radio where they were talking about trying to train dogs to help with screening tests, where they were trying to distinguish bits of body tissue that had cancer cells in them from ordinary bits, using cells collected from people in biopsies that were taken from lumps they'd found in places where they shouldn't have been, and that kind of thing; and they wondered if dogs would be able to tell which ones were the cancerous ones by sniffing the samples to see if the ones with cancer cells in them smelled a bit different, since dogs have a much stronger sense of smell than humans . . . I'm not saying the dogs actually ate the samples, by the way. At least I hope they didn't.

"I'm not sure what the dogs did every time they thought they'd found a sample with some cancer cells in it. But the trainer was giving them dog biscuit treats every time they detected one, to show them that that's what they wanted them to do and encourage them to do it some more. I think the dogs did quite well at it.

"I'm pretty sure there are no plans to use dogs to replace humans who look at cells to see if any are cancerous, or anything like that. But maybe the idea is that if they're good, one day dogs could help to double-check samples or something.

"Anyway, when the report about the dogs was on the radio, they played the sound of someone opening a packet of these dog biscuits, and I reckon something in my brain must automatically respond to noises that sound like packets of biscuits and sweets and things being opened by thinking, 'Yum!' because I found myself thinking, 'I fancy some of that!'

"Then I realised what I was thinking, and thought, 'No I don't!' "

They laughed. Colin grinned and asked as a joke, "Would you like to eat dog food stew, or dog food pie?"

Suzy smiled and said, "Imagine if someone invited a group of friends or work colleagues and their boss around for dinner, and when they got there, they said, 'I've made a nice dog food pie for you all!' "

They grinned, and Sarah said, "Talking of arguments, like we were just now, that might cause a few! Anyway, it's interesting about the thing about dogs being trained to detect cancer cells in body tissue samples."

The others agreed. But then Mya smiled and said, "Imagine if dog food was served at a royal banquet, with lots of international guests, like top politicians and royals and foreign diplomats! I wonder if they'd complain, or whether they'd be diplomatic enough to just keep quiet and eat it!"

Jackie giggled and said, "Imagine what a scandal it would cause if the press got to hear about it! Imagine the Queen being asked to come on a BBC news programme on the World Service or something, so she could be asked to explain why she'd ordered dog food to be served up at an international banquet!"

(This conversation took place several years before Queen Elizabeth died.)

Kirsty said, "Imagine if she hadn't known it was going to happen though, but it was all the idea of the cooks, who thought dog food ought to be the latest food fad or something. I wonder whether if the person serving up the food loudly announced to all the guests that the highlight of the meal was going to be dog food pie, the Queen would cause a scene in front of the guests by protesting, or whether she'd pretend it was just normal to eat dog food at banquets so as not to embarrass the person who made the announcement, and tuck into it herself, as if she just expected everyone to do that, and she'd only afterwards complain in private."

James said with a grin, "I can imagine it causing a few arguments when she did complain! Not to mention a few staff dismissals!"

Colin sniggered and said, "Just imagine the Queen sacking some of her staff by email. You hear about people being sacked by text message sometimes, don't you. Imagine if the Queen emailed her butler and said, 'I simply can't tolerate the fact that you served me up dog food the other day; you're fired!'"

Emma giggled and said, "Yeah, and just imagine if the butler didn't even realise that the meat he'd served up was dog food, because it hadn't been announced publicly till after the meal when he wasn't there, and he didn't even know it had happened! He might just think the Queen must be going mad. He might email her back, saying, 'I'm sorry to have to say this, Your Majesty, but I think you're going a bit nuts!'"

They laughed.

Then Kirsty grinned and said, "Yeah, imagine if the Queen sacked the butler, when all along it was the idea of the cooks; and imagine if no one else was told till after they'd eaten it, when they came in and told everyone they hoped they'd enjoyed it!

"Actually, talking about blaming someone whose fault it wasn't for something, I can understand how easy it is to do that; the other day, it was colder than normal, and I like to open the window in my room for fresh air, so I opened it that day too; and it started to get really cold in my room; and I got annoyed with the window for a second or two, and said to myself, 'I need to shut that flipping window!' as if I was blaming the window for it being cold, when if I hadn't been daft enough to open it, or if I'd shut it already, it would actually have been protecting me from the cold!"

The students chuckled, and Jackie jokingly asked with a grin, "Were you thinking the window was a person then?"

Kirsty giggled and said, "No! I didn't mean that!"

Heather said, "Oh well, at least windows can't get offended by what you think about them ... Actually, it would be spooky if they not only got offended by what people said, but they could get offended by things people even just thought about them, wouldn't it! Well, I suppose if they all did it, we'd all be used to it, so no one would think it was weird – or they might, but scientists would have come up with an explanation for why it happens, so then we'd all understand. Mind you, it would be spooky if no one had ever heard of that happening, and then a window suddenly seemed to come to life and get offended by something you just thought one day, and then it yelled at you, or banged itself shut or something!"

Becky grinned and said, "Imagine if you got annoyed and blamed the window for it being cold or something, and just after you thought something bad about it, a gust of wind banged it shut! I wonder if you'd worry that it had come to life and developed spooky mind-reading powers, and that it was annoyed with you for blaming it unfairly for you being cold, since you were the one who'd opened it!"

The students laughed.

But then Heather said more seriously, "At least you know really that if you insult a window without thinking, it's not going to bear a grudge against you. Not like humans! I think it can be awkward talking to people sometimes. One or two people said earlier that maybe we ought to be more careful about what we say to people; and that might help sometimes; but sometimes, people get offended by things you'd never get offended by yourself, so you can't stop that by just being careful what you say, because you just wouldn't expect them to get offended.

"I mean, here's something that happened to me: I once said to someone that I didn't understand the reasons why people do a couple of things she does as hobbies. I wasn't criticising them, just being a bit puzzled and curious about why she likes them, since I wouldn't have any interest in them myself. I mean, really, what's the point of chasing dogs to see if you can catch them so you can pull their tails, or daubing your initials on park benches with your own ear wax? . . . No, she doesn't do those things really; she does other more normal things.

"But anyway, she made some comment when I said I didn't understand why people do them, and we laughed, and I didn't think anything more about it. But then months later, she told me I'd once made a couple of 'very hurtful remarks' about not understanding the purpose of her hobbies, saying she'd laughed them off at the time, but hadn't liked them. I didn't understand it. Not long after that, she said she didn't see the purpose of something I like, and I didn't give a bean! I mean, why would you expect everyone to like the same things?

"But in the meantime, she'd probably blabbed to other people about how I'd made hurtful remarks to her, making it sound as if I'd done it deliberately; and they probably thought badly of me because of it!"

"Aren't people rotten!" said James with feeling. Then he joked with a grin, "I know: Let's all go and live together in a secluded cave to escape them! . . . Ah, no, but hang on, if we all did that, the cave would be packed full of people, wouldn't it! Yikes!"

The students chuckled.

One Student Teases Another One in Fun About Her Alleged Hobbies

But then Suzy said to Heather, "Hang on, you didn't only say you didn't see the point of that person's hobbies, did you. I suspect that what offended her was when you said you didn't understand why on earth anyone would want to do archery like she does, and you asked her if she liked doing it because she fantasises about killing people . . . Actually you said something a bit worse than that."

Heather blushed a bit and said, "Yeah, perhaps I shouldn't have said that; but I thought she knew I didn't mean it all that seriously. I just didn't understand why such a thing would appeal to her."

Suzy joked, "Well anyway, it's a good thing you don't care what people think of your own hobbies when they're so strange, isn't it! I mean, you can't expect everyone to like your attempts to make your room look like an exotic cave, hanging strings of dead starfish and long strands of seaweed from the ceiling, having big bowls of seawater on the floor with stones and barnacles in them to simulate rock pools as best you can, having a thick layer of seaweed instead of carpet, sticking seashells all over the walls, and having that dead fish-odour air freshener you use to make the atmosphere more authentic!"

"Oh yuck!" laughed Heather. Then she said in a mock commanding tone, "Silence! People will believe you!"

They all laughed.

Suzy made another joke, saying, "It's just as well you don't really do that; I mean, imagine going for a job interview or to hear a famous person who'd come to speak at the university smelling of fish-odour so-called air freshener, and having long strands of seaweed caught in your hair and hanging down your back that had fallen off your ceiling without you realising!"

The students chuckled again.

One of the Group Tells the Others About Strange Funny Things They Heard Happened At Job Interviews

Then Jackie said, "Talking about daft things that could just possibly happen at job interviews reminds me of an article I read on the Internet about a survey that was done where job interviewers sent in their stories about the strangest things that had happened at the job interviews they'd done. One said an interviewee chewed bubble gum and blew bubbles all through the interview. Another one said a woman came in and started eating a burger and fries, saying she hadn't had dinner. According to other interviewers, some things that happened were even weirder: One candidate interrupted an interview to phone his therapist and ask for advice on how to answer certain interview questions. One man stood up and started tap-dancing around the office when the interviewer asked him about his hobbies. Another one got up and started bouncing up and down on the carpet, saying the interviewer must be highly thought of by the management to have such a thick one . . . None of these people got the job, by the way.

"If all these stories are to be believed, another candidate had a little pinball game and challenged the interviewer to play it with him. Another one whistled when the interviewer was talking. One woman was sick on an interviewer's desk, and then started asking questions about the job as if nothing had happened. One woman had headphones on and was listening to music, and said it didn't matter because she could still hear the interviewer talk. One man who was going bald suddenly got up in the middle of the interview, went out, and came back a minute or two later wearing a hair piece to hide it. Another candidate challenged the interviewer to an arm wrestling contest during the interview. Another one went through the interviewer's bag at the end of the interview, took out a hairbrush, brushed their hair, and left.

"And there was another one who got a phone call during the interview. It was from his wife. His end of the conversation went, 'Which company? When do I start? What's the salary?' The interviewer said to him that he obviously couldn't want to finish the interview since it had turned out that he'd got another job, and the man said he was still interested, as long as the interviewer's company paid him more. The interviewer didn't give him the job, but later found out there hadn't really been another job; it was a scam to try to get a better salary offer!"

The students were silent for a few seconds, some grinning, and some looking surprised, taking that in.

One Student Tells a Story He Read About an Attempted Scam That Backfired on the Scammer

Then Stuart said, "You know, I read a funny story on the Internet about a scam that backfired on the scammer ... Well, it's a little bit funny. It doesn't sound like it at first, but it is in the end.

"A delivery driver in a van had stopped behind a line of cars that had stopped in a traffic jam. Suddenly the car in front of him started, went into reverse, came straight for him, and rammed his front bumper. Then the man in the car that had just done that jumped out screaming and yelling that he was going to sue the delivery driver for every penny he was worth, for ramming his car and causing a whiplash injury to his neck, which, if the claim was true, would have meant his neck had jolted forwards and back again so hard and quickly because of the force of the collision that it was injured. I've heard that some people deliberately cause crashes and then claim it was the fault of the drivers they've crashed into, to get money from the other people's insurance companies, and that doing that's on the increase nowadays, and sadly sometimes the innocent people who get crashed into or drivers near them end up badly hurt, so it can be a horrible crime.

"But anyway, this time, the delivery driver who'd been the intended victim, staying as calm as could be, said, 'That's not what happened and you know it.' The yelling man gloated that the delivery driver couldn't prove it, and that no one would believe someone would deliberately put his car in reverse to hit a vehicle, especially one driven by someone he didn't know, so it couldn't even be as if he was motivated by having a grudge against him. The delivery driver just smiled sweetly.

"The police arrived and took statements. The delivery driver was still calm.

"Then he went to his car to take out something little, and went to hand it to the police. The yelling man jeered, 'What do you think you're doing? Are you seriously trying to bribe the cops?'

"The delivery driver said he wasn't doing that at all, but just handing them the memory card from the camera he had attached to his dashboard.

"The yelling man went pail. The police looked at the camera footage and found out what had really happened, and the yelling man ended up being arrested for fraud; and they found out he was guilty of several other driving offences too. So he got what he deserved."

One of the Group Talks About Romance Scams, and Tells a Story About a Man he Thinks Tried to Scam a Friend of His, with Amusing Results

Some of the students smiled with satisfaction. But then Colin said gloomily, "I've heard a lot about scams. There are loads of different kinds out there nowadays. The scammers don't care a bit about the feelings of people on the receiving end.

"Someone I know used to post on an Internet forum till recently where I posted for a while, and this man from some developing country kept telling her he was attracted to her, and then he started asking her for her real name, and saying he wanted to go on a date with her, and he asked her to phone him up. She wondered how on earth he imagined they were going to be able to go on a date with each other when they lived thousands of miles apart. He never explained that one. When she wouldn't give him her real name, and refused to phone him up, he got nasty, saying a load of abusive things. So much for being attracted to her! She told him to get lost in the end . . . Well, she told him something along those lines anyway; perhaps it was more like, 'You are a gangrenous belching smut-hound, an offensive-smelling glob of congealing squashed cockroach pie, and I don't want anything else to do with you!' But I can't quite remember now.

"But I think he might have been like one of these scammers you hear about who go on dating sites and pretend to be in love with some of the women there, and they start phone conversations, and then the men lie to them and tell them tragedies have happened to people in their families, like accidents they need medical treatment for, and say that because they live in a poor country where they don't get free healthcare, they need loads of money for the treatment. Quite a lot of women who think they're starting a loving relationship with them feel sorry for them and send them a lot of their savings, which the men probably really spend on parties and designer clothes and things!

"And if they think a woman's a good payer, they tell them other bad things have happened, and get more money! And they carry on doing it! They've been featuring that kind of thing on some consumer programmes on telly recently.

"There are probably quite a few variations on the techniques the scammers use. But I think one reason some women fall for the scams is that the scammers flatter them and make them feel attractive and loved at first, and some women can be especially susceptible to that, perhaps because they're lonely, because they might be newly divorced or widowed, and their kids might have recently left home, and that kind of thing. I wonder if people who've had a lot of companionship they enjoyed and then lost it will often be quite a bit lonelier than people who've always lived on their own, because they'll miss what they had, especially because there'll be quite a contrast between their old life and living alone. If that's the case, then that might make some of them more eager to get into new relationships than a lot of other people might be at their age, so they're more likely to fall for these things, if they sometimes prioritise getting into a new relationship over being choosy and waiting till something that seems more ideal comes along. I don't really know about that.

"But anyway, I heard that the scammers tend to go for women over forty, probably partly because they're more likely to have accumulated some decent savings in the bank by then, and partly maybe because they'll be especially flattered if someone makes them feel really attractive when they're at the age when their looks are fading, and they don't expect so many people to be interested in them, and some might need cheering up because they've gone through stressful divorces, and they're lonely, and that kind of thing. Maybe the scammers think younger women who can afford to be more choosy because more men will be interested in them will be harder to attract. Mind you, some of them might go for them, I don't really know.

"But actually, I've read that when people are feeling a bit vulnerable, they're more likely to get sucked into other things that aren't good for them, like cults, and bad or quack therapies. You know, I suppose if you're feeling perfectly alright, you might hear about something like that, and just be a bit curious and wonder whether it'll be good or whether it's a con or something; but the more stressed and upset you are about things, the more desperate you'll probably be for things to change in your life, so the more you might be interested in things you're offered by people who tell you they have the solutions to life's problems, and things that can make people happier, and that kind of thing.

"And I think one technique cults can use to recruit new members is called love-bombing, where some of the members make efforts to be especially supportive and loving for a while.

I've heard that the kinds of people most likely to be recruited into cults are people who've recently had upsetting experiences, so they'll especially appreciate it if someone tells them they could join a group where they could find out about some really good ways that people can change their lives for the better, or if they go to a meeting where people seem to be really caring towards them.

"... Wouldn't it be awful if someone got depressed because they'd just been defrauded by someone doing one of those romance scams on them, and they met someone who told them they were from this really supportive community where they could find a lot of answers to life's problems, so they joined, and it turned out to be a cult, and when they realised, they left, but then they decided they needed therapy to get over it, and ended up going to a really bad therapist who charged them loads of money for years to talk about their problems, but they never got any better!"

The students smiled, despite thinking that would be a bad situation to have got into.

Then Mya said, "I read an article about that romance fraud the other day. It said that besides the scammers from abroad, there are ones who are local to the people they're deceiving too, who'll pretend to be very rich or minor celebrities to attract women, and they might act all loving and often give gifts at first, but they really just want to deceive victims into paying for things for them. Like they'll go on dates to restaurants and places, and they might sometimes tell a date that they've accidentally forgotten their wallet, or have some other excuse for not bringing money, so their date has to pay. They might promise luxurious holidays, and even claim to have private jets and to own wealthy businesses, or impressive things like that, just to attract the women they're targeting. The article advised that anyone starting to date someone who makes those kinds of claims should try to get proof of them before they get the least bit serious with them, such as by asking to see any private jet someone claims they own."

Colin said, "This scammer who might have been going to try to scam my friend claimed to be some kind of celebrity in his country, but we reckon he was just doing that to try and impress her, maybe thinking that would mean she'd be more likely to do what he wanted, whatever that was.

"She actually got quite fond of him at first, because he wasn't nasty at first, but they just had some fun joking around with each other. They used to tease each other playfully. But she did think it was weird, the way he kept saying he was in love with her when he hardly knew her. One day, they were teasing each other as usual, when she linked to a love song on YouTube about regrets about a relationship break-up, teasing him that it should be the national anthem of the country he came from, because the chorus kept saying, 'I should have tried a little bit harder', and she teased him that it would be appropriate to be played at sporting events where his country was playing, because they might keep losing, and want to tell themselves they should have tried harder. But she thought he might not have got the joke, because he seemed to want to believe it meant that she herself was sorry for anything she'd done that stopped him wanting to give her so much attention, and that she must want him to tell her he loved her some more. Well, he started telling her he did anyway.

"But he got nasty too at the same time as he started telling her he loved her even more than he had before, as if he thought that since he'd found out that she loved him, he could get away with being nasty and still get whatever on earth it was he wanted, which he never seemed to realise would need to be explained if he had any chance at all of getting it, which actually, he didn't, since it was probably something to do with her money, unless it was that he was expecting her to fly halfway around the world to give him a few cheap thrills or something.

"I think the reason he might have misunderstood what she said wasn't because he came from another country – after all, he seemed to be from the privileged elite, because he said he was sent to school at a posh boarding school in this country. I think he just assumed she just must be in love with him, because he was one of these strange narcissistic kinds of people, who seemed to think he was fantastic, and that anyone who had any sense would just be bound to admire him, and that anyone who didn't just had to be an idiot. That was the impression we got from the way he talked about himself.

"My friend thought he was just being humorous and tongue-in-cheek at first when he started going on like that, and she laughed, and that was partly why she got to like him; but later, when he got verbally abusive towards her, she realised he was pretty much being serious when he talked about thinking he was fantastic! And he seemed absolutely convinced that she was grovellingly infatuated with him, and kept ordering her to stop playing hard to get, as if he was convinced that she was only failing to declare her love for him and beg for his attention because she was playing some kind of teasing game with him!"

Colin paused to finish his drink, and Emma said, "I don't think it's just men whose English might be a bit poor who can get the wrong idea and think things that women do or say mean they fancy them, when really they're just trying to be nice, or they just want to have a laugh or something! Actually, I think it's quite common for men to think mere friendliness means something else."

Colin looked a bit embarrassed and said, "Maybe. But this man was something else! He didn't want to leave my friend alone. Just telling him to go away after he got nasty didn't work, so she thought she'd just have to try something more creative.

"She had a go at getting rid of him in style in the end! She wrote a funny story on the forum that she said she wished could really be about him, where he was launched up into the clouds in a big balloon made of his own ego, full of hot air from all the rubbish he talked. I thought the story was a laugh. He did seem to have a massive ego, judging by the fact that he kept boasting about supposedly being better than most of the other people on the forum.

"Anyway, this story she wrote said a sonic boom was heard as this man broke the sound barrier, as the masses of hot air in the ego balloon propelled him up faster and faster. I'll tell you the rest. It says that then the ego balloon hit the jet stream, and was carried along in it in a powerful wind. The man was experiencing the worst wind he'd ever known!

"He didn't know whether he was still alive or dead. But then he was relieved when the ego balloon started going down again. Eventually it hit the ground, and it would have burst with the force of the collision if his ego had been a bit more fragile.

"The story went on that he didn't know where he was, but when a horrible-looking creature came up to him and greeted him, he told it to go to hell, and ordered it to bring him a cool beer, since he'd landed in a hot place.

"The creature said it was pointless telling him to go to hell, since they were already there, and he was the devil, so he wouldn't take kindly to being ordered around!

"The devil ordered the man to get out of his ego balloon, and punished him forever and ever.

"Strangely, the story just convinced this possible scammer all the more that my friend was in love with him, for some reason, as if he thought any attention at all must be good attention! He gloated about how women were always falling over themselves to get to him, and called her some abusive names, and told her he knew she was infatuated with him, but that she'd have to wait for his attention till he'd finished playing with his other women. She said she didn't care if she had to wait forever!

"Then he sent her a picture of a rose, and told her he loved her really. She realised he hadn't got the message she'd been trying to give him, and wrote another story about how his ego appeared in the shape of a massive balloon above him, and got so full of hot air from the things he said that it lifted him off the floor, right up into the air, and then bruised itself when it hit the ceiling.

"Another reason he seemed to have a huge ego was that he was always boasting about how good he was at attracting women, so she wrote another story joking about it. I'll tell you what it said, since it's a laugh:

"It said that one day, all the women he'd done wrong got together and chased him out of town, yelling insults at him. He ran away from the angry mob of females, faster and faster, and then he took off and went into orbit in space, carried up and along by the massive ego balloon above him.

"Soon, he was sure he spotted a black hole in the distance. He was being whisked towards it, but he couldn't steer himself onto another course. He didn't mind though. His ego was so huge that he felt sure black holes would be no match for him!

He felt sure that with just one wave of the claws he had for hands, and maybe a few punches and kicks and piercing warlike shrieks, the black hole would collapse in on itself like a deflating beach ball, and he would be gloating in victory!

"So he went closer and closer to the black hole, challenging it to come out and fight him. He saw space debris being sucked in mercilessly and scrunched up to almost nothingness; but he thought that must just be wimpy stuff, and that the black hole would just shrink in terror before him when he got near it, since after all, it simply must have heard about his fearsome reputation for conquering everything in his path!

"He was still jeering at the black hole when he got right up to it, at first not realising he was being remorselessly sucked in himself. But then he screeched in agony as he suddenly realised he was being crushed.

"The black hole squished him to the size of a mouse dropping, which was kind of appropriate, since he had resembled one in some ways on Earth.

"Then it spat him back out into space, dead! That wouldn't be normal behaviour for black holes, but this one had a bit of class, and didn't think it would be able to tolerate having him around, even a mouse dropping-sized version of him. A spaceship was going by at a safe distance at the time, and the occupants saw what happened. They reported the news back to Earth. It was on the news all over the world, and there was great rejoicing everywhere, with huge parties to celebrate his demise, since he'd pestered women all over the world!

"Anyway, for some reason, the possible scammer didn't realise the story was wishful thinking, even though my friend told him it was a few times, and he felt sure it meant she must be trying to flirt with him. He said a female who wrote stories like that about him just must be in love with him. So he tried again to bully her into phoning him up and flirting with him, calling her abusive names again, and saying she was really privileged that he was going to let her phone him.

"She got fed up, and thought a poem about her skipping around in delight as she witnessed him being gruesomely killed might work better than a humorous story. She wrote one. She enjoyed it so much she wrote another one, about him being killed in a different way and people cheering; and then she wrote another one quite like it, and then another, thinking she might be becoming addicted to doing it. He finally realised she might not be pining with love for him after all, but seemed to imagine it must only be a temporary thing.

"He wrote his own little story, about how she was being mean to him but then he apologised to her for having said the things that had offended her and it melted her heart, and she loved him again so she did what he wanted, and it meant he could be nasty to her again, without her deciding she didn't want to be with him. Wishful thinking or what!

"A few minutes later he did apologise for being abusive to her. It made her think he must think that what happened in his story would happen for real. She'd thought he could say phoney things for some time – like using apologies like coins you might put in a vending machine just so you can get out what you want. Ka-ching! – Or should I say, the noise things make when they plop into the part of a vending machine where people can get them out. Plonk, maybe! But she didn't think it was very bright of him to actually write a story that nearly amounted to admitting that he was about to apologise just to get what he wanted!

"He got abusive to her again soon after that, proving his apology was fake, and she said he'd better be careful or he'd be banned from the forum. Then he started mocking her, telling her that if she was so much of a wimp she couldn't take a bit of fun, and was going to go running off to the forum moderators to report him and get him banned, he wasn't going to come and chat to her any more because she was so pathetic. She hadn't actually said she'd report him herself! But she thought, 'Hey, progress! He's finally going to hopefully do what I've been wanting him to do all this time!' But soon he started telling her he loved her again, and insisting she tell him her real name. She refused again.

"Not long after that, the forum owner must have got sick of all the nastiness on the forum – it wasn't just those two, but most people were horrible to each other there. The owner suddenly just closed the place down. The possible scammer had no way of contacting my friend after that. She still isn't quite sure why he kept trying to make her phone him up. But some things he said have made her think he didn't get a joke she once made, and mistook it as meaning she was very rich, or has rich relatives; and also he once boasted that he'd persuaded a 'chat bitch', as he called some woman he'd met online, sadly for her, to send him some money. so she's pretty sure he wanted to either try to get her to send him money, or to invite him over to where she lives and treat him to a bit of the high life. He'd probably have got a bit further with a scheme like that if he'd actually thought to go to a dating site to find someone, instead of pestering someone on an ordinary forum all that time!"

The Students Discuss Dating Scams, and Then Some Other Kinds of Scams

Sarah said, "Wow, it just shows you it's worth being careful not to get too friendly too quickly with someone on the Internet, because you don't really know what kind of person you might be talking to!

"I watched a television programme that said some dating sites themselves run scams. Some of them draw people in by advertising that people who join the site can look at other people's profiles for free. It turns out that if you actually want to communicate with anyone though if you like their profile, which is, after all, the idea of joining, you have to pay. Well, I think that one's just a sales trick, not a scam.

"But people who join certain dating sites – I can't remember if any names were mentioned in the information I heard – but people who join whichever ones they are often get messages from supposed people who are supposedly interested in them, but it turns out that the people are made-up, and the same messages they get are sent to lots of people; and the pictures of the supposed message senders can often be found elsewhere on the Internet in random places; sometimes they're pictures of semi-famous people, who didn't give their permission for them to be used, or don't even know they're being used. I think some dating sites do that to make people think they've got more chance of finding someone nice than they really have, so they'll be more likely to pay to stay there. I don't know what happens if people reply to the messages; maybe they just don't get replies back. I'm not sure."

The group of students began to feel a bit angry. A few other students passed by, saw them all scowling, and thought they'd better avoid them for a while, assuming they must all be arguing or something.

But oblivious to that, they carried on talking.

Kirsty said, "I can believe some things aren't all they seem on some dating sites; I know someone who went on one for a little while, and she got lots of messages saying, 'You look stunning!' But she hadn't even put her picture on there! Maybe some desperate men were sending the same messages to everyone without even looking at their profiles."

Some of the students sniggered. But then Jackie got serious, saying, "Talking about scams and people's identities being used by other people reminds me of something I read about. Not about dating, but about something else: I got an email once when my older brother was on holiday. It seemed to be from him, and said he'd been mugged, and that he'd lost all his things, including his phone and plane ticket, and desperately needed money to get back home, very quickly since his flight was only in a few hours. But I phoned his mobile, and he answered and said he was having a lovely time, and nothing bad had happened at all!

"I looked on the Internet, and found out it's a common scam that plays on family members' anxieties and wish to help a family member in need. Scammers can hack into the emails or Facebook accounts of people, and when they go on holiday, if the scammers can get hold of the phone numbers or email addresses of their family members and others who know them, they ring or email them, pretending to be the family member, telling them they've got into some kind of trouble. They get a lot of money that way, because people are worried, and want to help out quickly. The scammers often phone old people, pretending to be their grandchildren; if the grandparents haven't spoken to their grandchildren for a while, they might not quite remember their voices, so they might not be as suspicious as someone more familiar with them would probably be.

"The scammers find out information about the person and their family from reading their Facebook messages or other things, so they sound convincing; they'll know family names, and details about their holiday. The website I got the information from says it's best to call the family member's mobile phone number if someone claims to be them with a story like that, to see if they're really in trouble. The scammer might say they're ringing on behalf of the relative and tell them to ring some other number instead, telling them they can get more information about the person's problems there; but that phone number will really go to a fellow scammer, who'll say they know the family member, and repeat the scam story, and might give the person a bank account number to transfer money into, or ask for their credit card details so they can take some out themselves. Or the first scammer might do that.

"The website with that information on it says that one idea is that to help identify whether a suspicious caller's genuine or not, they could be asked a question or two about things the real friend or family member isn't likely to have written about on their Facebook page, that some random scammer wouldn't be likely to know, like names of pets when they were a child, funny things that happened on old family occasions, or other things like that. I know people aren't going to feel like doing that kind of thing if they suddenly get bad news that sounds urgent; but if something seems a bit suspicious, it's worth spending a minute or so doing, although that could get a bit worrying if someone says they're ringing on behalf of the friend and says they'll go away and ask them, and never rings back. It's probably best to try ringing the friend or relative personally.

"Also, it's best if people have their Facebook privacy settings set to friends only, since if you have yours set to share with the public, anyone can read what you say and use your information!

"There are lots of other Facebook scams around, not just the holiday one, like some where a scammer makes a Facebook account with the name of the person whose relatives they're thinking of scamming, and then messages them asking for money for some other reason, like saying that something they really need has broken and they need a new one, like a laptop they need to do their coursework on at university or something."

James said with a smile, "There are some horrible people around! It would be good if they could all somehow be transported back in time, to a time when this country was swarming with dangerous wild animals, and hardly anyone lived here to scam! I'd like to see them try to scam the dangerous animals instead!

"I remember going on holiday when I was little, and we went to a museum one day that had big plastic dinosaurs, maybe to show people what dinosaurs were like. I sat on one for a while, as if I was going to ride it. Imagine if scientists managed to bring real dinosaurs back to life, and people started having them as pets. I wonder if someone would dare try to scam the family of someone who said on their Facebook page, 'I'm going on holiday to the seaside tomorrow. We're taking the dinosaur. I've hired a special big lorry to take him down there, and he's going to sleep in a massive kennel outside the hotel'."

Suzy chuckled and said, "I don't know, but I bet no one on the holiday with them would dare scam the dinosaur owner!"

The students giggled. But soon the mood grew serious again, as Matthew said, "I've heard there are quite a few scams that people going on holiday need to watch out for. One is websites that pretend to be offering cheap holidays when they're not really. They're after people's credit card details. People can put them on the websites if they think they're booking their holiday. I've heard it's best to book up with an organisation that's well-known, or to make sure a website's at least part of one of the travel companies' associations that are respected, like ABTA or ATOL, although I've heard that some websites say they are when they aren't, so it's probably just as well to try and find out if they are from elsewhere."

The students began to feel gloomy. But Jackie said, "Imagine if there was a disease that made people tell the truth all the time, without actually realising they were doing it, so if someone went to a fake holiday-booking website, and the person who'd put it up had the disease, it might say, 'This is a scam website designed to take your money by stealing your credit card details. Please put them in the boxes below and pay us lots of money so we can buy the expensive cars we've been longing for.'"

The students smiled. But they soon got serious again, as Matthew continued:

"As well as fake websites though, I've heard that when people are actually on holiday, there are quite a few scams they might be the victim of. There's one where sometimes when holidaymakers hire a car, they bring it back, only to be told they have to pay for damage to it, even though they didn't damage it. It can be damage the people hiring the car out knew was there before, but didn't get fixed, so everyone who hires the car can be charged for it, because the people at the car hire company claim each one of them must have done it when they bring it back. So it's recommended that people look over a car really well before renting it, and point out any damage they find, or rent a different one.

"And then there's another scam, where someone in a taxi tells people who are about to go to a famous site that it's closed, but that they can take them to a better one. If they get in the taxi, the driver really just takes them around expensive shops, and pressures them to buy things, perhaps because they've got an agreement with the shop owners where they take a share of the profits if they bring in customers; and the passenger can end up buying lots of stuff they don't want, because they're worried the taxi driver will abandon them if they don't and they'll be lost.

"There are lots of other scams too. I think everyone should look on the Internet for information about them."

Mya said, "I once met someone who used to go on business trips abroad, where he used to negotiate about some things with the owners of some foreign businesses. He said the foreign negotiators were always friendly. But I was asking him about whether he used to stay in the countries long enough to do sightseeing, and he said not really, but he said there was one time when he was in Egypt, and he had a few hours free before his next meeting, and he thought it would be nice to go and see the Pyramids quickly. So he asked the person at the reception desk in his hotel to order him a taxi. They did. But the driver turned out to be a scammer. I don't know if the person at reception was in on the scam at all, being paid to select that particular taxi driver or something. Maybe, maybe not.

"But anyway, the taxi arrived, and this man got in, and the driver took him most of the way there, but then stopped. He said taxis and buses weren't allowed to go further, but that he had a cousin who could take him the rest of the way with a pony and trap. This supposed cousin turned up, and he took him to the Pyramids. When they were there, this man saw taxis and buses quite close to them, so he realised it couldn't be true that they weren't allowed there.

"Anyway, when the supposed cousin started taking him there, he asked him how much it would cost, and the supposed cousin kept assuring him it would be free; but he said that when they got back to where the taxi had left him, he'd have the choice of whether to give him a donation.

"When they did get back, the man gave the supposed cousin a decent amount of money, only to hear him say it wasn't enough! The man asked him how that could be the case, since before, he'd kept insisting that it would be free.

"The supposed cousin just kept insisting that he was going to have to pay more if he wanted the taxi to take him back to his hotel.

"The man got angry, and protested to the taxi driver. He must have been in a bit of a hurry by then.

"When he got angry, the taxi driver said it would be OK, and he would take him back to his hotel, but that it would be nice if he'd allow him to show him a couple of shops on the way back. The man said that would be OK. He thought that at least he'd get back to his hotel that way.

"Then the taxi driver started taking him back; but suddenly he turned off to the left, instead of carrying on to the hotel. He stopped near some shops, saying another cousin of his worked in one, and he'd like him to meet him. Then a man came out of one of them, and greeted the man in a really friendly way. He said he was sure he recognised him. The man said he couldn't really, since he'd never been to Egypt before. Still enthusiastic, the new supposed cousin said he was sure he'd at least met someone who looked like him, and asked him if his father had ever been to Egypt. It so happened that the man's father had; he'd been stationed there for a while in the Second World War. So he told him that, thinking he might really know his father.

"It would be surprising if the supposed cousin could really be sure he recognised him all those years later, but still! The man was invited into the shop. He ended up buying quite a lot of stuff.

"He realised afterwards that he'd probably just been manipulated by salesman talk.

"I think he said the taxi driver stopped at another shop as well before he drove him back to his hotel!

"I don't know how much that kind of thing goes on. Maybe a lot. I think he at least did make it back for his meeting."

Suzy said, "It's a shame there are people like those scammers, especially because I've heard about people from developing countries who've been genuinely friendly, even making sacrifices for people, like sharing their food with people from the West who are visiting their countries, with no guarantee of anything in return, even though they've hardly got anything themselves! It seems the scammers might ruin things for other people, if people start suspecting that anyone who seems to be being kind is probably really up to no good!"

A gloomy thoughtful mood came over the students again.

It only got worse when Becky said, "Don't forget it's not just scams that can end up with you losing your money. My uncle Steven was in France once on a school trip, and two pickpockets stole his wallet. He ran after them, but they kept throwing it from one to the other, and then they ran off in opposite directions, and he didn't know which one had it, so he didn't know which one to run after. He never got it back."

The students were angry that some people would do that kind of thing. Silence came over the group for several seconds, as one or two hoped hell was real, so criminals would get their comeuppance, while a few others reflected that it would be a good idea to buy clothes – or at least coats – with pockets that zipped up, or else had buttons that did up over the top of them in future, to make it harder for pickpockets to steal from them.

The Students Tell Each Other Funny Stories They've Heard About Attempted Crimes Backfiring On the Criminals

Then Colin said, "It's not fair that people do that kind of thing! But hearing stories like that, I do get a sense of satisfaction when I hear stories about the times when a crime goes wrong for a criminal, or about stupid criminals making mistakes that mean they get caught. I once heard about two robbers in America who tried to pull the front off a cash machine by attaching a chain to it, and attaching the other end to the bumper of their pickup truck, and driving it a bit to try to pull the cash machine hard enough to break the front of it off. But instead of doing that, their efforts ended up pulling the bumper off their truck. They were worried, and drove home in a hurry, leaving the chain still attached to the cash machine on the wall, with

213

the bumper still attached to the chain, with the licence plate still on the bumper. You can imagine how easy it was for the police to find them!"

Mya said, "Oh I've heard stories like that. I read about a burglar who raided a butcher's shop, and he took his dog with him and opened a packet of meat for him to eat while he was stealing things; but when he'd finished the raid, the dog was enjoying eating it so much he refused to leave. The burglar was still by the door calling him when the police came.

"And I heard about a burglar who broke into a furniture shop, but then felt tired and fell asleep on a bed, and was still there when the shop opened, and the police were called and came in."

James said, "I heard about a burglar who broke into a wood sales company's premises and broke open a vending machine to get the cash in it, only to find it took tokens instead of money. It actually said that on the front of the machine in big letters. But still, it was night-time. Then the burglar stole a mobile phone, which it turned out afterwards only worked in the grounds of the company, and he took an electrical screwdriver, but he forgot the batteries and charger. Then he had a drink of a can of coke he found in one of the offices, but it was twelve months past its sell-by date! The police said they were looking for a stupid burglar who should be easy to spot, since he'd be the one who was looking as if he was feeling really sick and sleep-deprived, and carrying around a load of useless junk."

Stuart said, "I heard about some men who tried to steal a cash machine from a restaurant, only it had been out of order and empty for two years. The company that had installed it had gone bust, and it never got filled up after that. The thieves ripped it from bolts sticking it to the floor, which must have taken some effort! The restaurant staff said the thieves actually did them a favour, because they'd been wondering how to get rid of it. One of the thieves got arrested, since the cash machine wouldn't fit in their car, and they drove away with it sticking out the back, and got chased by the police."

Kirsty said, "I read about a thief who snatched some jewellery from a market stall, not realising he was surrounded by police on motorbikes who were in the town for an international police convention. He got arrested pretty quickly!"

Becky said, "I heard about a car thief who got locked into a car he was trying to steal and couldn't get out, and was arrested trying to hide on the back seat. The car had a security device that locked the doors when the alarm went off. There was a button next to the driver's seat that released the locks, but he didn't use it. A policeman said he ought to go looking for a decent job, since he was so bad at stealing things."

Matthew said, "I heard about a violent robber who tried to steal a van, not realising it belonged to a judo team, who'd come to the neighbourhood to teach a self-defence course. He asked one of them for money, and then reached into the van to try to take the keys. Needless to say, he came off worst; he ended up on the ground, being punched and roughly held down by about six people till the police came."

James said, "I heard about a bank robber who took the money and stuffed it down the front of his trousers. Unbeknownst to him, it was given to him with an explosive dye pack that would spray out all the dye when it exploded, to mark the money and the robber, to make it easier for the police to find them. I've heard that banks use them sometimes, and there's a transmitter on the bank door that somehow detonates the dye pack, and it'll explode about ten seconds later. The robber hadn't gone far when it exploded in his trousers. Police caught him a block away, looking in pain and walking funny."

The students giggled.

Colin said, "I remember hearing about a robber who went to the effort of hiding, waiting and then jumping out at someone and brandishing a gun, only to find himself stealing a chicken sandwich and chicken fingers, worth about £2.40. The victim was a restaurant employee who was carrying them out in a small bag after he finished work in the early hours of the morning, because he wanted to eat them. Perhaps the thief thought the bag contained all the money the restaurant had made that day. After he demanded the little bag at gunpoint, not realising he was going to all that effort just for a bit of junk food, he ran off with it.

"And I heard about another thief who demanded a bag of dog mess. He didn't realise it was dog mess at the time, but the woman who'd been going to put it in the bin happily handed it over, and the thief ran off with it."

Kirsty said, "I heard about two robbers in Australia who drove a van into a petrol station, and demanded two bags of rubbish at gunpoint. A man was carrying them to the bins. He told the thieves it was rubbish, but they didn't believe him and demanded it anyway, and drove off with it.

"And I heard about a man who tried to rob a shop, and ended up £5 worse off than he was before he went in! He handed over a £10 note, and asked for some cigarettes. When the shopkeeper opened the till for change, he put his hand in it, hoping to steal all the money in it. He grabbed a few pounds, and shouted a demand for the rest. But she slammed it on his fingers, and told him where to go. That was despite him having a hammer. He ended up running off with just the few pounds he'd managed to grab. Later she said she'd had a shock, but that the robber was £5 worse off than he'd been when he came in because of the ten pounds he'd given her to start with, and he hadn't even taken his cigarettes."

The students were enjoying the stories. But Stuart said, "Something I don't like is hearing about burglars and other criminals being taken to court, only to get really lenient sentences, like suspended ones they'll never serve if they manage not to get caught again for the next year or two or so. It can't make anyone feel safer, especially since I think most burglars don't get caught for most of what they do. Still, you hear funny stories to do with that kind of thing too. I heard about a judge in court who said he was 'absolutely staggered' that the man being tried in front of him, who kept committing burglaries and was in court for nearly thirty of them, had been let out on bail three times in the past year, so he'd been free to burgle again all that time; and the judge demanded to know who the 'idiot' was who kept just giving him bail, only to realise later that it was himself – he was the one who'd done it."

The Students Talk About Punishments For Criminals, Starting Off Being Serious, But Then Having a Laugh and Telling More Stories

The students laughed. Then James said, "I wonder why not more burglars get decent prison sentences, and why more aren't remanded in custody while they're waiting to go to court. Well, I admit I don't know what the statistics are for what percentage of them get treated leniently; but it's just that judging just by things you hear on the news, it does seem as if quite a lot of burglars get sentences that are way shorter than they ought to be, when you think about public safety, and that too many get let out on bail, when it's predictable that they'll probably take the opportunity to commit more crimes before their trials.

"I actually watched a television programme where some young offenders were being interviewed, and they were all saying they thought people like them deserved to get tougher sentences, to put them off committing more crimes like the ones they'd committed before. If even criminals themselves say that, well they must know what they're talking about. I heard that there are about half a million burglaries a year in this country! If burglars got longer prison sentences when they were caught, I bet that figure would go down, simply because the ones in prison wouldn't be around to burgle for so much of the time. A lot of them probably come straight out of prison and go right back to burgling again."

Dave said, "I wonder if the main reason they don't get longer sentences is because there aren't enough prison spaces available. Maybe they ought to build more prisons. They could even have prison ships. I think it would be good if they brought back transportation, so they could take criminals far away! I suppose the problem is that no one else would agree to have them nowadays. Hey, imagine prison spaceships that transported criminals to another planet, or to the moon!"

Suzy said enthusiastically with a playful grin, "Hey that could be good! Just think! They could send a load of criminals up there, give them about two months' supply of oxygen and food and water, and some other essential things they'd need, and tell them they had all that time to make the moon a place where humans could live. They could be given a big instruction book on how to mine minerals, and be told that if they managed it, they could sell the minerals to Earth, and might make loads of money. They could be encouraged to think that instead of stealing things from other people and selling them to make money, they could all spend their time snaffling minerals from inside the moon, and selling those to make money.

"They could be told that in the unlikely event that they managed to make the moon habitable, the whole moon would be theirs! They could own it and rule over it, and no matter how much money they made from mining minerals, even if they found some really precious ones and made loads of money, they could keep it all. That would be an incentive for them to work hard and try to make things work out.

"They could be given a big book on do-it-yourself spaceship making, and be told that if they succeeded, they could bring the minerals to Earth to sell them, and that they might even make money from just selling moon rock here. And they could be given a big book on do-it-yourself terraforming, so they could get to work to make the moon habitable for humans if they could, making the temperature nice, and doing something to make it so there was oxygen and good drinking water on the moon."

Matthew said, "I wonder how things would end up if the entire community of moon men was made up of criminals. They wouldn't like it if they started burgling from each other! Well, that's if any of them had anything worth stealing. I wonder if they would eventually get so annoyed with each other for stealing from and harming each other that they'd kill each other off, or whether they'd realise that for the community to survive, they'd have to stop being criminals and be nice to each other, and they'd set up a police force to catch anyone who refused to stop committing crimes. Maybe they'd eventually want anyone who did commit them to be transported to other planets, and the process would begin all over again."

Kirsty said, "I wonder if it would be possible to grow food on the moon. If it wasn't, the criminals would have to come down to Earth every few weeks or something and sell their minerals, or whatever goods they'd made with them, and buy food with the money, and load up their spaceship with it to take it back home to the moon. But then, people on Earth might not want any criminals coming to Earth in case they stole stuff while they were here. Maybe someone would have to develop a new technology where they could shoot the food up to the moon with a missile system. The trouble is, if it didn't quite reach the moon, all the food might shoot off into space, and orbit the sun forever, or until it biodegraded. Imagine tins of ham and pints of milk and bunches of grapes and things flying around space for years and years!

"Mind you, it probably wouldn't be so bad if they stayed in space, but just imagine if one day a hundred-year-old carton of milk fell to Earth like a meteorite! I suppose scientists might have an interesting time examining it . . . although they might have to put clothes pegs on their noses to keep out the smell! Imagine what they might say! 'Yuck, this is a smelly meteorite! . . . Oh hang on, no, it's a smelly ancient carton of milk.' Mind you, it would probably be even worse if it was a chunk of ancient meat or something!"

Jackie said, "Actually, something like that would probably burn up as it re-entered the atmosphere."

Kirsty said, "Oh yeah. But just imagine if its remains still came down to Earth! Scientists might think it was someone's ancient burned dinner. They might say, 'So some people must have been just as bad at cooking in ancient times as my mum was when I was growing up!'"

The students laughed.

Emma said, "Imagine if one of them said that in an official paper he got published in a science journal, or on television! I don't suppose his mum would be very happy with him when she found out!"

They giggled again.

Then Becky said, "That reminds me: I heard about a burglar who got caught because he left a trail of ham that led from the shop he broke into right to his home. He burgled a shop in Hamburg. The police came and saw several bits of ham on the ground outside the shop, where he'd smashed a window to get in; and then they found more ham and some footprints that led them to a house close by. They rang the doorbell, and a man who was a known burglar opened the door, and they arrested him."

Matthew said, "I heard about a burglar in America who got caught because he accidentally left his false teeth at the crime scene. He stumbled after he broke into a house and they came out of his mouth. He didn't stop to pick them up. A relative of the person whose house he broke into found them the next day. The police had searched the house, but missed them. So had the home owner. The police found out who the false teeth belonged to, because in that part of America, there's a law that says false teeth have to have the name of the person they belong to written on them."

Suzy said, "I read about an armed robber who dropped his mobile phone during a robbery, and didn't stop to pick it up. The police found it. He kept committing other robberies, and police soon caught him, and matched his description and the gun he had on him when he was arrested to a picture he'd had taken that was on his own phone, of him posing with the same gun.

"And I read about a robber who went into a bank and accidentally handed the person behind the counter a demand note with his name written on it! The note was written on the back of a printed online job application form, with his username and password on it, and maybe his address. So it turned out to be easy for the police to catch him! The person he handed the note to was sitting behind bullet-proof glass, so they didn't feel the need to give him any money. Then he ran away, leaving his application form behind."

Colin said, "I read about a robber the police thought they wouldn't be able to catch at first, because the CCTV camera images outside a shop he'd just stolen from weren't very clear; but then they found a photo of him on a camera in the shop; his accomplice had taken a picture of him on one of the digital cameras on display, and forgotten to erase it before they stole stuff and left. He was easy to catch after they found that."

Suzy said, "I heard about a woman who wanted to make some money by defrauding her insurance company into paying her money she said she wanted to spend on going to university; so she went to the police, and told them her skis and expensive ski-wear had been stolen. But she was actually wearing her ski trousers at the time! When the police pointed that out, she remembered and was embarrassed, and confessed that she was making a false claim."

Matthew said, "I read about two young men in Germany who felt hungry after a night out, so they kicked in a shop window, and stole handfuls of Easter bunnies and chocolate eggs. They lived right next-door to the shop! The police found them easily, by following a trail of Easter bunnies and eggs they accidentally dropped as they went home."

Dave said, "I heard about three burglars who got arrested when they went back to ask for receipts for the things they'd stolen. They went back and said they were struggling to sell what they'd stolen because people wanted receipts for the things, so could they have some? When they rang the doorbell, the owner of the house called the police, so they came and caught them there."

The Students Start Talking About Scams Again, Starting off Passing On Serious Information But Then Finding Something to Laugh About

The students sniggered. They were enjoying the stories and the joke ideas some of them were coming up with.

But then there was a pause in the conversation, and then it got serious again for a while. Anne, who'd rejoined them after having been to the boring psychology class she'd been complaining about earlier, said,

"Talking of receipts, I heard about a horrible email scam, where people get an email with an attachment that's made to look as if it comes from a supermarket, saying the attachment's an online receipt for the things they bought. The attachment's often a zip file, and if people open it, they discover it really contains some virus or malware that infects their computer. The email address it came from might look genuine, but it'll often have letters or numbers added to the name of the supermarket it supposedly comes from, or it'll be from an address like Hotmail rather than an official one. I've read that real supermarkets or official companies won't have addresses like that.

"And it's best not to open email attachments from anyone who could be a bit dodgy, in case they're viruses. There are other scams like that too. I read that some scam emails claiming to be from supermarkets tell people there was a problem with processing their money, and that they should go to a website they link to to sort it out. People often assume the link goes to the website of the company that supposedly sent the email, but really it's a link to another website that's disguised as the company's one, where the scammers try to get people to type in their credit card details, so they can steal money from them."

The students were angry. Then Matthew said, "I've heard about shopping scams. I think there are quite a variety. I know there are some where you get an email that falsely claims to be from an auction site like eBay, telling you the person who put in the highest bid in an auction you've just been in has pulled out, and that your bid was next highest so you've won the right to buy something you wanted. They say you can buy it by just putting your credit card details into a form they provide or something; but if you give them to them, they'll take as much of your money as they want, and you won't get a thing.

"Or some claim you have the chance to work as a mystery shopper, where you'll be going around finding out how prominently shops are displaying various products certain companies are selling, and things like that, and they promise you quite a bit of money after you've found out those things, but say you have to pay them money upfront for an employment pack first or something. So you pay money, and then nothing happens, or it does and you end up even worse off, because they say they want more money for something or other, so you pay them more, and I think it goes on like that, till you end up paying them more money than you ever get from them; or you do some work for them, only to find you don't get paid at all. Genuine offers of mystery shopper jobs won't ask people to pay money before they can get the job. That's what I've known them to say on consumer programmes on television and consumer advice websites. I think people ought to find out more about scams, to make sure they don't fall for them. I think there's quite a lot of advice about them on the Internet."

Jackie said, "I've heard that scam messages sent by text message to people's phones are increasing. A lot of scammers just send them to a load of random numbers, so even people who've just bought new phones that they haven't even used yet can get them.

"There's one where people get a message claiming to be from a mail delivery service like Royal Mail, saying there's a parcel they couldn't deliver, or that the person who sent it didn't pay the full amount, and it says they'll deliver it if they're just paid a small delivery charge. They never ask for much money, I don't think, but they say people can pay if they go to a website they link to, which has the name of the company that supposedly sent the text message, but it actually has extra numbers or letters in it, or it's a different domain name to theirs. But people can be fooled into thinking it's theirs, and then when they go there, they're asked to type in their bank details, and then the scammers take as much of their money as they want.

"Even well-educated people like doctors have been fooled by it. Obviously they weren't educated about scams like that! Not that you'd expect them to be at medical school. But it's easy to be fooled if you're expecting a parcel at the time, or you often get sent them.

"I read that the Royal Mail say they never just text people to say a parcel's been undelivered; they'll always put a card through people's letterboxes.

"It's best if people look online if they get a message they're unsure about to see if it's a known scam."

The conversation was turning gloomy! Perhaps it would have been appropriate, in a twisted kind of way, if they'd eaten a gloomy meal to go with it – maybe cold lumps of fatty meat with cold stringy runner beans and over-cooked Brussels Sprouts or something. But then maybe they'd have forgotten where they were and thought they were back at school. Then they might have felt even more gloomy!

Kirsty said, "I've had a couple of dodgy emails claiming there's 'suspicious activity' on an account I supposedly have, according to the email, which claims it's from one of these companies you can sign up with and then easily buy things online from, where you can put your credit or debit card details in the first time, and then it remembers them so you don't have to put them in every time you buy something. Maybe these scammers are trying to worry people into wondering if some-one's stolen their credit card details and they're using them to buy stuff for themselves.

"Anyway, one or two emails said my eBay account had been disabled temporarily because of this supposedly 'suspicious activity', and that I would be permanently locked out of it in twenty-four hours' time if I didn't go to the web page they linked me to and put my details in to confirm my identity. I didn't go there, but I'm presuming they would have asked for my credit card details and that kind of thing if I had, so they could steal my money. Thankfully I knew better than to take the email seriously and do what they wanted. That's partly because I haven't even got an eBay account! The scammers must just send these emails out randomly to people, hoping for the best.

"The funny thing is, the emails that said that weren't even well-written; they had quite a few mistakes in them! I expect the real eBay's fraud department at least employs people who can write emails that actually look official! Funnily enough, both the emails I got said, 'Dear costumer' instead of customer, as if they thought they were writing to someone who works in the costume department of a theatre or something! But you'd have thought that if they really knew there was 'suspicious activity' on my account, they'd at least know my name, so they'd address me by name in the email, instead of thinking I'm someone who works in a theatre or circus, or a fancy-dress shop or something – I don't think I've even been to a theatre, actually . . . Well, they either thought I was a costume designer or something . . . or much more likely, they somehow thought that's the way to spell customer, or it was just a typo they were too high on drugs to notice or something."

The others chuckled.

Then Kirsty carried on, "Anyway, I've heard that if you get an email like that, saying your account's been disabled, and you wonder if it really might be from a genuine company you're signed up with, it's best to go to what you know is their official website and see if you can do anything with your account, to prove to yourself that it's still working really, or else contact them directly and ask if there really is a problem with your account, or look online to see if there are websites about hoaxes and scams that say emails just like that are doing the rounds and they're from criminals trying to steal your money, or look for online articles about the kinds of techniques email scammers use."

Emma said, "Yes. My grandad might have got scammed, if it wasn't for my older sister and brother warning him off. I heard about it later. He got an email saying it was from eBay, saying his account had been suspended because of outstanding payments they were owed that needed to be paid immediately if he wanted his account to work again. He emailed them back and argued with them, saying he knew he'd paid everything he should have done. He thought it really was eBay emailing him. The scammer emailed him back, and a bit more arguing went on.

"He told some of my family what was happening, and my brother and sister told him it was a known scam and that he should stop arguing with the person and just delete all their emails. My brother asked him if he'd given the scammer his credit card details and he said no. They were worried he'd either done that, or clicked on a link in an email the scammer had sent him and it had downloaded malware onto his computer. He said he hadn't done that either.

"My brother looked at the emails they'd sent him, and told him they were full of clues that it was a scam. For one thing, the first one didn't call him by his name. It said 'Dear' . . . and then some identity number he had on the eBay site that it was easy for anyone to find.

"My brother said another clue was that there were one or more mistakes in the English. And the email said they wanted to ask him a question, and then asked several! One was what payment method he was intending to use, so they were trying to get his credit card details right away.

"And there were other things that were clues that it wasn't genuine, such as that the email supposedly came from ebay.com, when it would have come from ebay.co.uk if it was really about his eBay account, since that was the site he used. But my brother said that in any case, it's possible for scammers to spoof email addresses, so their emails make them look as if they're from legitimate addresses they're not from really.

"He told my grandad to go to the actual eBay site himself to check his account wasn't really suspended, not by clicking on a link he'd been sent in the emails he'd got, which might really go somewhere completely different even though it said it was a link to eBay, but by typing the eBay address into the address bar of his Internet browser. Then he could tell if his account really was suspended or not, because it would say so if it was, when he put his password in, or when he made as if he wanted to buy something, (which he could do without actually buying it), or if he went to his account settings. He went to eBay, and his account was working as normal.

"He was angry, and said he was going to reply to the email he'd been sent and threaten to get lawyers onto them. But my brother and sister told him not to have anything else to do with them, but just to delete all their emails. So he did."

Suzy said, "Someone tried to scam a relative of mine not long ago. She'd decided to sell some of her furniture, because she was moving house, and she knew it wouldn't fit in her new place. She sold it on a website where people advertise things for sale. She got it sold in the end.

"But the first person who offered to buy it was a scammer pretending he wanted it all, at the full price. He sent her an email, that was made to look as if it came from PayPal, supposedly transferring the money to her. Then the scammer asked if she could refund a bit of the money, saying he'd have to use it to pay a certain courier to come and collect the furniture for him.

She looked at the address of this supposed courier, and he turned out to live in Nigeria! That would have been a long way to come, just to pick up some old furniture! The scammer was asking her to refund him about £314 to supposedly pay this courier. If the courier could get from Nigeria to her door and back for £314, I think it would mean he'd discovered a miracle form of transport that we could all do with knowing about!

"But she thought it must be a scam, and didn't give him any money. The email that was supposedly from PayPal transferring money to her later turned out to be fake. But when she wouldn't pay, she got an email from the scammer, threatening to report her to PayPal if she didn't pay him, saying he'd get the police onto her. She just ignored the email. Then a few hours later, she got another one, saying he'd reported her to PayPal, who'd said they were going to call the police if she didn't pay very soon. She ignored that email too. Nothing happened after that.

"She phoned up PayPal, getting their official number from somewhere else; and when she told the man on the phone that she'd been told she'd been reported to them and what had happened, he laughed!

"It's not nice that scammers try to scare and con people like that! At least she wasn't scared into paying! But maybe some people are."

Dave said, "Yes, it's not nice, is it! And it's not nice to know that things like this are going on right in your doorway . . . I mean at your doorway . . . no, on your doorway . . . no, what do I mean – on your doorstep – that's the phrase I was looking for!"

The others giggled.

Matthew smirked and said, "Only, the scammer wouldn't really have got anywhere near this relative's doorstep, if he came from Nigeria!"

There was more giggling.

Then Suzy said, "The story didn't end there. About a month after she had the problem, my relative wanted to sell a very old sewing machine that someone had given her in her will years before, since it wouldn't fit in her new house, with all the other things that she was planning to move in there. So she advertised it, quite cheaply, and a woman said she wanted it. She spoke to her on the phone, and the woman asked if my relative could sell it a bit more cheaply. She agreed, but then the woman asked her if she could post it to her, since she lived at the other end of the country, almost, so it would be a long way to drive to collect it. My relative refused, since it would have cost loads of money to send through the post! So this woman asked if it would be alright if her husband came and collect it in that case.

"My relative said yes; but when she thought about it, she wondered why on earth someone would spend all the money they'd have to spend travelling hundreds of miles just to pick up an old old sewing machine! She had a look for information about the make of it on the Internet, and she found out it was an antique, worth quite a bit of money! So she realised this woman must have thought she was on to a real bargain, and that maybe she often browsed websites where people sell things, just so she could spot antiques and buy them cheaply from people who didn't realise what they were selling was valuable, and then she probably sold them on for a massive profit!

"So my relative decided not to sell the sewing machine to the woman after all. She phoned her up and told her she'd changed her mind about selling it, and the woman was angry, saying she'd arranged for her husband to collect it. But my relative still said she'd decided not to sell it.

"But then she decided to sell it on a different website where people advertise things they want to sell. And guess what! That man who'd tried to scam her before on the other site got in touch with her and said his sister desperately needed that sewing machine to work on, so could she have it sent to Nigeria! She laughed and told me she didn't understand why anyone would desperately need to use an ancient sewing machine, and couldn't get one any closer to home! She just ignored the man.

"Mind you, she said she has managed to sell a lot of things successfully online since she started trying not long ago, so it's gone well most of the time."

The students said they were at least pleased about that.

Then Dave said, "This subject reminds me of those scams that quite a lot of scammers from places like Nigeria are famous for pulling, where a scammer emails you pretending to be someone who's got loads of money in the bank, who needs to get it out of the country, but can't without someone's help, for some reason; and they promise that if you help them, you'll get a percentage of the money. If someone shows interest, the scammer ends up telling them that before they receive the money, they have to pay a certain amount in bank charges or bribes so it can be transferred. When people pay, they never hear from the scammer again. And it can be even worse, because some actually get people to travel to some far-away country where they can supposedly meet them to give them the money, and then they steal all their things so they're stranded, or they do worse things."

Catherine said, "Oh I've heard of those scams. I think the worst of them are ones where the scammers promise to donate all the money they supposedly have to a charity the person they're emailing's running. The others just try to appeal to people's greed or hopefulness, but those ones play on their generosity."

Colin said, "I've read about people who string those scammers along and get them to do funny things, wasting hours of their time that they might otherwise be spending scamming other people. People do need to be careful if they do that, since I've read that the scammers are dangerous criminals. But some of these people who mess them around make up false names for themselves, and send replies to them from email addresses they specially make up for the purpose, so they're not using their official ones, and so they can just delete them if the scammers get too annoying or nasty; and they pretend to be interested in what the scammers are saying; and they can correspond for quite a while before a scammer realises they're just wasting their time.

"I read about some of the things they do. Some pretend to be scammers too, who've been at it for longer and can give advice. They recommend to the scammers that they say things to possible victims like, 'Take this offer of mine with a huge grain of salt', telling them it's a common English idiom that means, 'This will be the chance of your lifetime and I'm very serious about this.' The scammers don't have the expression about a pinch of salt in their language, so it's possible they'll believe it and use it. Or if a scammer sends them a fake document like a photocopy of their passport, for supposed verification of who they are, if it looks obviously fake, the person pretending to be their victim tells them it looks really good and it's really helping them to trust them, so they might send ones that look just as fake to their real victims, who might realise they're fake and stop trusting them.

233

"Some people who play scammers along have persuaded them to travel thousands of miles to meet them, because they promise they'll hand over a lot of money in person when they do; but they don't turn up at the airport to meet the scammer, and later make some excuse for why they weren't there, having told them to hold up a sign at the airport with something they've told them to write on it to identify themselves. Some have persuaded scammers to hold up signs saying things like, 'Hopscotch is my favourite game' or, 'knitting is an aggressive male sport', or rude things, and scammers have been waiting for hours at the airport holding those signs, waiting for intended victims who don't turn up. And the people who play scammers along dupe them into doing all kinds of other funny things too."

The Topic of Conversation Turns to Good and Bad Ways of Handling Money

The students grinned. But then the conversation turned serious again for a while. Sarah said, "It's not just where other people try to take your money that you can end up a lot worse off. I've heard that some people end up making themselves poor by their own behaviour. I read a book called *You and Your Money* by someone called Alvin Hall, who did several series on television where he tried to help people overcome their money problems. I watched a few of the programmes. It was interesting that the reasons why the people he helped were always short of money had a lot to do with attitudes and habits they had that they didn't even realise were causing a problem, rather than because they just weren't earning much, or that they'd come from a deprived background so they had a bad education and couldn't get a good job afterwards, or that try as they might, they couldn't get any kind of work. I'd assumed they'd be about things like that before I started watching, and was a bit surprised that they weren't.

"The programmes were all about the author Alvin Hall giving people advice about changing their behaviour, and showing them how much what they were doing was causing problems for them, in dramatic ways to bring it home to them, such as making a massive pile of pound coins, to illustrate just how much money they were really spending when they would buy something with a credit card with barely a thought.

"He said there are quite a few different attitudes to money that are actually self-defeating, because people think they're using it in their best interests when really they're not.

"In the book of his I read, he says one self-defeating attitude is where people are always treating themselves and other people to things, whether they can afford it or not, because they think they ought to have them. They keep buying stuff they feel like getting but can't really afford, justifying it by using the old saying from those adverts about how they're worth it. They reckon they deserve it. But the author says when he's asked them why they deserve it any more than anyone else does, they don't know. Anyway, they buy things they think will make them happy, but because they don't stick to buying just what they can afford, they're really dumping a load of future anxiety and misery on themselves without realising it, because the time will likely come when there's something they really need to pay for, but they can't, because they've frittered their money away."

"I know someone like that," said Jackie. "She's always buying expensive things for herself and someone she loves, and then she gets scared and upset when she can't afford something she needs to pay for. The other day she fancied buying a big takeaway pizza, because she wasn't in the mood to cook; but she wasn't sure whether to buy one, because she couldn't really afford it. A few people told her to go on and buy it because she deserved it. She did. But sadly for her, she fell asleep halfway through eating it. Her head fell forward as she nodded off to sleep and plonked right in it. Oddly enough, she didn't wake up for a while. When she did, the pizza was cold, and she didn't fancy it any more. So she didn't eat the rest."

"I'd have eaten it!" said Dave, who had a special reputation for enjoying food.

"What, after someone's head had been in it?" asked Mya with a grin.

"Yes!" proclaimed Dave, and they laughed.

"Ugh, hairy pizza!" said Heather, and they cringed. Then Emma said, "Or even worse, pizza-splodgy hair! Imagine the person who fell asleep in it walking around the street afterwards without washing her face and hair first!" They giggled.

Sarah wanted to carry on what she was saying, so she continued,

"Anyway, the author who wrote this book about some reasons people end up poor says some other people who bring financial trouble on themselves in the end are really dreamers who fantasise about how nice the things they want would be, without counting the cost; or they have big ideas, but they don't plan them through well. They can start businesses or pay for expensive holidays, or do other things that cost them a lot of money, because it seems like a good idea at the time, but they haven't thought things through properly, or found out how things might possibly go wrong in the future and planned for what to do if they do, so they can end up seriously in debt, or being a burden to other people by borrowing loads of money from them all the time, if things don't work out the way they want. Or they borrow a load of money in the first place to get what they want, assuring people they'll be able to pay it back, but then they don't, because they've just been having unrealistic dreams about how the money will start flowing in once they start their business or whatever.

"And the author says some people take risks just for the sake of it, because it gives them an adrenaline rush they're addicted to. So they can end up in the same situation, because they blew money on things that didn't have a high chance of working out, or they gambled loads of money away. Spending it makes them feel good in the short term, but they end up in a whole load of trouble for it; they can sometimes lose relationships because their partners can't stand the worry and insecurity of living with their behaviour and what it might mean if bad things happen because of all the debt they're in; and other bad things can happen."

Mya commented, "I've heard that some people who get addicted to gambling, or drugs and drink, get into those things because they've got personalities where they love taking risks. I've heard that some people spend thousands of pounds on gambling! But surely you don't have to spend that much money if you want to take risks so you get the adrenaline boost! I mean, you could just get it by getting too close to geese in the park, or . . . well, I don't know, annoying your wife till she yells at you or something. Or you could join the army and become a bomb disposal person or something; that way people Pay you to take the risks!"

A few of the students grinned. Then Sarah said seriously, "Talking of addictions, the author of this book says some people are addicted to shopping. They buy loads of things, because it makes them feel good at the time; but they're often things they don't really need, and might not even use. And then they can get just as miserable in the future, when they find themselves in debt and can't afford things they would really love to have, that would actually be really useful to them. And if people they're married to can't cope with their money habits, they can lose good relationships too.

"The bloke who wrote the book about all that says a lot of people who spend money recklessly have a deeper emotional need for something that isn't being satisfied in their lives, and they spend money as a substitute for it, sometimes without realising that that's what they're really doing. So for instance, a mother who wants her family to have a high standard of living might go out to work to earn enough money to help them get one, but then feel as if she really ought to be with her children, but she might not want to sacrifice her career. She might feel guilty about depriving her children of the time and love she'd be able to devote to them if she wasn't working, so she might get them lots of toys and other things all the time instead, some of which they might not even play with or use.

"But maybe trying to arrange to work part-time, and doing more enjoyable and educational things with the children so as to give them attention and fun, and also guidance that'll help them in the future, would be a better solution."

"Giving them guidance and educational things? What kind? I bet some parents' idea of giving their kids that is standing over them nagging them to do their homework!" said Dave, with a half-smile. "That never did me any good."

"Oh yeah? How did you end up here then?" asked Stuart.

"My dad ended up doing all my homework for me," joked Dave with a grin . . . At least, the students all assumed it was a joke.

"Actually," said Sarah, "I think the idea of mums spending more time with their children would be for them to do things like, say, play ball games with them, and teach them about being sensible with money and things."

"How does playing a ball game teach children to be sensible with money?" asked Dave as a joke.

Sarah screwed up her face at what she thought was the cringeworthiness of the joke, and said, "Oh, you know what I mean!" Then she continued:

"Anyway, the author says the reason some people make bad decisions about money isn't even because they've made a deliberate choice to live as if they can do what they like with money, feeling sure it won't cause a problem, but they've just got into bad habits with it, because their parents didn't handle it well, and they automatically learned from them and imitated them; or they didn't like the way their parents handled money, and they've over-reacted by going to the opposite extreme, like feeling so deprived because their parents hoarded money so they couldn't have everything they wanted that they never wanted to be like that, so they've made life one continual treat-fest, or they were so disgusted with a parent who wasted all their money on things they didn't need that they decided they never wanted to be like that, and got into hoarding theirs.

"The author says that when people realise they're only behaving the way they are because things in their past got them into the habit, they can stop feeling as if something in their gut's telling them it's important to handle their money the way they do, and start being more sensible with it, because they realise it's only some impression they got when they were being brought up that's made them feel like doing what they do, and not something important really."

Mya said, "I used to hoard sweets when I was younger. At least, that's what my mum called it. I called it collecting them! I used to buy little treats every now and then, and put them in a tin under my bed till I had lots. I might have kept some for months. My mum told me it was babyish to hoard sweets, and said I shouldn't. But I was keeping them because I wanted to have feasts with my friends, and I enjoyed knowing I had lots of sweets. I had a couple of feasts with a few people, but I still had quite a few sweets left that I was hoping to have more feasts with, and then my sister started stealing them! I was unhappy about that! Now she's a lot fatter than me, and she's trying to lose weight, but she's finding it difficult."

Mya continued with an evil grin, "I like to tell her for a joke that some of the fat she's got comes from the sweets she nicked from me years ago, and that she wouldn't have so much of a problem if she hadn't done it, so it's fate serving her right."

"I bet you're popular with her!" said Jackie sarcastically, sniggering.

"Actually yes, we quite like each other really," said Mya. "I mean, you can tell, because we give each other big boxes of chocolates at Christmas . . . Come to think of it, maybe some of her fat comes from those."

She joked with a smile, "Perhaps I ought to give her a bag of salad leaves instead, or a cabbage or something."

Sarah was still feeling serious, and said, "She isn't the only one who could maybe do with cutting down on things. Well, we all probably could. And not just food, but spending too much. Everyone probably does, to some extent. I mean, you've got to enjoy life a bit; but it is important to save money too."

Dave said, "You're beginning to sound like a parent or a teacher!"

Sarah joked, "Well, I've been around parents and teachers for most of my life, so maybe that's where I got it from. Just be thankful corporal punishment's illegal in this country nowadays, or I might have given you the cane for being cheeky enough to say what you just said!"

The students grinned.

Then Sarah said seriously, "Anyway, that book by the author Alvin Hall says a bit more about the reasons some people spend a lot more money than they should. It says that sometimes, it's because they feel under pressure to buy expensive things, because they're overly worried about what people will think of them if they don't, or they're so concerned about looking good, and envious of people they think are having a good time, that they want to buy all the things they think the better-off people around them have. So they blow a lot of money on evenings out with friends, or expensive holidays and cars and things. But they can end up regretting it when they're in debt, ending up with a lower standard of living than they could have had if they'd saved more of their money to buy things they actually need. And all along, it might be that the people they thought were better off than them have gone into debt to pay for what they have, and are always feeling anxious about it, so spending all that money isn't really making them happy after all.

"And some of the people who the ones buying expensive things are trying to match by showing that their tastes are just as expensive as theirs in case they look down on them might really wish they didn't feel they had to spend so much money to keep up appearances; maybe they're doing it themselves because they're worried about being looked down on or thought of as mean if they don't. So they might really appreciate it if people around them who've been feeling under pressure to spend lots of money start suggesting they do things together that don't cost so much, instead of doing the expensive things they might have been doing up till then, or if people start daring to be different and shopping around for cheaper things that are really just as good as the expensive things they've been buying; when one person in a group dares to be different, it might sometimes encourage others to, and then they might feel better for it."

"Oh yes," said Suzy. "That reminds me of something I heard on the radio, where a woman was complaining about the amount of money she felt pressured by the expectations of people around her to spend, going to expensive hen party after expensive hen party after expensive hen party for people in her office. They would all go on weekends abroad and things. It made me wonder, 'Just how many hen parties do these people have? How often do they get married? Do they all have about six husbands each or something, or do they keep divorcing after their honeymoons or something, perhaps just so they can get married again so they can have more of their beloved hen parties?'"

The students laughed. Dave said, "That reminds me of an old joke about someone who's had six husbands, with people around her having a theory that she only keeps marrying new ones because she likes wedding cake so much . . . Actually, I've never found that joke funny, so I don't know why I just bothered mentioning it. Perhaps I'm going nuts."

They grinned.

Then Sarah carried on talking. Some students wondered why she wanted to tell them all of what she was telling them, thinking it was beginning to sound as if she must suspect some of them of being just like the people in the book she'd read, so she thought they needed the lesson. But whatever the reason was that she was telling them, she said a few more things. She said:

"Anyway, another thing this Alvin Hall says is that some people spend loads of money because they're defiant and angry with people around them, like their parents, for any number of reasons, or with a system they don't think has given them their fair share in life, whether it has or not; so they spend money on themselves to get back at them or the system, having to borrow more and more from their parents or others, or scrounge from the system more, while they're thinking about how to live for the moment, instead of planning how to make their lives really worthwhile. They might not think of themselves as spending to get back at people or the system; but sometimes in counselling, when they think about it, they can realise that that's basically what they're doing.

"If they carry on, it'll mean that despite all the things they're buying, they'll always b bitter and unhappy sometimes, brooding on what they think is unfair; and in the end, when they haven't got the money they would have ended up with if they'd actually saved some and been more sensible with it, they'll feel even more bitter, on top of all the misery they've brought on themselves throughout life, when they realise there are things they'd really like that they can't afford, and by then never will be able to. They'll blame the system for that too, according to this author Alvin Hall, instead of realising they should have been wiser with their money.

"Then you get the people who go to the opposite extreme and hoard money; so they're always less happy than they could be, because they deprive themselves of the happiness they could have if they would spend a bit more money on what they want and need.

"So anyway, whatever scams do to deprive people of their money, it seems that a lot of people can lose all their money without being caught up in any of them; their money problems come about because they're doing things that really amount to scamming themselves."

That made the students thoughtful.

The Students Discuss Teaching School Pupils About Scams, Joking About Which Lessons Could Be Replaced to Make Room For the Subject

But then Emma said, "Still, at least if it's your own attitude that needs changing, it's within your control, at least from the time you realise what you're doing wrong. If someone's out to scam you, you might not be wise to it till after the event, when all your savings have gone in one go. I think it would be good if schools taught pupils about how to avoid scams."

"That would be good! But I'm not sure when they'd teach it," said Becky thoughtfully. "I mean, the curriculum's already full of stuff."

"They could teach it instead of a lesson that doesn't really have a purpose," said Emma enthusiastically. "Like maths, for example," she said as the idea made her face light up with joy.

"But maths is useful!" said Matthew, who liked it for some reason. "After all, we need it on this course, for when we learn stuff about statistics and things."

"Yes, but we can do a lot of that on the computer, letting the machine do the work for us . . . or at least I hope we can!" said Emma. "And anyway, I'm sure we could scrap Most of what we learn in maths at school; I can't imagine ever needing to use it in my life!"

"Maths is used for a lot of things you wouldn't expect," said Kirsty. "I heard something about it on the radio the other day . . . I can't remember what they said it was used for now, but I know I was surprised."

"You might be surprised to learn that I used my maths notes for lining my rabbit's hutch," said Jackie. "When I finished my school exams, I thought about having a special celebration to rip a lot of my notes up. I thought I'd especially enjoy ripping all my maths notes up; but then I thought, 'No, why not let my rabbit do it! That'll be even more satisfying, knowing he'll cover them in droppings first! Just the kind of thing that ought to happen to maths notes!' So I kept them in a pile, and put a fresh wad of them in there every time I cleaned the rabbit's hutch out, before I put new straw and things in there! You're supposed to put newspaper or sawdust or something like that at the bottom of the hutch before you put the straw in, to soak up all the wee the rabbit does in there. But I put maths notes there instead. It was quite satisfying knowing they were going to be destroyed by being weed on and ripped up!"

Becky said, "I remember someone telling me that when she was at school, for a few weeks there was a song in the charts called 'Rip It Up And Start Again' by an old band called Orange Juice; and one day, her maths teacher said that would be a good maths homework song."

"He knew people like to rip up their maths homework then?" asked Dave, grinning.

Becky said, "No, I think he was thinking that they often ought to do that to their homework, because they'd done such a bad job of it."

Colin said, "Someone told me he fed his maths homework to his pet goat once. He said the goat enjoyed it. He said he was dying to tell his teacher his goat ate it, but she never asked why he hadn't done it."

The students giggled. Then Jackie said, "Oh well, if schools wouldn't get rid of maths – more's the pity – Maybe we could replace some English literature lessons with lessons about scams instead. I mean, we learn a ton of rubbish in that! All that turgid horrible poetry we had to wade through, and Shakespeare! I've never understood what the point was of studying that!"

"Some of the stuff we had to do in those lessons was alright though," said Heather. "I quite liked the Charles Dickens novels we had to study."

Suzy smiled and said, "I remember our English teacher telling us she was once at a lecture where the lecturer said, 'Today we're going to study Dickens.' There was someone there from a foreign country, who'd probably never heard of Charles Dickens, and it seems he assumed the S on the end of the word Dickens signified that it was a plural word, and he asked, 'What's a dicken?' "

Becky said, "Just think: If an English literature lesson was replaced with a lesson on scams, but the teacher didn't tell anyone that was going to happen before the lesson itself, so the pupils just weren't expecting to study them, the teacher might start the lesson by saying, 'Today we're going to study scams', and someone might assume that must be an author, and ask, 'Who's Scams?'"

They laughed. Then Emma got serious again and said, "It would be nice if they could find somewhere in the curriculum for a lesson or two about scams anyway."

"The thing is though, new ones are always being invented," said Matthew. "So their information would always be going out of date. I mean, a few years after you'd been taught about them, the ones you'd been taught about might be out of fashion, and a load of new ones would've come along."

"Still," said Kirsty, "they could teach people about the main kinds of cons out there, and advise people to check things out more, like telling them to go on the Internet sometimes to find out if there's any information about new kinds of phone calls and emails and letters and things they might get from scammers. And they could give people some basic rules that would protect them quite a bit of the time, like never giving passwords or bank details to anyone who contacts them out of the blue and says they're their bank or some other official organisation, since banks and other official organisations just won't ask for details like that by email or over the phone."

The Students Talk and Joke About Ideas to Try to Teach School Children to Become More Caring People

Anne said, "I think people should be taught to be good citizens at school. Then maybe not so many people would scam other people and do other horrible things in the first place. I heard about a school where teenagers were sent out to do some kind of work in the community for a number of weeks, like serving dinners to old people who were no longer well enough to make them for themselves, and things like that; and by the time their work experience ended, they were much more caring than they had been before. I think it might be a good idea if all schools had schemes like that."

Dave said with a wry smile, half-joking, "But I bet doing that for old people wouldn't make you more caring, Anne! I bet you'd come away complaining, 'It's so depressing being with those old people; they just want to talk and talk about the bad things in the news, and things like that!'"

Anne blushed. While she was thinking of an answer to that one, Mya said, "But what if some scammers start scamming early; they might think of working for needy old people as an opportunity to scam them, or just to steal from them, instead of it making them more caring!"

Anne blushed even more. She said, "Yeah, well maybe they could select the most trustworthy students to work with the most vulnerable people, and the others could maybe just help raise money for charity, finding out a lot about what people's needs are, but just not meeting them."

"Presumably you mean not meeting the people, rather than not meeting their needs?" said Stuart with a smile.

Anne looked dismayed and said, "Yes, that was what I meant."

Emma said, "Wouldn't that mean that the people who got to do the caring work would be the people who were the caring ones anyway? And as for the others, is there any evidence that raising money for charity and finding out about people's needs can make people more caring?"

Anne looked just as embarrassed as she had before. But she said, "I don't know. But still, I think it's an idea worth thinking about. Anyway, there will likely be signs that a teenager's a budding scammer who might exploit people they're sent to help, because they'll probably mistreat other pupils in some way at school; and people like that can be excluded from schemes where some of the class goes into the community to help people; but most pupils will probably fit somewhere between caring and bullying, so schemes like that might help those ones get to be more caring. But anyway, if it turns out that there is real evidence that people can become more caring by helping other people, whether in person or even just by learning a lot about people with various kinds of problems and doing things to raise money to help them, I definitely think it should be made part of the school curriculum.

"And whatever reasons there are why people start turning to crime, I think schools and governments should do something about those, to try to stop people becoming criminals. I think there should be systems in place to try to stop people becoming criminals in the first place; I don't think the authorities should only try to change people once they've become criminals."

All the students agreed.

The Students Start Talking
Seriously About Scams Again

Jackie said thoughtfully, "I wonder if it would help if victims of some crimes went into schools and talked about the effect they had on them, to help pupils understand that a crime can really mess up a person's life. It might put at least some pupils off committing them. Mind you, it might make any psychopaths in the class think they'll enjoy committing crimes more, feeling joyous about the emotional pain it'll cause, for whatever reason they enjoy causing it. And actually, I suppose telling pupils about scams might give any psychopaths in the class new ideas about how to scam people. Still, it might put some people off getting into crime if victims told classes how it affected their lives; and I'm sure it would be worth warning pupils about the scams out there, since budding psychopaths who want to commit crimes will probably commit them anyway. I think school pupils should at least be given some basic rules that can help people avoid scams, such as that if an offer seems too good to be true, it probably is.

"I mean, one thing I've heard about is that a lot of people get these letters in the post, telling them they've won loads of money or valuable things in prize draws and things, or that they have a good chance of winning one, or that fortune has somehow smiled on them and they've been entered in a lottery they've never heard of and they've won, and that they'll get their prize if they only send a certain amount of money, for some supposed reason I can't remember now. I was surprised to find out that loads of people fall for that kind of thing, and how much money they can spend! People can spend thousands of pounds over time, not just replying to one letter, but lots, since when they reply to one by sending money, their names and addresses get passed around criminals who have what they call 'sucker lists' of people they think of as being gullible enough to fall for their scams, and then more scammers start sending them letters claiming they've won things, and that they just need to send money to get the prizes, and things like that. That's what I've heard.

"People can be sucked in, partly because some get an addictive adrenaline buzz from the letters, because they love the thought of winning stuff, and they're always excitedly anticipating that the very next letter they get might be the one with the big cheque for millions of pounds or whatever the prize is in it. But it never comes. People have ended up getting sackfuls of letters a day, because more and more criminals think they're a good source of money, so they keep sending them letters with promises of prizes in them that they just have to pay a bit of money to receive, that they'll never really get!"

The Conversation Turns to Daft Driving Mishaps, As the Students Tell Funny Stories and Make a Few Jokes

Heather said, "Why do people fall for scams like that? I mean, no company's going to send random strangers prizes out of the goodness of their heart, are they. Why aren't people on the lookout for the catch with these things?"

"I don't know," said Jackie. "Maybe some people are too trusting, like some people I read about the other day. This wasn't to do with scams, but sat navs, where some people obey their instructions even when they should be able to tell it's not a good idea. I don't know why, but for some reason, it seems sat navs sometimes tell people to do things that really aren't sensible.

"I read about a German man who drove on to a building site, up some steps, and crashed into and knocked over a portable toilet, later saying his sat nav had told him to do it. And another driver drove down a flight of steps, with his boss in the back of the car, saying his sat nav had told him to do that. And there's a place called Crackpot in Yorkshire, where several drivers have driven down a narrow muddy private road after their sat navs have told them to, despite a sign saying it's a no-through road; and they've got stuck on an awkward bend, and had to be rescued by farmers with tractors.

"I'm guessing that driving with due care and attention's more important than obeying the sat nav … That's if the sat navs really did tell them to go in those directions, and they weren't just making up excuses, or misunderstanding the instructions, like if a sat nav told them to go right at the next turning, meaning the next road turning, not the next turning no matter what it happened to be, but the driver took the instruction so literally they turned right at the very next place it was possible to go right at, even though it was a daft place to do that."

Dave said, "Yeah! Imagine those drivers trying to explain their behaviour, insisting: 'I drove up some steps and knocked over a toilet because my sat nav told me to do it'!"

The students laughed.

Then Dave said, "Actually, that sounds like some of the strange things I read that some people have written on insurance claim forms after car accidents to describe why they happened, like:

"'I pulled away from the side of the road, glanced at my mother-in-law and headed over the embankment.'

'The other car collided with mine without giving warning of its intention.'

'I had been driving for 40 years when I fell asleep at the wheel and had an accident'.

And, 'In an attempt to kill a fly, I drove into a telephone pole.'"

Suzy said, "Oh yeah, that reminds me of one I heard once: 'I had been shopping for plants all day and was on my way home. As I reached an intersection, a hedge sprang up obscuring my vision and I did not see the other car.'"

Kirsty said with a grin, "Imagine how scary it would be if hedges really could instantly spring up in front of people! Maybe no one would ever risk driving. Or maybe cars would be equipped with instant hedge destroyers, that would automatically sense when a hedge was springing up and blast it into oblivion! Mind you, I suppose that could be dangerous, if everyone's vision was suddenly obscured by little bits of blasted-to-bits hedge flying through the air! They might cause more accidents than they would have done if the hedges weren't destroyed!"

The students giggled.

The Students Discuss Dangerous and Distracted Driving and the Main Causes of Car Accidents

Then the conversation began to become serious, as Heather said with a smile, "Yes! Instantly-appearing hedges would make driving risky whether the car was equipped with those things or not, wouldn't it! . . . Mind you, I suppose it is anyway."

Emma said gloomily, "Yeah, well sometimes it's a lot more risky than it needs to be! I once heard these two nutters – or at least that's what they sounded like – saying they actually loved driving badly and taking risks; one said he loved to overtake people dangerously because it gave him an adrenaline buzz, and the other one said he loved to drive too close behind other drivers because it gave him a feeling of power that put him on a high, thinking about how much he must be annoying people. There must be less risky ways to get adrenaline buzzes!

"They didn't seem to have much imagination, or they would have been able to imagine what it might be like to have a car accident, and end up in hospital in severe pain for some time, or permanently disabled, in a wheelchair for the rest of their lives or something, not feeling powerful at all, having to have lots of things done for them, on other people's time too instead of just when they wanted them, so they'd have less control of their lives, and they couldn't do a lot of the things in life that they'd have liked to!

"Or even worse, maybe if they've got enough of a con-science, they'd feel guilty all their lives if they had accidents that actually injured or killed other people!"

Mya said, "I was in a psychology lecture once, where the lecturer, who was also a psychotherapist, said a woman once told him that she heard a lecture he gave one day, where he talked about how emotions like impatience and irritation and anxiety about being late can flare up and make people like car drivers decide to take dangerous risks on the spur of the moment, like overtaking people in traffic when they haven't got a good view of what's in front of them, so they can't be sure they won't be about to drive into an oncoming car; so their emotions make them do things that risk their lives, just to save a few seconds!

"He said that the day after she heard that lecture, the woman was driving to work when the traffic lights turned green, and the car in front didn't move. She felt impatient all of a sudden, and was tempted to nip around him, driving into oncoming traffic to pass him and save time. Then she remembered what she'd heard, and realised the same thing applied to her, and saving what would likely be only seconds wasn't worth risking her life and the life of other people for by suddenly driving out into oncoming traffic. She'd never thought about it like that before, but she realised she really would be risking her life, all for the sake of saving a few seconds!

"And I heard someone say there are people who try to run across level crossings when they see the gates are about to go down, because they want to save the couple of minutes they'll have to wait if they don't; but if they don't make it and a train comes and hits them, again, they'll be sacrificing their lives, just for the sake of that couple of minutes of time they wanted to save.

"The psychotherapist I heard talk about the woman who decided to drive more carefully after hearing the lecture he gave where he mentioned the dangers of giving in to the temptation to take risks on the road said he was once talking to a man who said he got really frustrated when he was driving and he had to stop at traffic lights. He was always bothered by thinking they were going to make him late for whatever he was driving to. The psychotherapist gave him a bit of advice, recommending that instead of thinking of traffic lights as a pain and a hindrance, he started thinking of every time he had to stop at them as 'me time', when he'd have the chance to do something to relieve the worries of his day – while obviously still keeping his eyes on the road – like taking slow deep breaths and relaxing.

"He said the man took his advice, and he spoke to him a while later, and he told him the advice had worked, and he'd actually managed to make stops at traffic lights quite pleasurable."

Matthew said, "That's good! And maybe calming down made him a safer driver as well as a happier one. I read a couple of articles once about the most common reasons for car accidents. It was quite depressing reading really. I can't remember everything they said, but one said thousands of accidents had been caught on camera and analysed to find out their causes, and there were some kinds of errors that happened again and again:

"One was drivers falling asleep. One of the articles said there was a survey that found that over a third of the drivers who were asked admitted to having fallen asleep at the wheel at least once in their lives, and over a tenth said they'd done it in the past year! Hopefully with most of them it was at least only for seconds! But it said it's possible to fall asleep for a short time and then wake up and not even realise you've just had a sleep, because of course you won't realise time's passing when you're asleep, and also you can't necessarily predict when you'll drop off to sleep. People don't always feel sleepier and sleepier for a while before they finally fall asleep; people can feel fairly alert one minute, and fall asleep the next sometimes. Sleeps of just a few seconds are called microsleeps. The article said that about a fifth of all car crashes where one or more people died involved drivers who were sleepy.

"It recommended that people do their best to get more than seven hours' sleep on a night before they drive, and avoid driving late at night if possible, especially without caffeine. A person might prefer to struggle on to their destination than to delay their journey by stopping for a sleep; but if they fall asleep and end up in the hospital, they'll be delaying it for a whole lot longer!

"Actually, sometimes I've been in a car, and the driver's opened the window, and I've been a bit cold and felt like asking them to shut it, but then I've thought, 'For all I know, the air coming in might be helping them to stay awake!' So I haven't said anything. I once heard a couple of people being interviewed on telly, who'd been driving back from a nightclub in the early hours of the morning. The driver had had her music up really loud, and the other one had been in the back, and asked her to turn it down because he wanted to go to sleep. She did turn it down, but they both wished she hadn't later, because she'd fallen asleep too, and the car had crashed and she'd been seriously injured. The loud music might have been what was keeping her awake before.

"Anyway, one of the articles I read said another fairly common cause of accidents is people losing control of their cars, for reasons such as that they went around a bend too fast and then couldn't stop in time when something they didn't expect loomed into view, or something happened unexpectedly that meant they had to swerve, and because of the panic and wanting to move the car really quickly, they've moved the steering wheel too forcefully so it's turned too far, so the car's turned too far the other way and driven into oncoming traffic or something else. And sometimes it happens because rain or snow or fog or high winds are causing hazardous driving conditions, and people are driving as if they expect everything to be alright, till a car in front gets into difficulties, or something else unexpected happens, and they're driving too close to them to stop in time before they hit them, or they're the ones who have the problems, such as if they skid on ice.

"So the article recommended that people drive more carefully so they get more warning if they encounter other drivers or pedestrians doing things they shouldn't, and drive more slowly in bad weather.

"It said another cause of accidents is people turning to drive past other vehicles when they can't see if anything's coming towards them, because the vehicles are blocking their view. Or they can disobey traffic signals like stop signs or red lights, just hoping nothing will be in their way. Or they can try to rush through amber lights, hoping to make it across places like busy intersections where traffic's coming from different directions before the lights turn red, and they don't make it in time and hit something.

"One of the articles said that most car accidents happen at intersections, where driving suddenly gets more complicated, because cars are coming from more directions than normal. So it advised people to take extra care and slow down in places like that.

"The other article I read said one cause of car crashes is when people want to turn at an intersection, and they look one way to make sure nothing's coming before they pull out, and then they turn back to look in the direction they want to turn in, but when they last looked that way the road was clear, so they don't expect anything to be there, but while they were looking the other way, a pedestrian or cyclist or something else came along, and when they turn back, they spot them in the way, but because they're all set to move in that direction, not expecting anything to be there, and they're still thinking of what they've just seen in the other direction, they start driving, because they haven't been thinking about whether an unexpected hazard's suddenly appeared since they last looked, so their reaction times are slower than they might have been otherwise, so they hit them. It said that's another reason for people to go slow round corners like that, since people are less likely to be killed by a car travelling slowly.

"And it said people often drive too close to the driver in front, so they can't stop in time if the person in it brakes, so they hit the back of their car. It said about a third of all car crashes happen because of that! It said a lot of them aren't serious, but that some of them are.

"And it said it's easy to get distracted and stop paying attention to what's going on on the road for a few seconds every so often, since it's actually very difficult to concentrate on the same thing non-stop for ages, so it's easy for people's minds to wander, or for people to stop paying attention to their driving because something on the side of the road has caught their eye, or because they're paying attention to something going on in the car, or they take mobile phone calls or something. When people aren't paying attention, they can veer into another lane or even off the road without realising till it's too late. So it said that anyone who can foresee that something might cause a distraction will be making themselves safer by doing something to try to stop it causing a problem before it happens, or to pull over to deal with it when it does, if that's possible.

"I actually heard about an experiment where somehow they managed to set things up so the same things drivers were seeing were transmitted by some kind of video calling system to people they were talking to on their mobile phones, so they could see the traffic too; and the experimenters found out that when the people on the other end of the phone calls could see what was going on, they didn't talk about just anything like they would do normally, which might have distracted the drivers, but especially if the drivers were travelling into awkward conditions that they needed to concentrate even more than usual on, they stopped talking or warned the drivers when something that might get dangerous looked as if it was happening. So that makes you think that having normal conversations on mobile phones while you're driving might sometimes be risky, because of the possibility of getting distracted from concentrating on the road."

Suzy said, "I overheard someone talking about how she'd been in a minor car accident because she'd got distracted after some impatient idiot started honking his horn and making rude gestures at her because he thought she needed to hurry up and turn, when she was waiting till the right time came. It had made her angry, and she started making hand gestures back, to try to communicate that she was waiting for a good reason; but she felt under pressure to hurry up, so she did, and had this minor accident because of it. No one got hurt, but someone's car got a bit of minor damage, so she felt guilty for a while afterwards, and she thought that in future, she ought to just ignore idiot car drivers who might make gestures that make it obvious they think she's stupid and annoying for not doing what they want. She probably looked upset after the accident, because she said the woman whose car she hit was actually more concerned about whether she was alright than she was about her car; but she still felt guilty.

"But she said it's not easy to keep your cool on the spur of the moment when car drivers try to bully you into doing things and it catches you off guard. It would be nicer if there weren't drivers around who behave in distracting impatient ways like that. Maybe people ought to bear in mind that they could end up causing problems if they get tempted to behave like that, so they'll hopefully think better of it. I don't know how much hope there is of that kind of thing happening with some people though."

The students sympathised with the woman in the story.

Then Heather said, "I read this really boring book we were told to read for a course I did at school; but occasionally it got more interesting, and one interesting thing it said was that even when people know getting distracted on the roads makes them more likely to have accidents, it's still easy for them to get distracted, especially if there are other people in the car, joking or doing who knows what else, or if they start enjoying themselves chatting and laughing or whatever, so they stop concentrating so much.

"It said teenagers are more likely to get killed in car accidents if they're driving on their own than the average person is, and the risk goes up if they're with someone, because they might get more distracted, and the risk is more than double if they're with more than one person so they can get even more distracted, like if they start joking with each other, and they're having such a nice time that the one driving feels as if they're enjoying themselves too much to want to stop the fun, so their concentration goes down.

"I don't know how much of the increased risk is to do with people being inexperienced drivers, and how much it's to do with them being more likely to do things that stop them concentrating so hard, or being a bit more reckless or something.

"This book said that maybe cars should have sensors in them that can detect when teenagers start driving badly, that can trigger things to happen that they don't like, such as making some kind of automatic phone call to their parents, or making classical music blare out at them till their driving gets better."

The students smiled.

But then Anne said, "I heard about a car with a police camera in it that drove around filming people's behaviour while they were driving, and they found that lots of people did things that were bound to distract them so it would make their driving more dangerous. A lot of people sent texts on their mobile phones while they were driving, or did their hair, or put make-up on, or even browsed the Internet! It seems some people somehow just don't realise how dangerous getting distracted from driving can be, considering that unexpected things can happen! Even talking on a mobile phone can be dangerous if it means a person's mind isn't on the road."

Dave, who'd only been half paying attention, joked, "Ugh! A person having their mind on the road? What a horrible thought! Surely that's Not something you want! People would say, 'Oh look, that must be his mind on the road . . . or at least bits of it.'"

A few students cringed, and said things like, 'yuck!' Some grinned despite themselves. But Colin elbowed Dave and told him it wasn't a funny joke and to be quiet, making a face.

Kirsty teased, "Come on! If someone said, 'Keep your mind on the road', they wouldn't mean it literally! They'd mean concentrate on it! Maybe if you heard someone tell someone to keep their eye on something, you'd think they were asking them to actually take one of their eyes out. Like if someone was cooking vegetable soup on the stove and didn't want it to boil over and they asked you to keep an eye on it for them, maybe you'd be shocked and horrified because you'd think they were asking you to take one of your eyes out and put it in the soup!"

Stuart joked sarcastically, "Eye and vegetable soup! Yum!"

Colin said with a grin, "Hey imagine if someone tried to convince you that vegetarians' eyes were suitable for vegetarians to eat, saying that since the vegetarians would only have eaten things made of vegetables, and our bodies must be made of what we eat, then everything vegetarians are made of must be made of vegetables, so it would be alright for vegetarians to eat other vegetarians."

The students laughed, and Catherine said, "If someone tried to sell vegetable soup made of vegetarians, advertising it as suitable for vegetarians to eat, maybe it would be a bit like one of those scams we were talking about before, since they'd be conning people."

The Students Discuss more Scams, and One Receives a Funny Phone Call

Jackie said, "Talking about scams again, I've heard about people who get scammed over the phone."

"Wow, that would be a double whammy!" said Stuart with a grin. "Imagine the hazards of being distracted from driving while being scammed at the same time on your mobile!"

Some of the students couldn't resist a chuckle. Then Jackie said seriously, "Yeah! I bet most people get scammed via their landlines though. It's shocking how much money people can lose. I didn't realise till I heard.

"Some fraudsters even trick people by telling them they're from their bank, and that they're trying to protect them against fraud! So the people are reassured. A scammer tells people they're phoning from the bank to tell them there's been some unusual activity on their account that looks as if a criminal's taking money from it, and they say they'll have to transfer money from it to a safe account. They can reassure the person they're not a fraudster themselves by telling them to put the phone down and ring the number of their bank so they can tell it's really their bank they're speaking to; but the scammer doesn't put the phone down at their end, which means the line's still open – (that's the way it works at the moment anyway, although I've heard that phone companies might change that one day so the line gets cut off when just one person puts the phone down.)

"But the line staying open now means that scammers have used it to abuse the system; when the person rings the number of their bank, the scammer can pretend to pick the phone up, and they say they're someone from the bank.

"Then they say it's true about the suspicious activity on their account, and ask for the person's bank account numbers, saying it's to confirm the person's who they say they are or something; and then they ask for other details they say they need to transfer money from one account to another, like their bank sort code and online banking password. Then, unbeknownst to the victim, they transfer their money into their own account!

"People who give advice about how people can protect themselves against scams say it's best to wait five minutes or so before phoning out if you get a phone call from someone advising you to ring your bank, so as to be able to tell they're not a fraudster, because the line will likely have genuinely been cut off by the time you do, because the scammer will probably have got fed up with waiting and moved on to someone else by then; or another thing they say you can do is to phone the bank from another line, or a mobile phone; or if you're phoning from the same phone, to make sure there's a clear dialling tone first, although some scammers play a recorded one to fool people."

Just at that moment, Heather's mobile phone rang. It would have been a strange coincidence if it had been a scammer; it might have seemed as if fate had determined that it would be good if the students got a practical lesson to go with the discussion about how to deal with scammers, and she was going to be the one to get the practice. But instead it was her boyfriend, who'd decided to playfully announce to her that he'd just had a counselling session and discovered his inner child, but that immediately the child had pestered him to go to a local restaurant and buy a huge burger they were advertising, and he might have to skip all the rest of the afternoon's lectures because it would take him all afternoon to eat it. Then he said his inner child was begging him to skip lessons for the rest of the week, and as he'd heard so much about how inner children should be taken care of, he was just going to have to give in to it.

"Stuff your inner child back where it came from!" was Heather's advice.

He pretended to be shocked, and said, "What? I thought you trainee psychologists were all supposed to advise people to pamper their inner children and give them what they want."

"I'm not going to be the kind of psychologist who believes in people letting their inner children loose," said Heather.

Her boyfriend was an engineering student. For some reason, he found the idea of her doing a psychology degree amusing, and he would often phone her up to tease her playfully and make jokes about psychologists and psychology he'd made up or come across, just as he was doing then. He didn't seem to have a very high opinion of psychologists, perhaps because he'd heard a bit about quack outlandish psychological theories and therapies, and thought all psychology must be like that. A few days earlier, he'd rung her up to tell her he'd read a joke on the Internet about an engineer and a psychologist who met on their 20-year college reunion, and the engineer said he was surprised the psychologist wasn't covered in wrinkles after listening to people's problems all day for years. The psychologist replied, "You think we listen?"

But Heather got her own back on him in a playful way, ringing him sometimes to tell him engineering jokes she'd found or made up. Only a few days earlier, she'd asked him, "Is it true that if you only get a mark of 80 per cent for an engineering course project, you might design a bridge one day and it'll have a 20 per cent chance of falling down, because you don't know 20 per cent of what you're supposed to?"

He'd joked in reply, "I'll tell you what: When I'm an engineer, I'll only design footbridges, and you can always test them before anyone else is allowed to walk over them. I'll stand underneath waiting to catch you if they break. Or better still, I'll hire a bouncy castle each time you test one and put that underneath it, although if you put on weight, you might break that too!"

They made each other laugh by teasing each other, and had fun together.

When their phone call ended and the students had had a laugh about what was said, Jackie continued:

"Anyway, people who give advice about dealing with scams say people should ask a lot of questions whenever they get an unexpected offer, or when someone asks them to do something that just might be a bit dodgy out of the blue, instead of just accepting things. I mean, for one thing, why would someone from a bank ask for a person's bank account numbers and want their help to transfer their money, when they should have the details right in front of them if they really are the bank, and the bank can transfer money themselves, without the help of the person it belongs to!

"And in fact, it would be worth asking why they even want to do a transfer at all, instead of just checking that what seems to be suspicious activity really is unwanted, and then preventing whoever's causing it from withdrawing any money from the account, in whatever way they do that kind of thing. I'm sure that's more like what a bank would normally do.

"Mind you, I think some people say it's best not to get into a conversation with people who you suspect of being scammers at all, but just to put the phone down on them, or walk away if you're talking to them face to face, because if they're good at conning people, the more you talk to them, the more opportunity they have to try and talk you into believing they're genuine.

"I think people are caught off guard because they're phoned up in the middle of doing other things, and they're not really given time to think. It's easier to make bad decisions on the spot. It might be best if people ask for at least several minutes to think about it if they get a call asking them to do something, and they're not absolutely sure the caller's genuine, maybe telling the person they'll call back at some point later if they think they need to. and then they can look on the Internet and find out if other people have been asked to do the same things as them, and whether it turned out to be a scam.

"I heard that a survey's been done to find out who the people are who are most likely to fall for scams, and it found that it's people who've recently had some kind of upheaval in their lives that's caused them some kind of distress or worry. It's because if people are feeling anxious to start with, it'll be easier for scammers to stir up their emotions, which is just what they'll be trying to do, because when people get into a state of emotion, it's a lot harder to think calmly and carefully, because the emotions are making people feel as if they just want a problem fixed as quickly as possible so they'll feel better; so when the scammer promises they can solve the problem if they do what they tell them, they're more likely to agree to it. So scammers deliberately try to make people scared, because they know that.

"It's crueller than it sounds, really, because imagine lots of people slogging away for years, maybe in jobs they don't like, day after day, going in to work and getting bored or stressed, maybe having to deal with nasty people around them, so they can build up savings, partly because they hope to do something nice and live comfortably when they've retired and haven't got as much money coming in, only to have their life's savings swiped away from them in one day by a scammer or a fraudster, after all those years of hard work! It's horrible really!

"And I think another way some frauds work is creating a sense of urgency, so people don't think they have time to think, like if a scammer says money needs to be transferred to another account quickly to prevent any more being stolen.

"Actually, I think some ordinary companies do something a bit like that quite a bit too, making offers that sound great, often online, and people don't realise there are catches in the terms and conditions that mean they're not such good offers as they think; I've heard that people often don't bother reading terms and conditions – Well I don't read them very well, for a start, because they're often just plain boring, and so long!

"But I've heard that sometimes, people don't read them because they think they need to hurry up and accept an offer or it'll end. So that works to the seller's advantage, and companies can design things like that deliberately, knowing customers won't have good grounds to complain that they're getting a bad deal if they're caught out by something that was in the terms and conditions all along but they didn't read them, such as if they're booking what seems to be a bargain holiday, but they don't realise that it says in the terms and conditions that they won't get any money back if they cancel it, and then they have to later, and only discover it then, or if they buy something and it turns out to be faulty, and they want to return it, and they find out they have to pay quite a bit to do that, and it says so in the terms and conditions, but they didn't realise because they didn't read them.

"Mind you, it's no wonder people often don't read terms and conditions properly; I think the BBC did a test once, and they found out that some were so long, they literally took hours to read! I think they said that some companies deliberately make them long and boring, in the hope that people won't bother reading them. I can't quite remember what they said now though.

"But talking about looking things up on the Internet, I've read some useful information about scams and things on there; but maybe one problem is that I think a lot of the people who fall for scams are old people, who are less likely to use the Internet. Maybe social services or some other organisation ought to send people information leaflets warning about scams every so often. I've heard of people losing all their life's savings because they fell for some scam offer, where they were phoned up and told they could invest some money in some scheme and end up getting a share of the profits and getting rich, or other things like that, so they did, but they never saw their money again, or the profits were never going to be anywhere near as big as they were told. They can be sent impressive-looking certificates that help convince them their investments are genuine; and these scams can go on for years, with people being persuaded to hand over more and more money over time."

The Students Talk About Rogue Traders, Unfair Customers, and Other Such Subjects

Becky said, "That's bad. Still, at least there are some television programmes on with information about scams like that, as well as ones about those rogue traders who say they can mend things in your home or make improvements, or fix your car, and end up making things worse, but charge you loads of money anyway, saying they did what they could, and that if you don't like it, it's your problem, or that they'll do more work on them for a price, or things like that. Or they replace expensive parts of broken things that don't really need replacing, assuming most people won't know enough about what's causing the problems to realise they don't, when really the things just need a slight fix; so the rogue traders can charge you more for the work they do on them that didn't really need doing, because they charge labour costs by the hour, and they spend a lot longer working on the broken things than they need to. And that kind of thing.

"I've heard about people phoning plumbers up to come out and mend a leaking tap, or other minor things like that, only to be told they have to pay loads of money because their entire water tank needs replacing, when it doesn't really, and things like that. Or people can take their car to the garage with a minor fault, only to be told it's got such serious things wrong with it that it'll need days of work done on it, that'll cost loads of money, when the work doesn't really need to be done! And people who haven't got any expertise in those things won't necessarily know they're not being told the truth, so they can be defrauded out of loads of money!

"What kind of person does that kind of thing! I mean, imagine how it must feel to wake up in the morning assuming everything's fine, and by the evening, you think you've got to pay half your life's savings or something, so you can have something you rely on to make your life easier or more comfortable fixed, say even like a boiler that hasn't really got much wrong with it at all, where you've got no hot water or heating till it can be fixed and turned on again. It wouldn't be nice at all to suddenly have to put up with that kind of thing! These rogue traders ought to try thinking of what it must be like from their customers' points of view! I mean, they wouldn't like it if something like it happened to them, would they! They can't care about their customers at all!

"At least there are lots of articles on the Internet about things people can do to try to stop themselves being ripped off, and about what they can do if they have been. And it's best if people can get recommendations from friends who've had work done about who's trustworthy, if any of them have found anyone good."

Emma said, "I agree. Actually though, it's not just a case of some tradesmen ripping customers off; I heard about how a lot of tradesmen who go out to do a good job are cheated by customers, who don't pay them, or don't pay for ages, sometimes pretending there are faults with the work that don't really exist, just so they've got an excuse, and that kind of thing. And it's really bad, since I heard that a small minority of traders have nearly gone out of business, and some companies have had to delay paying some of their workers or make them redundant, or delay paying companies they get supplies from for their work, because they're short of money because customers haven't paid them.

"I mean, imagine if everyone treated tradesmen like that! They'd all go out of business, and then there would be no one to ever mend things when they broke, or anything like that. It's a bit like shoplifting; some people might say they only steal a small amount in comparison to what's in the shops they're stealing from, but if everyone took that attitude, there would soon be nothing left! And the more that gets nicked, the more the prices of other things have to go up to make up for the money that's been lost by the shopkeepers paying for things they didn't get the money back on because they got stolen; so everyone gets affected! And if it happened a lot, a shop might even lose so much money they had to go out of business, and that might really inconvenience people who relied on it."

James said, "Let's hope it doesn't start happening any more than it already does then!

"Mind you, it's not just criminals like shoplifters or scammers and rogue traders who do things that make people lose money in ways that seem a bit unscrupulous; I've heard of respectable-sounding companies doing it; I mean, I don't suppose any of them go out to take away people's life's savings, or anything anywhere near that bad, but still, people can end up paying them quite a bit more money than they expected to, especially if they aren't wise to what they're doing; I mean, I've heard that one thing that can happen is that directory enquiries services can find a phone number for you and then ask if you want them to put you through to it. You might say yes, not realising that all the time you're going to be talking to who you want to speak to, you'll be charged the amount you're being charged per minute while you speak to the directory enquiries person, which is a lot! I think people have ended up getting phone bills that tell them the cost of their call was £75, and amounts like that!

"So it's best to just write the number down when they give it to you, put the phone down and ring the person yourself."

The Conversation Becomes Amusing, as the Topic of Mistakes and Prank Calls Comes Up

The students were annoyed. But then Kirsty said, "Wow, I remember when Directory Enquiries was free! At least, I think it was. Once when I was little and went to brownie camp, I tried to phone my mum from there, and for some reason I got through to Directory Enquiries instead. I was surprised, and told them I was trying to phone my mum up. A man just told me to redial. It would have been funny if instead of being surprised, I'd said, 'Dad! How are you!' and refused to believe he wasn't my dad, and kept asking why he didn't want to speak to me but was telling me to put the phone down. I wonder what he would have done!... Well, he'd probably have just put the phone down on me in the end.

"I did accidentally shock some poor man once; I was thinking of doing a few weeks' voluntary work in the holidays, and I was given a number by someone who told me it was a charity that might give me a job for a little while. I'd never heard of them, so I wanted to know a bit about them. I phoned the number, and the person on the other end just said hello. Afterwards, it occurred to me that if it really had been the charity, they'd almost certainly have said its name when they said hello. But I didn't think of that at the time, but just said, 'I'm calling to find out some information about you.' The man sounded shocked and said, 'I'm sure I don't know who you are!' I don't know what kind of spy he thought I might be!"

The students giggled. Then Mya said, "That reminds me of those prank calls some people make. I don't like a lot of them, because I feel sorry for the victims, but some are funny. I heard that some people phone up a random stranger and say, 'Can I speak to Mr Wall?' When they're told they've got the wrong number, they say, 'Is Mrs Wall there?' When the person says no, they say, 'Are there any walls in your house?' The person will usually say no, and then the prankster says, 'Then how does the ceiling stay up?' "

Stuart said, "I've heard about some prank calls people have made on scammers, and ways people have tricked scammers who phoned them.

"One that really made me laugh was some joker who got phoned up by a scammer who told him his computer was being infected by viruses and he was from Windows Technical Support, and he'd phoned up to help. Windows Technical Support won't really phone people up out of the blue and tell them their computers have got viruses. But these scammers do, hoping you'll give them permission to use a program they've got to nose into what's on your computer and control what it's doing. Then I think they sometimes actually secretly put viruses on your computer, and then tell you they've found a virus on it, and try to sell you something to get rid of it.

"They don't know who they're phoning at first; they just phone random numbers, so they don't even know if you've got a computer. They just assume people have, or phone someone else if someone says they haven't got one. I think they can sometimes persuade people to hand over credit card details, or if they've got online banking, to go to their account, and then the scammers transfer money from it into their own one.

"Anyway, when this scammer phoned the prankster and told him his computer was infected, the prankster sounded shocked and said, 'Oh no, what shall I do?' The scammer said something about Windows, and the prankster said, 'What's that? You want me to throw my computer out the window? Alright. I'm taking it to the window now. Are you sure I need to throw it out the window? Won't it hurt someone if it lands on them?'

"The scammer didn't know what to say, and then the prankster said, 'OK, I've thrown it out the window now. It's on the ground outside. What shall I do now?'

"The scammer didn't know what to say again, and hung up after a few seconds."

The students found that amusing.

The Students Talk Seriously About Scams and Fraud Again, Except When One Tells More Stories About Pranksters Scamming Scammers

Then Colin said, "The other day I was browsing the Internet, when suddenly a spooky message popped up that said something like, 'Warning! Your computer has just been infected with a virus! Criminals are now stealing your credit card details and financial information.' I thought, 'They'll have a job; I haven't got a credit card!' I've got a debit card.

"But this message continued, 'If you leave this page, your computer will be disabled to protect the network from the virus spreading onto it!'

"I thought, 'My computer isn't on a network!'

"Anyway, then a voice suddenly started talking, repeating this message over and over again, telling me not to leave the page or my computer would be disabled, but to phone this number to get Windows to advise me on how to fix the problem. It said it was an alert from the Windows Defender program. It sounded a bit strange to me, and I wondered if the message was some kind of scam, because I thought, 'Surely Windows would just send down an update to their virus definitions or its operating system if a virus came along that they knew would affect machines with their systems on them.' So I tried to leave the page anyway. But it wouldn't let me. It wouldn't close when I tried to close it, and when I tried to navigate away from it, it asked me if I really wanted to, and then wouldn't let me, regardless of me keeping on telling it yes.

"My music was playing in the background while I was doing

my best to leave it, so I had this inappropriately cheerful music playing while this dire warning message kept telling me that thieves were stealing my passwords and financial information, and that I'd better phone this number before I left the page or my computer would be disabled.

"Then I went into Windows Task Manager and closed my browser that way; and guess what: My computer wasn't disabled! I decided to do a quick virus scan with Windows Defender just to check there were no problems there. So I updated its virus definitions and then did one, and it told me my computer was running normally! I know anti-virus programs don't always pick up every virus around, so they can sometimes tell you everything's alright when it's not really; but considering that it was actually Windows Defender that this virus alert supposedly came from, you'd have thought it would have found this virus if it was really there!

"Anyway, I thought that to make absolutely sure, I'd do a full computer scan with it one day, since I think the quick one just scans the files to do with the working of a computer, but the full scan scans every file you've got. So one day when I went out, I put it on this full scan, which takes a few hours. When I came back, it was nearly finished. And when it was, it still said that no unwanted or harmful software had been detected and that my computer was running normally!

"So that message must have been a scam virus alert! Thankfully, it hasn't come up again. I don't know what the phone number I was ordered to ring really was. Maybe it would have gone to some criminal who would have said he'd have to sell me a program to get rid of the virus, and would have asked for my credit card details, and stolen money from me if I'd given my debit card details to him, I don't know.

"I'd never come across something like that before, although I have come across these horrible advert-type things that pop up and say they're offering you the chance to download a free anti-spyware program; but I've heard that some of them are spyware themselves, so if you download them, you're downloading spyware!

"Anyway, tell us more about those pranksters who try to trick the scammers."

Stuart said, "OK. Another trick was played when a scammer phoned someone who pretended to be an old woman. The scammer started the call by telling her – well, I think it was a him really, just pretending to be a woman – but anyway, the scammer said she'd purchased a service to stop nuisance calls that cost £49. Never mind that you can join a service that does that for free! I suppose anyone who didn't deny they'd purchased it at that point in the call would probably be an old person whose memory was going, so they would be thinking they just might have purchased such a thing and forgotten, so the scammers would think they might be easier to scam.

"Anyway, the scammer was really just trying to get people's personal details, like their bank account numbers, so he could steal their money. He kept on and on telling this person who was pretending to be an old woman to verify her address so he knew it was really her he was talking to, and she kept saying, 'What have you got written down, dear?' When he wouldn't say, she would say, 'How can I verify it if you haven't told me what you've got?' He didn't answer that – well, he probably couldn't! But he just asked for her address again. A lot of these scammers don't really know who you are, so I've heard; they're just hoping they can persuade you to tell them, by saying they know already and they just want to be sure they're talking to the right person.

"Then the scammer said he wanted to 'verify' her bank details, but again he almost certainly didn't actually have them, and was just hoping to get them so he could steal money from her. He said he wanted her debit card number, and she said, 'Debbie, you say? What's that about Debbie? I've got a niece called Debbie.' He asked her which bank she was with, and she mentioned one that probably hasn't existed for about 100 years. He said, 'Which bank?' and she said, 'The Which bank? No, I'm not with that one.' Then she gave him a number that she said was her bank card number, but really it was something really unlikely, and he got fed up, and hung up.

"And then there was another prankster who got phoned up by one of these scammers who try to convince you you've got computer viruses and tell you to do things that really end up with you downloading their malware onto your computer; the prankster pretended he was talking on a really bad line; he kept only saying half of each word, so it would sound to the scammer as if the sound kept cutting out. And he pretended he couldn't manage to do what the scammer was asking him to do; at one point, he kept saying he couldn't see what the scammer said should be coming up on his screen, and eventually said, 'Oh sorry, it's because I've got my hand over my eyes.' The scammer lost his temper in the end, and threatened to blacklist him from his company, and the prankster said, 'Thank you, that would be wonderful!' "

The students laughed.

But then Mya said, "Getting serious again though, sometimes you can get defrauded by people you'd never think of as scammers. I've heard of people you might think of as respectable conning people, such as dentists who do things like giving people fillings they don't really need, to get more money."

Dave made a face and said, "I'm not sure dentists can be called respectable; I mean, what kind of person wants to go into a career where they're inflicting pain on people all day for years?"

Some of the students grinned. But Mya said, "There is that. You know what I mean though, people in Jobs that are actually thought of as respectable. I've read about some dentists doing all kinds of work on people's teeth that they don't really need, just to get money. I don't know how widespread that kind of fraud is, but I'd hate to be a victim of it! That's if I haven't already been!"

Some of the others cringed.

Then Jackie said, "You know, the other day, I heard about some companies that aren't even genuine! I don't mean dentists' companies – hopefully there aren't many of those around, if any! I mean other ones, that give the impression they're real when they're not.

"I heard about some fake companies that get set up so the people running them can scam other people, where they pretend the companies are modelling agencies. They advertise that they can get some young people flashy careers in the modelling business, and some teenagers think it might be a brilliant opportunity to get into modelling or make money, so they apply to be interviewed, and people from a fake agency really flatter them, and take photos of them and show them what they'd look like on the front of a magazine, and say they've got real talent and could have a really good career. So they really build their hopes up, and then they say it'll cost hundreds or thousands of pounds to get them started, and the teenagers can plead with their parents to spend it, because they think it's a brilliant opportunity for them.

"But if their parents do give the company money, they wait to hear from the agency, but they don't; and when they try to contact them, they can't. So in the end, they realise it was a scam and they've lost their money.

"I've heard that some people wonder how other people could fall for scams like that. But I don't suppose it's all that hard, unless you know all about them. I mean, if you really want something, and someone's flattering you, making you feel really good, telling you you could have it and really make it big, you're going to be carried along on a wave of enthusiasm and hope and excitement; and in that mood, you're just really going to want to go for it; you're not going to be in the mood to sit down and think, 'Hmmm! I wonder if this could be real, or whether it might be a scam!'

"And anyway, the fake agencies deliberately don't give people time to do that, because they try to hurry people to make a decision about whether to pay the money and sign up, because they say there are other people there waiting to be interviewed so there isn't much time, and things like that. They do that deliberately, so people feel as if they have to make a decision quickly, before they really have time to think things through.

"And besides that, if the families have never heard much about scams, they might not even know it's common for fake agencies to try to scam people. And if they haven't had experience of being deceived by people from companies that seem professional, it's just natural to trust that people are who they say they are and that they're being honest, and that they're going to do what they say they're going to do. You can't blame people for falling for these scams. But I think scams like that should get a lot of publicity, so a lot of people hear about them and get warned off them. I heard that real modelling agencies won't ask for money upfront like the fake ones do, so that's one way it's possible to tell if you're talking to someone from a fake one.

"And there are other scams that get criminals money for flattering people. I heard there are puzzle scams, where people are invited to pay just a small fee to get sent a puzzle to do, like a word search game; and if they pay, they get one to do, and when they've done it, they send it back to be checked, and get told they've done a really good job and they're clever for being able to do it, and that if they pay a bit more money, they'll be sent a puzzle at the next level of difficulty, to see if they can do that. The same thing keeps happening over and over again, with them paying more and more money to get harder and harder puzzles and then being praised for being able to do them, which entices them to get more. And they're often told they'll get a certificate if they manage to achieve a certain number of levels of difficulty, and that motivates some people to carry on, because having a certificate gives them a sense of pride and achievement. Some old people have even paid so much money in the end to do more and more puzzles, they've had no more money left!

"maybe sometimes the attraction of scams like that is that some old people living alone are isolated and lonely and bored, and beginning to feel useless and worried about their health; and getting a letter telling them they might win a prize if they just send a bit of money to enter a competition, or that they can pay for puzzles to be sent to them every week or so to do and they'll get a certificate of achievement if they manage to do them, makes them feel as if they haven't been forgotten, so it feels like a bit of human connection; and maybe getting the chance to do puzzles, and being told they're intelligent for completing them, makes them feel as if they must still have some ability if they can do them, and being praised for it gives them a nice feeling of appreciation or accomplishment. I don't know. The scammers probably do though, which is how they know what'll work on those people . . . besides their experience of knowing it gets them a lot of money.

"And I heard that there are scam websites where people can download puzzles to do, but the downloads contain malware that can infect their computers and harvest important personal details like bank account information."

The students were angry when they heard about the modelling scam and all the other scams, and agreed that people should be told more about them. Catherine said, "I think it would be good if schools and other organisations did teach people to be more wary about scammers and about what risks are out there, like we said earlier; it seems there are so many conmen out there who try to get people's money that people really need to be careful. I've heard that one kind of scam is phishing scams, where scammers send people emails supposedly from their bank, saying something's wrong and they need to provide their password or PIN number or account numbers to get it fixed, and things like that, and they use the information they're given to steal money from people's accounts. I've heard that banks say they won't really ask for that kind of information via email."

The conversation got gloomier, as Becky said, "I've heard that some people do something like that in person, going to people's houses and persuading them they're from the bank, and that there's some suspicious activity on their account so they need to take the person's money out to check that the systems are working or something; and if people go with them to the bank and take their money out and let them have it, to supposedly check whatever they say they need to check, they steal it. It just shows you you can't trust everyone.

"And some people pretend to befriend and do some caring for old people, calculating that they'll be less clued up about scams and tricks than younger people are, and then they steal from them, or persuade them to go to the bank with them to take lots of money out of their account and give it to them, to pay them for something they say they've done for them, when they're just conning them really, because they haven't really done it, or it doesn't cost nearly as much as they say it does, and things like that."

The students were all angry that people would do that.

The Students Tell Each Other Stories They've Heard About Cows Getting Drunk, and Make Jokes

Then Stuart said, "It would serve people like that right if they got chased out of the bank by a pack of dogs or something! Well, maybe not a pack of dogs, because that would frighten the old people they were with."

"Not to mention everybody else in there!" said James with a chuckle.

Stuart became more playful and said, "Well, there is that. Maybe smaller animals then, like a horde of hamsters and Guinea pigs, who kept jumping up and nipping at the scammers' ankles or something!

"Actually, I heard about a cow that escaped from a wedding in Germany, that the bridegroom, who was a farmer, had taken it to as a joke, to treat his wedding guests to its milk instead of giving them champagne. It sauntered through the sliding doors of the local bank and looked around. After walking around for a little while, it walked out again. It was caught later, wandering through a car park. A staff member at the bank said the cow was a nice customer; they said it was friendly and behaved itself, and didn't even knock anything over.

"But wouldn't it be good if a cow walked into a bank where there was a scammer about to take someone's money, and for some reason it went right up to them and chased them away! Imagine if it fiercely chased them all around the town till they were tired out!"

The students giggled. Then Dave said with a smile, "But you never know what that friendly cow at the wedding might have done if it had gone around drinking people's booze before going into the bank! It might have chased everyone; or I wonder if it would have just got merry and started dancing around in there, doing a mooing karaoke to some cow song or other that was going on in its imagination."

Colin said, "I've heard of cows getting drunk. I heard a news story about this family who were having a picnic in their garden, when half a dozen cows that had escaped from a field suddenly came in and went straight for their beer, as if they knew just what they wanted! Perhaps it smelled more appetising than all the food, somehow. The cows knocked their beer glasses over, and lapped it all off the table!

"And I've heard about cows getting drunk on rotten fruit they've found, because it's started fermenting and gone alcoholic. I heard about a group of farm workers who were asked to pick up all the apples from an orchard, and then let some cows into the orchard to graze it. They picked up lots of apples, that were going bad by then, and put them in bags by the fence. When the apples were all piled up together, they started heating up, and fermented some more, so they got more alcoholic.

"When the farm workers let the cows into the orchard, they didn't eat the grass like they were supposed to, but went straight for the bags of apples, tore them open and ate all the apples in them. Then they were all drunk. They staggered and wobbled around, and couldn't manage to get back in their barn doorway for ages. And they were doing long moos all together like a cow sing-along.

"And then some other cows got drunk on rotten apples, but not as drunk as the other lot; they just lay down under the trees with daft looks on their faces.

"And I heard about a vicar whose two cows got drunk on rotten apples. He didn't realise what had happened, and thought his cows were behaving strangely, so he called the vet, who told him they were drunk. He looked around, and saw a corner of their field where lots of apples had fallen off trees at the edge of it and gone bad."

The students thought that was funny.

Then the humour became suddenly darker, as James said ghoulishly, "I wish cows could give scammers and other criminals mad cow disease, by just going up to them and blowing on them or something, without infecting anyone else."

"No," said Becky. "The NHS would spend loads of money treating them. They wouldn't be worth it! It would be far better if the cows somehow managed to just pick them up and hurl them into the sky, so high they might not come back! . . . At least, not alive!"

Jackie said, "You wouldn't even want them to come back dead, or they'd make a horrible mess being splattered on the ground. That's unless they'd been thrown up right into space and pretty much burned up as they re-entered the atmosphere, so they came down as little scammer fritters. They'd be interesting objects of scientific curiosity then."

The Group Talks About Fraudsters Making False Claims That Badly Harm People

The conversation turned gloomy again for a little while, as Emma said, "You know, I think the worst scams are ones where people claim they have cures for diseases, but they don't really work. I post on an Internet forum, where one person said his dad died of cancer, and that it was skin cancer, which is one of the easiest ones to cure if it's caught early, but that he refused to go for medical help, because he was convinced someone knew what he was talking about who'd written books about how just eating certain foods and avoiding others, taking certain herbs and vitamin and mineral supplements, and thinking positively, and things like that, could cure lots of diseases like cancer. He trusted what the author said so much that he didn't think it was worth getting proper medical treatment.

"Maybe lots of people were fooled by the books and ended up dying because they followed their advice instead of getting medical treatment. In the end, the author got convicted of fraud and sent to prison. It was found that he'd told lie after lie, like claiming that the drug industry was trying to suppress the findings that natural cures work, and saying lots of other things that aren't true.

"His books sold over half a million copies. They claimed that studies had found that cures like the ones he was recommending worked, but actually he was making that up. He claimed there were studies that backed up what he was saying, that didn't even really exist. And he quoted people who'd supposedly said they were cured by the things he was recommending, when they hadn't been. He got put in prison for a long time, which was good, because quite a lot of people might have died because they believed what he said. I even read that he one day said that if anyone was gullible enough to believe what he wrote, they deserved what they got. Nasty man!

"I think there are quite a few books out there that make false claims, either because the authors have somehow deluded themselves into really believing what they're claiming, or they're out-and-out con artists."

Becky said, "I read about a boy with diabetes who thought he'd found a cure on the Internet, and he was really pleased, because he hated having to inject himself with insulin every day, like people with type 1 diabetes have to, because it's a hormone the body needs, and people can get sicker and sicker and die without it, because the body stops making it when you've got type 1 diabetes. The website the boy found had lots of supposed testimonials on it from people who'd been supposedly cured, praising the treatment; and the website said people could pay to find out what the cure was and get it, and that it was a scientific breakthrough that drug companies didn't want anyone to know about, because if people were cured, it would deprive them of all the money they got by making insulin for people to have to keep injecting.

"But someone the boy spoke to said the supposed doctor advertising this cure might be a fraud, and he looked up his name on the Internet, and found some information that said he really was a fraud, and he found reviews from people who'd tried his treatment and it didn't work.

"The boy was upset to find that out. But that shows you how careful you ought to be, because there are lots of fraudsters out there trying to make money from people with problems."

"There's a lot of information about scams and fake or harmful therapies on the Internet that it's worth reading," said Kirsty.

Matthew said, "Some of the information warning about them might be fake though, you never know. Mind you, it's probably better to be safe than sorry, or at least to try to double-check the information you've read by finding an article about it on a website you know has got a good reputation.

"I think you can get fake scam warnings by email some-times, warning you about things that aren't really happening. It must just be some sick person's idea of fun. But you've got to be careful, because sometimes you might get warnings of things that are really happening, but one or two details make it look as if the story can't be true, so you might decide it all can't be true – you know, like if the person who sent the warning in the first place made a mistake in one or two details – or they didn't, but over time as the email's been passed along, one or two of the details have been changed, for whatever reason. Sometimes things aren't all true or all false; they're a mixture, but the main message is still worth taking seriously.

"One example was an email that got sent around saying there was a new bank scam around, and that one person who fell for it was an old woman who got a letter from her bank that said they'd transferred a lot of her money into an account where she'd be getting more interest on it, but that she'd only be able to take out a small percentage of her money every month; and the next day a man phoned her up claiming to be from the bank, and he asked her if she'd received the letter, and offered to cancel the account transfer for her, but said he'd need her bank details to do it, and she gave them to him, and later discovered he'd taken all the money out of her account.

"You might think, 'Oh that must be a hoax email! A bank would never transfer someone's money into an account like that without their consent, and then send them a letter just saying they'd done it; and how would a scammer know to phone someone up who'd got a letter like that from their real bank the very next day and scam them, when they wouldn't know they'd been sent it!' And you might rubbish the entire email as a hoax. But what if most of it was true, but the person who sent it in the first place had just made a mistake at the beginning of it, saying the letter was sent by the bank when it was really sent by the scammers, pretending it was from the bank.

"And I think other things like that can happen."

The students all began to feel a bit down . . . again.

There's a Pause in the Discussion, During Which They Hear a Funny Conversation Behind Them

Silence came over the group, and they overheard a few students who'd begun to lounge around behind them talking.

One of them, Robert, said, "Those students at those tables look miserable!"

Another one, Chris, said, "I recognise them – they're psychology students. They're bound to look miserable, having to deal with other people's problems all day."

"Not yet I hope!" said another student, Tony, feeling a bit worried. "That would be a bit like student doctors being allowed to do operations on patients, wouldn't it. I mean, imagine if a medical student who'd only been on the course a couple of months was allowed to do a heart transplant! They might take out the heart and accidentally put in a liver they'd mistaken for a heart, for all we know!"

The students he was with smiled. Then Chris said thoughtfully, "I wonder if a patient could end up with a spooky beating liver if a doctor did that. I mean, what powers a heart to make it beat? Does it do it to itself, or does something else keep pushing it around, so it would push a liver around if it was in the heart's place?"

The other students didn't know. Then Robert said, "If a doctor really did swap a heart for a liver, I wonder what would happen to the old heart. I mean, I wonder if there would be a chance they'd keep it just in case they'd made a mistake, so they'd be able to put it back if they realised they had and the mistake was ever discovered."

"No!" joked another student, Jonathan. "I expect they sell them off to university cafes to put in the food!"

Tony was shocked by the thought, and nearly dropped the food he'd bought! Then he began to look at it suspiciously, and said, "I hope this is animal meat!"

Jonathan joked, "Oh I expect so. I mean, apart from the fact that humans are technically animals, maybe student doctors make even worse errors, and sometimes mistake monkeys for humans, and take out Their hearts in some of their operations, so it's Their hearts that get sold to university cafes a lot of the time, and you're eating monkey meat!"

Chris pondered, "I wonder if they really could mistake a monkey for a human. I mean, imagine if they were taking a monkey down to the operating theatre, and trying to get it to understand that it had to have an injection for the anaesthetic! It wouldn't behave like a human, would it!"

Chris laughed and continued, "And they'd think its appearance was a bit odd, wouldn't they! Imagine if they went away and spent ages searching through medical libraries, looking for information on some strange rare disease that makes humans look and behave like monkeys, that they thought just must exist, because they were convinced the monkey they were trying to treat was a human!"

Those students moved away, and the psychology students with Becky started their conversation again.

The Students Have a Laugh About Amusing and Gross-Sounding Information They've Heard

Dave said, "Our conversation's turned a bit gloomy! Let's get back to eating eyeballs in McDonald's burgers like we did when we first came in here." (The first topic of conversation over lunch, hours before, had been some rumour he'd brought up that they contained them.)

Suzy laughed and said, "Oh no, please, let's not!"

Dave realised it had sounded as if he meant they should eat them, when that hadn't really been what he'd meant; and he joked, "Alright, let's just Talk about them." Then he said, as if he'd very patiently waited to pick up the conversation where it had left off hours and hours before as they discussed other things, "I once got an email that mentioned them, and I think it said that it was someone on the telly who first said McDonald's burgers contain them."

Matthew laughed and sarcastically said good-naturedly, "Oh well if someone on telly said it, it must be true! Who said it, a comedian?"

Dave didn't know.

A few students who'd started comfort eating when the conversation turned a bit gloomy some time before and had finished their food looked enviously at the food of others who'd been put off theirs when the conversation turned a bit gross. So much so that those with a lot of food left thought that eyeballs or no eyeballs, they'd better eat it quickly before it was snatched away from them. One or two started eating faster; but as if he was reading their minds, Stuart, who was one of the comfort eaters who'd looked at them enviously, reassured them that he wasn't going to steal theirs and gobble it up while they looked on, helpless to stop him. They slowed down again.

They were fairly soon to be put off their food again though. But first, they had a bit of a laugh.

Emma said, "Someone emailed me a funny story once, about how there was an ancient law at Cambridge University that said students were allowed to scoff cake and drink ale all the way through exams, and that in one exam not too long ago, one student got up in the middle and demanded cake and ale. The person supervising the exam was surprised, and said, 'I beg your pardon?' The student repeated what he'd said, saying he requested and required it; and then he showed the supervisor a piece of paper with the ancient law written on it in Latin, that said those who requested and required cake and ale could have it.

"His request was kind of granted – well, he was allowed a big cup of coke and a burger and fries. The thing is though that the supervisor told other staff what had happened, and it turned out that there was another ancient law, that said students had to dress in full uniform at the exams, and the student who'd requested cake and ale had just had his own clothes on. So they thought with a smile, 'If you want to use ancient laws, then you should use them all', and they fined him £5, which was the equivalent of what the penalty for breaking the rule about wearing full uniform would have been in the olden days."

"Ouch!" Dave said, but then said with glee, "Wow! Imagine if we were allowed to scoff cake and drink ale all the way through Our exams!"

Mya laughed and said, "You'd have to be careful though, or you might enjoy them so much you got distracted from the exams, and wouldn't get to write all of what you wanted to before time ran out!"

"Before time ran out?" laughed Stuart. "You mean there's something about exams that might bring on the end of the world?"

"Very funny! You know she just meant time to do the exams!" groaned Catherine, who then said with a mischievous smirk, "But it might be the end of the world for you personally if all that scoffing and guzzling meant you didn't get your degree . . . or at least it might be the end of your hopes of a good career!"

Heather said, "Yeah, and just imagine if the ail was really strong and we had lots of it! You never know what we might end up writing! What if one of us answered a question about the best ways of curing anxiety by writing, 'I can't remember what they are. I hate this exam, and I've decided studying for my degree was pointless, since we were hardly taught anything that was worthwhile, and I've forgotten most of the useful stuff we did learn! I know I should have revised to remind myself of it, but I forgot to do that too!' "

They all laughed.

Then Sarah asked if the story about the student requesting cake and ale was true. Emma said she couldn't be sure. Matthew asked, "Did you go to one of those websites that investigate stories that get passed around by email to see if they really happened?"

"Yes," said Emma. "But they said they didn't know if it was true or false either!"

The students giggled.

Then Catherine said with a little bit of irritation in her voice, "It can be fun to read funny stories like that. But I often get people emailing me hoax scare stories about new computer viruses and things that people have emailed them. It's annoying. I keep feeling the need to look on one of those websites that investigates urban legends and things when I get one to find out if it's true, and I often email the person back telling them the story's just made-up, and that they should look there first next time before passing on the rumour!"

Matthew said, "I do that. But I remember one day, I got an email saying there's a flavouring put in some foods that's made of a secretion from beaver glands that they use to mark their territory, and that some manufacturers put it in foods and then say 'natural flavouring' on the label, so you think it comes from strawberries or at least some plant or other, but really it's from a gland near beavers' bottoms, and the email said that sometimes little bits from their poo and wee get in it. I went to one of these hoax investigation websites, feeling all smug and arrogant, certain I was about to find the proof that the claim was false, so I could tell the person who emailed me they were silly to believe it, only to discover the website said it was true! Yuck! But it at least said companies don't do it much at all nowadays."

The students cringed and squealed, and Jackie asked, "Ugh! What do they use it in?"

Matthew said, "I'm not sure what, but things with vanilla flavouring. The secretions from the glands near beavers' bottoms must taste strangely like vanilla! But I think most companies use artificial flavourings instead, or more harmless-sounding natural things. I think the beaver gland flavouring's difficult to get anyway, because beavers have to be anaesthetised before anyone can put their hands next to their bottoms and squirt the stuff out. I'm not surprised!"

Some of the students laughed. But several were noticeably being put off their food yet again. Dave pretended to be sick in his, and James pretended to be about to throw his out the window in despair of ever feeling like eating it again.

Becky said, "You'd have thought whatever the secretion from the gland is would taste of poo, or at least a bit meaty or something. But then, maybe the people who make stuff with it in it only use a tiny bit, so no one really notices much of whatever flavour it really has above the other things in the food. I think that happens with nice things too sometimes. My uncle Steven said he was once at the house of a family where they cooked a meal with a few things he didn't like in it, but they were all mixed together with other things, and he found out he liked them in combination."

Heather said, "Yes. I've discovered that sometimes a dinner I've made doesn't taste very nice, but then I've added another thing, and it completely transforms the taste into something really nice – you know, like if I add a cup o' soup."

Dave grinned and said, "What's your dinner in the end then? Rice and cup o' soup or something? Sounds like the stereotypical student meal! I've had quite a few meals like that myself, actually."

The others giggled.

Catherine said, "It can work the other way around too. You know, mixing a lot of nice things together can make . . . well, I don't know about something horrible, but something not nearly so nice anyway. I mean, from my own experience, I like both nuts and chocolate, so some people assume I'll just love nut chocolate; but actually, well, I have tasted some that's really nice, but with some of it, it doesn't taste anywhere near as nice as nuts or chocolate do separately; the chocolate and the other stuff they put in it obscures the flavour of the nuts – and I think they might cook all the flavour out of the nuts anyway or something, before they put them in there."

Stuart grinned and joked, "Well I would hope they wouldn't be cooking it after they put them in there! Imagine what would happen to the chocolate then! Imagine if a manufacturer came up with this supposedly bright idea about how something made of chocolate would be a better product if it was cooked afterwards, so they cooked tons of the stuff, only to end up with a massive liquefied mess of melted chocolate all over their pans, instead of all the chocolate bars and sweets they'd made before they cooked them!"

The students laughed.

Then Catherine said, "Yeah, but I mean, I think chocolate and nuts often taste a lot nicer separately than they do if they're put together, when one thing obscures the flavour of the other, especially if there are other ingredients in it obscuring the flavour of them both!"

They were thoughtful for a few seconds.

Then Sarah said, "That reminds me, I've sometimes mixed raw vegetables that've got a really nice flavour in with rice dishes and things, thinking it would make them taste especially nice, only to be disappointed, because the flavour of the raw vegetables seemed to completely disappear."

Becky said, "I wonder why that happens! What a shame. Maybe it's to do with a more delicate flavour being obscured by a stronger one. Or if you cooked them even a little bit, just to warm them up, the vegetables might have lost their nice flavour, because vegetables do lose flavour when they're cooked. But I think some raw vegetables have got more flavour than other ones of the same kind anyway; like I think the freshest ones have the most flavour."

Matthew said, "Putting raw vegetables with another thing that obscures their flavour sounds a bit like the way they put something that comes from seaweed in ice cream, but you'd never know it."

"Seaweed?" a few of them groaned, making pained faces. Most of the students refused to believe it happened. But Matthew said, "It's true. I couldn't believe it myself at first, and went on one of those websites that investigates email rumours that get passed around; and, supposing you can believe that's accurate, it says they put a substance that comes from a type of seaweed in quite a few foods and drinks, including ice cream, because it stops it turning into ice when it's frozen."

"Wow!" said Stuart. They all thought it was interesting.

Becky said, "The thing is, we probably just think it sounds yucky because we're not used to eating seaweed. If we'd eaten it all our lives, we'd probably just be used to it and not think anything of it. They probably grow it specially in clean places

– or at least I hope they do! I don't suppose they just fish it out of parts of the sea where loads of people have been swimming and doing wees, and rubbing dead skin cells off their feet and things."

The students chuckled.

Then James said, "You know, it's not just emails about yucky-sounding things that get passed around; I remember getting one that said drinking water before going to bed can stop people having heart attacks during the night. I went to Google, really hoping to find a website with a good reputation saying it was true. But I just found these websites that debunk hoaxes all saying it was rubbish. I was so disappointed!"

Kirsty said with a grin, "If scientists found that eating a pound of seaweed before bedtime stops people having heart attacks, do you think you'd do it?"

They all laughed.

Then Mya said, "Why are you worried about heart attacks at your age?"

James said, "Well I'm not really; I just thought it would've been nice to know if the thing about drinking water really worked, for when I'm older ... if I can still remember it by then. I suppose it partly depends on which goes first, the memory or the heart! Actually, I did hear that when people get older, it's best if they keep some aspirin handy, and take one if they get severe chest pains, while they're waiting to be taken to hospital, since if it's a heart attack, it might make the blood a bit thinner, so it stops clogging the heart valves that might have got a bit too narrow over time so badly or something, since that's what can cause heart attacks. I can't remember quite what I heard now; but I know it was good medical advice, not something that just came from some random email. But anyway, if I heard from a good medical source that seaweed could keep me young forever, so I'd never be at risk of my bits failing, I might eat pounds of the stuff!"

They giggled.

Then Catherine said, making a face, "Fancy putting seaweed in ice cream though! Or at least a part of seaweed! You never know what you might be eating these days, do you! Oh well, at least I've heard seaweed's good for you."

"Yep, full of healthy minerals, so I've heard!" said Colin, who smirked as he then said, "As long as they clean it first to make sure there are no little fish still hiding in it, I don't see a problem."

The students chuckled and made faces.

Sarah said, "Seaweed's nothing! I was looking at one of those hoax debunking websites to try to find out if something someone emailed me was true, when I found out there's a tropical beetle that gets ground up for a kind of red food colouring that they call cochineal and carmine, and put in some sweets and fruit juices, and other things too, like some shampoos. The beetle comes from Central America, and they used to breed them in huge numbers and send boatloads of them across to Europe to be used! And there's another food colouring that comes from coal that they use. I suppose they must use it in such tiny amounts that people can't taste it. I remember making cakes with my mum when I was little, and we used to put just a drop of food colouring in, and it was enough for the whole cake."

Heather said, "Honestly, who would think of putting ground beetle in shampoo? What would make someone think to do that? But I suppose a lot of weird thinking must have gone on over the years, and some's led to good things. I mean, who would think to cook parts of animal for food? The first person to ever do that can't have known it would turn into meat they could eat."

James said, "I dunno. Maybe they originally just threw a dead animal in the fire because they wanted it to burn up so they could get rid of it, but then they noticed it smelled nice, and they were hungry, so they thought they'd see if it tasted nice, and it did, so they passed on the news that chucking animal parts in the fire was a great thing to do because you could eat some of them afterwards."

Emma said, "That's a bit like music on memory sticks, or on the radio. I don't mean you can eat that – imagine chewing your way through dozens of memory sticks every day! But I mean it's amazing that it's possible to get thousands of songs on a little bit of plastic you can hold in the palm of your hand; who would ever have thought songs and bits of plastic like that could be connected like that if they didn't know! Imagine if about 400 years ago, someone had said they reckoned it might one day be possible to have thousands of songs on a little thing that wasn't a musical instrument, that you could hold in the palm of your hand, and the songs could have full orchestras playing or all kinds of instruments and harmonies, without a single person being there while they were playing; people would think the person who said it was nuts, wouldn't they! Of course, they might have been nuts; but no one would have believed such a thing was possible, would they!

"And maybe in a few hundred years' time, things will be being done that we can't imagine could ever be possible, and if someone said they might be now, we'd think they were just nuts!"

James said, "I don't believe the world will last that long! I reckon we'll probably all be nuked long before then!"

"Cheerful, aren't ya!" said Stuart.

Suzy asked, "Hey, is it true that while radiation kills us, it makes some insects and animals swell up really big, so you could come out of a nuclear bunker in a nuclear war to find flies the size of rabbits buzzing around you and things?"

"Oh where did you hear that?" laughed a few students near her.

"I heard a comedian say it," she said.

Matthew said with a grin, "Oh well that explains things! He was probably joking! How could it possibly be true? I mean, swelling up to the size of rabbits would mean they swelled up to about 200 times their size or something! . . . Then again, there are probably celebrities' heads that've swollen up that much after they've become famous!"

One Student Tells the Others About Insects and Other Animals Being Able to Survive a Nuclear Attack Better Than Humans

Ignoring that joke, Suzy said, "OK. But does radiation have different effects on insects than it does on humans so they can survive better?"

Kirsty said, "Actually I've read an article that said some insects do survive better than humans. It said they couldn't survive a direct hit from a nuclear bomb, but cockroaches can survive 150 times the radiation that could kill a human. Fruit flies could survive 320 times what a human could survive! And it said some ants can cope with 450 times what a human could survive!"

"How on earth do they do it?" asked Suzy in surprise.

Kirsty said, "I think scientists don't really know, but they reckon it might be partly because each of their cells contains less DNA than human cells, and radiation kills by damaging the DNA.

"But I read that near Chernobyl, which is in Ukraine, I think, where there was a big famous accident at a nuclear power station a while ago, and lots of radiation was released into the atmosphere, humans had to be evacuated, but loads of animals made their homes there after the people had gone, as if they didn't mind the radiation at all. In fact, so many have gone to live there it's like a wildlife sanctuary, according to one article I read. It said a few species were badly affected, but most weren't.

"It said two scientists did a study that found that animals had all deserted the most contaminated areas, and birds refused to nest there, but the article said it was a badly done study, saying they only went to one of the five most contaminated areas, and then made it sound as if all the areas were like it, but that actually, that one area was so badly affected, the trees all got turned red because of the radiation after the accident, and they were all bulldozed and buried, and new ones were planted; but they didn't grow properly because of the radioactive soil and things; they just look like weird twisted bushes; so the reason birds won't go there now might be because it looks so strange and uninviting, not because it's radioactive. It seems it's so easy to draw the wrong conclusions with all kinds of things . . . I suppose it's possible that I drew the wrong conclusion that the article's accurate when it isn't or something.

"But if it's to be believed, if the scientists who did the study had looked at the next most contaminated areas, they would have seen loads of animals, surviving doses of radiation that would make humans ill.

"Apparently, when humans were evacuated from Chernobyl, the animal population there grew a lot. They'd be no good for meat, because their radiation levels are too high to be safe for humans; but most animals don't seem to be affected themselves. The article said a number of experts have challenged the findings of the study that found animals had deserted the place, and studies were done that tried to count the animals, and there were found to be as many as there might be in a nature reserve. So if that's true, why the animals aren't affected when we are, who knows!"

Matthew asked, "Can you be quite confident that's reliable information though? I mean, it sounds surprising. Are you sure it didn't come from . . . I dunno, the Chernobyl tourist board or something, wanting to convince everyone the accident wasn't as bad as it seemed?"

(The conversation took place over a decade before the barbaric Russian invasion of Ukraine in 2022.)

Jackie burst out laughing and said, "The Chernobyl tourist board! If there was such a thing, trying to make a profit for them would have to be one of the hardest jobs in the world! There can't be many people who want to go on holiday to a place where there was a nuclear accident!"

The students giggled. But then most of them were surprised when Colin said, "Actually, I've heard there is such a thing as nuclear tourism! Mind you, I think nowadays it's mostly about people going to museums about nuclear explosions. But I heard that in the 1950s in America, they did some nuclear tests, and groups of people actually went to watch them and cheer, from a distance, and they had parties to celebrate them, because they were excited about the new powerful technology. Maybe they didn't know so much about the harmful long-term effects of nuclear explosions in those days. I even read that there were beauty pageants where young women were crowned Miss Atomic Bomb, and they wore costumes with pictures of mushroom clouds on them, or crowns made to look like them."

Some of the students laughed, while others were mystified.

Then Kirsty said, "Anyway, I think there's quite a bit of information about animals living at Chernobyl on the Internet, so you can look it up for yourselves if you want, to see if you find articles that say the same thing, or different things. I'm only going by what I've read. But one thing I read says the reason there are lots more animals there than there used to be is that humans haven't been around to disturb them since they were evacuated, so they can live on the land and breed as much as they want, since no one will try to get rid of them. I don't know if they're really unaffected by the radiation; maybe there'll be reports of lots of animals starting to die of cancer or something one day, although maybe they don't live long enough for it to develop, and that's partly why they don't seem to have been affected badly like humans would be. Anyway, I wouldn't fancy eating any of them, that's for sure!"

The others agreed that they wouldn't want to eat any either.

Then Colin said, at first sounding as if he must have dropped off to sleep for some time and just woken up thinking they were still having the conversation they'd been having some time earlier,

"Someone sent me an email once that said McDonald's puts worm meat in their burgers, so they don't have to put so much beef in them! It sounded like a silly rumour to me, and I don't know why anyone would believe it; I mean, how many worms would you need to get enough burger filler to be worth it! Surely the amount of time and energy you'd need to find enough of them and dig them all out of the ground, and then prepare them, separating the minuscule amount of meat on each one from the rest and packing each bit up to send off, would be way more than doing it was worth! Imagine the labour costs of preparing all those worms! Unless they could grow them on worm farms or something, where there were loads, and they could get them easily; but even then, you'd get such a tiny amount of meat from each one that it just wouldn't be worth the money it cost and the time it took to get it, I wouldn't have thought! I don't know why people don't think of how likely a rumour sounds before emailing it to other people."

Then he joked, "Then again, maybe if the worm farms were in the areas that are contaminated with radiation, there would be loads and loads of worms, and they'd all swell up really big."

Jackie put on a dramatic voice and made pained faces, and pretended to tremble as she joked, "Maybe you'd have worms growing to eight inches, and then a foot, and then two feet, and then four feet, and then they'd grow the whole length of the worm farm! And then if there were any houses near the worm farm, maybe the worms would be so big and powerful they'd be able to wrap themselves around them and crush them if they decided to curl up or push in on the house walls!"

Heather joked, "Wow, if worms got to be like that, it would be a mercy if McDonald's did get people to kill them and put them in burgers!"

Emma said with a giggle, "Yuck! Actually it would be far more of a mercy if they were killed but they didn't go into burgers!"

The students laughed.

The Students Talk About safety, and Harmful Hidden Ingredients That Have Ended Up in Some Food and Drugs, Before Becoming Light-Hearted Again

Then James told them something that shocked them, saying, "You do hear some horrible food stories that are true though. I've read that in Mexico they sell a kind of vanilla that's really popular, but some of it's not the real thing, but contains a chemical that can cause organ damage.

"And I heard that in Victorian times in this country, when there were no regulations about food safety, all kinds of awful things were often added to food and drink by some unscrupulous people who sold it, to make it seem as if there was more of it, or to make it look nicer, so they could sell it for more money and make more profits, because the things they were adding were cheaper than proper ingredients, so they could put less of the real ones in, or make bigger batches of things with the amount they had, so it wouldn't cost them so much to make things with the substitute stuff in them, so they'd be keeping more of the money they sold the products for for themselves, because they weren't spending so much of it on the proper ingredients.

"I heard that bread often contained sawdust, or ground bones, or pipe-clay, or chalk, or alum, which is a kind of aluminium, I think, that companies often use in detergents today. Some bakers used it to make bread heavier and whiter, so it would attract customers more, who wouldn't realise the flour in the bread was being diluted with horrible things that weren't good to eat.

"Lead was added to some cheeses and sweets and other things to make them look nicer so they'd sell more; sand was often mixed with sugar; and all kinds of other nasty things happened. Food could often make people ill, and would sometimes even kill them, because of all the things added to it.

"It's a good thing we've got laws nowadays making that kind of thing illegal, and food inspectors who go around testing things! But I've heard there aren't enough food inspectors to do the job as well as it needs to be done."

All the students began to feel horrified or depressed, and one or two of them wished they'd left earlier, while others made a mental note to find out more about what went on out of morbid curiosity, or concern that some food could still be unfit for human consumption if there was really a shortage of food inspectors.

James continued, "I've read that even today, whenever there aren't enough inspectors and safety regulations, some companies and even governments will make decisions that make it seem as if they think that making profits or cutting costs is more important than people's safety. I'm not just talking about food, but all kinds of things; for instance, they can do that by selling or using building materials – or resisting pressure to make it illegal for others to use them – as part of houses that are being built or renovated, when they know the materials haven't got much fire resistance, or that they'll even burn especially quickly if they catch fire. Companies can know just how to make building materials fire-resistant, but still make some materials that aren't. And I think that goes for quite a few other kinds of products too, where making things that are as safe as they can be would cost a bit more, so some companies can make less safe versions of them, thinking that then they can sell them at a lower price so they'll probably sell more of them and make more profit.

"That's why we need governments that care about making sure there are good safety regulations."

The students felt angry and a bit upset, and Mya said, "Wow! Why would anyone be willing to have a company making products they know have got safety problems? I can't imagine doing anything like it myself if I was the boss of a company! Why would you be willing to sell a product, knowing it might be unsafe, when you knew you could make a safe version? I mean, if it's the case that upgrading older less safe versions to make them safe would be hard for the business making and selling them to afford, maybe they should be in a different business entirely!"

Dave said, "A trading standards officer came round to our school to give us a talk about what trading standards departments do once. It was interesting, all about how they investigate faulty goods. I can't remember much of what he said now, but it got me interested in the subject, and I looked on the Internet afterwards, on websites that I knew have got a decent reputation for accuracy, for information about the safety and quality of products that get sold, and I found out that there are shops, even nowadays, that sell drinks that have actually got chemicals in them that are used as part of substances that get used as fire retardants, although the shops might not actually know they're doing it . . . I mean, they might not know that certain kinds of drinks they're selling have got those chemicals in them, not that they might not know they're actually selling the drinks, as if they're selling them in their sleep . . . Well, I don't mean the shops themselves might be asleep and selling things, as if they're alive; I mean their owners."

James made a face and said, "Don't be so pedantic!"

But some of the others grinned, and Kirsty chuckled and said, "Wow, maybe firemen should use those dodgy drinks as well as water to put fires out then! 'Bring me more of those orange and lemon drinks,' they'd say. 'I need to fling them at this fire!' "

The students giggled. But Dave said, "It's serious though. I mean, you wouldn't want to drink one of them, would you. I'm assuming those chemicals aren't really fit for human consumption ... Mind you, I don't think what I read actually said that, so maybe they are. But they'd put me off anyway. I don't know why they get put in the drinks."

Colin said, "Come on! There are substances that get used in all kinds of ways, so you'd need to know more about them before making a judgment that they weren't safe. If a substance in cheese started being used in a product that was designed to lubricate the wheels on trains, and then you heard that cheese contains a substance that's used in that way, would you start thinking cheese must be unsafe to eat?"

Dave said, "Well, it might put me off eating it, whatever I thought. But I suppose you're right about how it's best to find out more about things before making a judgment.

"Talking of cheese though, I've read that there are brands of cheese that are partly made with vegetable oils instead of fat from milk, but some of the companies that make them don't declare that, and they use vegetable oils instead of making cheese the proper way to cut costs."

"Wow, they should tell people it's part vegetable oils instead of dairy fat as a selling point!" said Heather with a grin. "Imagine it being advertised as half-vegan cheese, for people who aren't quite sure if they want to be vegan, but who want to see if they can get into veganism gradually."

310

The students laughed.

Then Dave said, "Maybe the cheese really would still be popular if they declared what was in it. But it's nicer to eat something that really is what you think it is. I even read that some cheese on pizzas isn't even cheese at all, but something called cheese analogue, which is a mixture of vegetable oils and additives like flavourings. Apparently it's legal for it to be used, as long as its name's used on the label instead of it just being called cheese, but sometimes it is just called cheese."

Jackie said, "That's not so good; but still, would you prefer to eat something that's mostly derived from plants, or something that was once inside a cow? If people weren't used to eating animal products because most people in the world had never done that, and then a company started manufacturing food with them like meat and cheese, we'd probably all think that was yucky, especially if they didn't reveal that they were putting animal products in their foods, and it was only discovered afterwards by a trading standards organisation, after lots of people had eaten them."

Dave replied, "True, I suppose. But it's nicer if companies can be honest about what's in their products, especially because I don't suppose additives can be that healthy."

Jackie said, "Probably not. But sometimes they can be healthier than the alternative, like if they're preservatives, and not using them would either mean the food went off more quickly, or that companies would have to use more natural preservatives like salt, which isn't healthy except in very small doses."

Dave said, "I suppose so. But I think it's still worth investigating these things. Another thing I found out is that some brands of packets of frozen prawns can have a load of ice crystals in the bags, that are put there deliberately to make them heavier, so people will think there are more prawns in them than there are; and some companies can use a process where they can fill prawns with water so they swell up, so they seem bigger than they really are. So that makes a packet seem bigger and heavier as well, so they can sell it for more money. In fact, I read that even half the weight of one of those packets can be water.

"And another thing is that I read that there's such a thing as meat emulsion, which is finely ground meat mixed with a couple of additives that make it easier for other things to be added to it; and often, fat gets added and absorbed into it that would probably otherwise be thrown away. One way it's used is to be put into some kinds of ham, partly to make it look thicker, so people think there's more of it. But if they cook it, the fat will start coming out and it might shrink a lot. Well, ham probably does that anyway. I think it's quite fatty as it is. But it sounds a bit yucky that some people actually add fat to some of it so people think they're getting more meat, so it can be more expensive.

"So it seems it's important that there are Trading Standards officers and people like that to inspect food; but I read that sometimes, their budgets get cut by local authorities, that have had their own budgets cut by central government, so they have to make some of their inspectors redundant; so that might mean that more faulty or substandard food gets into the system, and more companies get away with making it."

Most of the students started feeling a bit worried. But Emma said, "Well, you can tell that most food must be alright, when you think about the fact that almost everyone in this country grows up to be fit and healthy. Maybe that's partly because there are still enough inspectors to do quite a good job of checking its safety; but it's probably also because there are lots and lots of manufacturers that do care about it."

The students were relieved to think about it from that point of view.

But then Anne said, "I wonder how much more bad practice would go on if there were no food inspectors around today though, so it might be more tempting for some people to try to get away with things they shouldn't. Mind you, sometimes you can think you're being conned when you're not really, because there are reasons why manufacturers do things that you don't know about.

"I remember I used to think packets of crisps weren't such a good deal as they seemed, because they've got so much air in them. I thought the crisp companies must just be putting the air in there to fool people looking at them in the shops into thinking there were more crisps in them than there really were, because the packets would look smaller if they contained crisps but no air. But I heard that manufacturers say it's not just air, but nitrogen, and they put it in them partly because it keeps the crisps fresher for longer, because other gases in the air can make them go soggy or stale more quickly than they do if they've just got nitrogen around them. Mind you, I don't know if they sometimes put more in there than they need to, so the bags look bigger and more impressive than they really are.

"But another reason they put air in them is because it means they're protected from being squashed when they're loaded up together; I mean, just imagine if there was no air in them, and a big box was filled with packets of crisps; when they started putting the ones in at the top, all the ones at the bottom might start getting squashed, and crumble up into little bits . . . especially if someone sat on them!"

Stuart said with a grin, "If someone sat on a load of bags of crisps as it is, they'd all pop! Imagine that!"

They all laughed. Jackie said with a chuckle, "I expect any employee who kept sitting on the boxes of bags of crisps and making them go pop would soon find himself getting the sack!"

The students giggled some more.

But then Sarah said, "It does seem that some foods aren't quite all you expect though. I once bought some scones that were called sultana scones, but there were only about two sultanas in each one! And I once bought a rock cake that was called a cherry rock cake, and it was a great big thing; but I think it only had about five bits of cherry in it! I wondered if the people who made them were deliberately skimping on the more expensive ingredients, and whether they're just allowed to do that kind of thing.

"I wonder if there's a set of laws buried in some official law book in parliament that says things like, 'It is permissible to call a food a sultana bun as long as it has no less than two sultanas in it'.

"Actually, these scones I had were called 'all butter and sultana scones'. They weren't 'all butter' either; but I'm actually glad about that. I mean, Imagine someone just picking up a big chunk of butter with a couple of sultanas stuck in it and stuffing their face with it!"

The students laughed, and Becky joked, "That would be a time when you'd actually be glad if the thing was diluted with other ingredients – at least if they were nice or normal ones, like flour and sugar, and other kinds of things that scones are supposed to be made of!"

They giggled.

Then Sarah said with a grin, "Imagine if a strange person who just loved the taste of butter on its own and enjoyed gobbling great globs of it down by the mouthful bought those scones, expecting that they really would be completely made of butter, and they were really disappointed when they found out they weren't! Really, I expect the label that said they were 'all' butter really meant that one ingredient was all butter, as opposed to being part butter and part margarine . . . I wonder if some people would think it defeated the object if you were to buy 'all butter' scones, only to go and put margarine on them instead of butter to make them moist enough to eat, so you were kind of diluting the all-butterness of them, rather than putting butter between the halves of the already-all-butter scones. Not that you'd ever guess that's what they were if you didn't know. Not only did those scones not taste of sultanas; they didn't taste of butter either; so I'm not sure what the point of them being all butter was.

"Imagine if there was a label on them that announced that you had to buy your own butter and put that on them if you wanted the full benefit of them being all butter, and you had to buy your own sultanas and stick them in the butter you put on them if you wanted the finest real sultana taste, and you realised when you started eating them that it must mean that's what you'd have to do if you actually wanted them to taste of those things at all!"

Matthew chuckled and said, "If you had to do that, it might almost make you think you may as well make your own scones from scratch!"

Dave grinned mischievously and said, "Who would want to eat scones made of scratches! Now that really would be a scary ingredient! Imagine it said on the news one day that it had been discovered that a lot of ingredients in scones were diluted with lots of old bits of scratches and scabs!"

They laughed and made disgusted faces. Stuart said with a grin, "Oh how could anyone collect enough of those to make it worth using them as a substitute for some other ingredient?"

That made the laughter carry on longer.

But when it died down, the conversation turned serious again, as James said, "You know, that stuff we were discussing about how some foods were often diluted with other things in the olden days sounds a bit like what happens with drugs such as cocaine and heroin. It seems that a lot of drug Users don't know what they're really putting in their bodies; I've heard that some illegal drugs can contain chalk, or talcum powder, plus other things, even much more unhealthy things, as well as other drugs that people aren't told are in them, but that can sometimes have some kind of effect that's a bit similar to the drug they're in, but are cheaper.

"They're diluted partly so people make more money from them, because then there'll seem to be more to go around so they can sell more. But they can cause health problems, even serious ones sometimes, partly because of all the extra things in them. I read a book by someone who used to be a customs officer, who said he's even known heroin to be diluted with rat poison! Why anyone would want to make it more likely that they'd kill their customers, goodness knows! If someone took pure heroin, as long as they managed not to overdose, he said they could stay healthy; but heroin users can often get ill because of the toxins and other rubbish bad batches can be mixed with."

Heather asked, "I wonder if cocaine and other drugs should be legalised then, so the government could make laws about it being illegal to put stuff like that in them, so they could inspect them to make sure they hadn't been diluted with unhealthy things, so they would at least be of a good quality?"

Emma said, "Well, it's possible that that might help, but illegal drugs are illegal because they themselves cause problems. Anyway, if a heroin user one day took a dose of pure heroin, it would kill them, at least if they took the same dose as usual because they weren't expecting it to be a lot stronger than normal, which it would be if it was pure. I mean, think about it, if you've been used to taking heroin that's really diluted with stuff, you'll get used to taking a certain amount, and then if you took that amount when it was pure heroin, because you didn't realise that much more of that amount than normal was heroin, you might be really taking, say, double or treble the amount of the drug that you normally would, or more, even ten times the amount, so you'd overdose.

"People can do that now, because different batches of heroin are different strengths, because some's diluted more than others, and because different ways of manufacturing it means some of it's stronger than others. Even if it was always all pure, so people were used to it, it would be easier to overdose on it, because people would have to take more care when they were injecting themselves with it, because dangerously high levels would be reached more easily. I mean, there might be a way around that. But it might not be easy."

That was a sobering thought. Most of them had finished eating some time earlier, although some had been snacking throughout the day. Catherine said sarcastically with a smile, "Right, thanks, you lot; since I've been here trying to eat things, we've talked about death, war, crime, radiation poisoning, drugs, cockroaches, worms, cow's eyeballs, crushed bugs in food, and other horrible things! Who started this rotten conversation?"

"Becky!" said several students loudly in unison, grinning and pointing at her.

"Oy, don't blame me!" Becky said, laughing. "I didn't start the bits about those things. The fact that I started the conversation in the first place doesn't mean I'm responsible for the whole of it! This is like when my mum accuses me of using up all the hot water when I happen to be in the shower when it runs out, despite the fact that she had a shower before me, so she must have used up some of it!"

The students grinned or laughed.

Most of them had had no lectures that afternoon, and no plans for the evening. It was just as well. They realised it was pitch dark outside, and that the place was becoming emptier. James looked at the time, and was surprised to realise how late it was! He joked, "Hey, if we don't get out of here soon, we might get locked in . . . or thrown out! Look at how late it's getting!"

They all decided to get up and go. They'd had an interesting lunch break. And it had been some lunch break! They'd been engrossed in conversation for over ten hours!

Most of their discussions weren't anywhere near as long as that. But Becky and the others had several during her time at university.

About the Author

Diana Holbourn has written self-help articles and is the author of *The Early Life of Becky Bexley the Child Genius* and other books about the same character. Taking short psychology courses, working on a helpline and reading psychology books has prepared her for writing the self-help information that appears as part of the story in the Becky Bexley series. Diana lives and works on the south coast of England, where the sun shines . . . sometimes.

For more about the author and her books, visit:

www.DianaHolbourn.com

Other books in this series
Becky Bexley, Book One

Even from the moment she was born, it was clear that Becky Bexley was not like other children. Her family were shocked by her behaviour!

Just a few years later, and she's in secondary school, often seeming wiser than her teachers. She does her best to help people, whether they like it or not. She has advice for her teachers when they want to give up smoking, gives a boy advice he uses to stop himself being teased, and even gives the headmaster some advice on improving the school's anti-bullying strategy.

She helps people outside school too, including rescuing her mum from a con artist. She even gets to go to the White House, where she ends up giving the president advice about his behaviour!

He invites her to help some politicians with the depression they have. But will a few tactless remarks she makes and their own fierce disagreements unwittingly stirred up by some of the insights she tries to pass on ruin her efforts?

Becky's advice is based on genuine therapy techniques and psychological research, and the books in this series combine humour with handy information.

Becky Bexley, Book Two

Becky Bexley the child genius goes to university at a much younger age than most people do. She copes with the coursework, but has a few unexpected difficulties. Things begin well, as she makes friends she has fun with, and finds herself giving one of her psychology tutors some psychological help. She has a laugh working on a local community radio station with other students, and interviews the brother of a founder member of the pop group Fleetwood Mac. The paranormal comes up for discussion after a student tells the others about scary night-time experiences he's been having.

However, at a Christmas party in the psychology department, a succession of stressful events begins involving tutors behaving badly that makes Becky worry she risks being thrown out of university.

Becky's advice is based on genuine therapy techniques and psychological research, and the books in this series combine humour with handy information.

Printed in Great Britain
by Amazon

25946185R00189